Nous Nous

Nous Nous

A Novel

John Vanderslice

BRADDOCK AVENUE BOOKS

UNCOMMON BOOKS · UNCOMMON READERS

Printed in the United States of America
10 9 8 7 6 5 4 3 2 1

ADVANCE REVIEW COPY, August 2021

ISBN 10: 1-7328956-9-0
ISBN 13: 978-1-7328956-9-0

Book design by Savannah Adams

Braddock Avenue Books
P.O. Box 502
Braddock, PA 15104

www.braddockavenuebooks.com

Braddock Avenue Books is distributed by Small Press Distribution.

I am poured out like water;
all my bones are out of joint;
　　my heart within my breast is melting wax.

My mouth is dried out like a pot-sherd;
my tongue sticks to the roof of my mouth;
　　and you have laid me in the dust of the grave.

—Psalm 22

This book is dedicated to the different men and women who have taught me something about true religion. These include, but are not limited to, the late Sister Pauline McShain, Sister Carmen Gillick, the Reverend Thomas Pettei, the Reverend Teri Daily, the Reverend Greg Warren, the Reverend Peggy Cromwell, the late Reverend Doctor Linda Brown; and, last but not least, my late father, Joseph T. Vanderslice, the maverick with his heart in the best place.

Nous Nous

A Novel

John Vanderslice

1

When the man came through the doors of the church, her first instinct was to run to the bathroom and hide, but instead she established herself in the office and behind her desk as quickly as possible. There were certain exaggerated people that in Elizabeth's experience as rector made her believe that even a priest has limits. *You mean,* she said in her head—she supposed to God—*that I am actually expected to sit at a desk across from this person and listen? Are you fucking serious?* She edited the f-word from her mind, but she refused to jettison the question. Indeed, she would ask it more fervently. More than once, she'd left a meeting and proceeded straight down the hall to the chapel where she sat in a pew, lowered the kneeler, put herself in a position of supplication, and waited for God to provide her with strength. Occasionally, that happened.

There was the blue-eyed, pale-skinned visitor, his face as narrow as a blade of grass and fiendish as a cockatoo. A man who'd come to Sunday services exactly one time and then corralled her for an hour afterwards, arguing as to why he should be allowed to leave his wife for a woman who lived on another continent. Finally, Elizabeth had to say, "Do whatever you're going to do; just realize God sees all the way into your heart." She'd thought of it as an effective blow-off line, a fork into his conscience; but only five minutes later she realized he would take her to mean that God read all the love in his heart for the new woman and would thus approve of his abandonment. *Smart, Elizabeth. You just extended church sanction to adultery.*

Then there was the possibly still worse meeting with the minister from Second Baptist, a soft-spoken older man, with a narrow but square chin, reserved manner, and dignified haircut, who asked her quite kindly if her church would consider shutting its doors since—apparently without realizing it—it was doing the devil's work. Ordaining homosexuals and all that. The only thing she could never understand about that particular meeting was whether the minister actually expected her to consider his notion or whether, under the camouflage of gentleness, he just wanted to toss theological grenades.

And of course this reckoning did not even begin to include all the ordinary, disheartening meetings with members of her own congregation: those eager to tell about the affronts perpetuated by other members, or report on the ridiculously paltry sums a certain individual or two contributed to St. Thomas's each month, or to suggest that one person or another should be officially sanctioned if not formally removed for sins as variable as anal sex, gum chewing in church, voting Republican, or watching reality television. *What is this, high school?* she complained to the Almighty. *Are we just nosy fifteen-year-olds, desperate to rat on each other to Mama?* She wondered if any of the last three rectors at St.

Thomas's—all men—had had to put up with quite so much tattling, or whether it was a function of being a woman and thus (according to theory) more approachable. She liked to think the former might be the truth, but she was all but certain it was the latter. And if so, she decided that henceforth she would reverse feminist theory and try to prove herself a horrible exemplar of its tenets. She was going to drive all those tattlers away like Jesus did to the moneychangers in the temple, except not with physical violence but disdain.

So far, however, she had been unable to bring herself to do this. She worried that the reason for her caution was the fact that a few of the tattlers were also among the biggest donors to the church. To forcibly end their gossip might mean to put her own salary in jeopardy to say nothing of the salaries of the office staff and the parish mortgage payment and St. Thomas's pledge to the diocese. No, she could not do it. Day after day, sometimes hour after hour, her life was nothing but a string of disheartening sessions with both strangers and friends.

But when this new visitor walked through the doors into the lobby, she took one look at him and was certain she'd reached an absolute impasse. It was not that he was dressed shabbily—an olive-green parka, presently unzipped to show a white oxford beneath; khakis; loafers—or that he moved with any sort of menacing, aggressive gait. He carried no instrument of violence. What caught her attention was his face. The man had what looked like a bad rash or an inherited skin disease that colored nearly half his head the shade of a wine stain. Worse were his gray-green, reptilian eyes: focused on her, only on her, as if she were the prey he'd set his sights on many long hours ago. Once behind her desk, she found the sharpest object available—a letter opener—and kept it out, as near to her hand as she could leave it without raising suspicion. She also checked to make sure she had 911 on her cell's speed dial. She did, so she left the phone out too, with its screen showing her list of contacts. Finally, she readied herself, turned her face to the open office door, and forced herself to smile when he came through, just as she knew he would.

"I need to talk to you," he said.

Before she could stop herself, Elizabeth said, "Why?"

"Because I'm thinking of killing someone."

She blinked. "That's a fairly serious problem."

"I know. That's why I'm here."

"You mean that you want me to talk you out of it?"

His head reared, his lizard's eyes narrowed. The weak fluorescent light in her office didn't quite cancel the late winter murk outside; perhaps this was the reason his eyes, in that moment, seemed closer to charcoal. Or maybe there was another reason. "Not in the least," he said. "I just want to know what you have to say about it."

"Why?"

He grimaced, showing his teeth like a dog giving a warning. "I guess I thought it would be fun."

Okay, so he really was just playing with her. "I can think of a lot of things more fun: eating a steak, hugging a baby, seeing a movie . . ."

She was trying to get into the spirit of the encounter, to loosen the guy up so that he would move on to what he really wanted to talk about. But he only stared at her now for a long moment; then he waved his hand. "I don't think you understand. I think I might be in the wrong place."

"That's possible. What brought you to us anyhow?"

He turned his head slightly. "You know. Grapevine."

"What did the grapevine say?" About this, she was genuinely curious. Even if the speaker was a crazy person. She could not help but wonder—every day, all the time—how St. Thomas's was perceived in the community. And she was nervous about it too. Because it had everything to do with whether or not they survived. For the six years she had worked as rector—and for as long as anyone here could remember—St. Thomas's had operated with deficit budgets. Last year's deficit was $55,000. Desperate emails had been sent to the congregation, warning speeches from various vestry members had been delivered weekly from the lectern, repeated and soulful urgings by her to "please pray about their level of commitment" had been issued. All their different savings accounts had been used up and various fundraising tactics tried.

The bishop, meanwhile, had forbidden them from using a line of credit. In the past, he had expressed dissatisfaction with the church's lackadaisical growth, but never as much as he had lately. And he appeared to have Elizabeth directly in his sights. "You're the only church in this town delivering our particular message," the bishop had told her more than once in their face-to-face meetings. "People ought to be fighting for seats on Sundays."

They were not fighting for seats on Sundays. And Elizabeth feared that some morning she would arrive to find that a FOR SALE sign had been hammered by some diocesan hit man into the grass by the sidewalk. And maybe a hand-scrawled note taped to the front door: *Closed for lack of support.* And, the final blow, a voicemail from the bishop on her cell explaining that, oh, she was officially relieved of her duties as rector. *Think of this as an opportunity to reconsider your calling, dearie. Maybe you were never supposed to be a priest to begin with.* Of course, the scenario was not possible—for one, the bishop would never call her "dearie"—but that didn't mean she couldn't fear it.

The strange man blinked at her. "You don't back down. You tell it like it is. You get hurled at, and then you hurl back."

About her. That was what he meant. That was what they said about her. In the grapevine. Not about St. Thomas's, but about her. "I don't know," she said. "Sounds like a soccer match."

He shrugged. He did something with his hand. "But sitting here, looking at you, I think you might not be up for it. You strike me as tired. More tired than you even let yourself realize." What the man said, or maybe the way he said it—as if it were a simple fact—caused goosebumps to rise on her forearms. She turned in her chair. She turned back.

"I don't think I know what you're talking about."

"I know you don't. But maybe that's what's fun."

Now, that just made her mad. "Look, Mr. . . . ?"

"Rouse," he said and blinked again.

"Mr. Rouse, today is just that kind of day. I have several more meetings, and some important business off site." The former statement was a lie, but the latter at least was true. Robert Lemons—a member of St. Thomas's for 42 years—was in Caddo Regional with serious heart trouble. The family had asked her to come. "How about we store this discussion for another time?"

"You don't think I'm serious."

"I think you're testing me."

"That must mean you don't think I'm serious."

"I think you're serious about testing me. And I'd like to know why."

The man smiled again, but he kept it inside this time. He showed no teeth. He turned his head to her office window and laconically observed the church parking lot. In that moment, even with his half-and-half face, he suddenly appeared ordinary. Not a predator, but someone lost in a maze. From Elizabeth's experience, everyone was lost in a maze. "Maybe I need to know if I can trust you," he said. He looked at her again.

"Well," she started, "on one hand, I can understand that. There's no communication without trust. But, on the other hand—" She paused a second too long.

"What? Say it. Let me have it." He was actually pleading.

"Killing someone is nothing to joke about. I mean, if that's what you think is a fun discussion, I'm going to have to ask you to leave." She saw a new bitterness enter his expression. Maybe she'd been too blunt. Her eyes darted to the cell phone, to the letter opener. Right where she'd left them.

"You haven't even asked me why I would want to kill this person."

"Right. I haven't. But no matter what the reason I'm afraid I can't sanction murder. As a Christian, that's just one place where we can't—"

"As a Christian?" Now he was furious. Every last shade of green left his eye to be replaced by gloamy black. His shoulder muscles tightened; his elbows flared; his neck went stiff; his hands formed into claws. The ancient fight reflex evidenced itself right before her eyes. *Maybe he wasn't kidding, after all.* Now her chill went well beyond goosebumps. "As a Christian, you say?" He spoke the word as if it were the most ignominious in the language, as if he were saying *retard* or *bastard* or *nigger*. "I find that hilarious." There was absolutely nothing hilarious about his body language.

"Sorry, but it's true. Old Testament and New. God gives life. It is not our place to take it away."

Now he just sat there and grimaced. She couldn't tell if the expression was a demented smile or the prelude to crying. His eyes were slanting and filled with hurt. Oceans—waves—of acute, unarticulated pain. Something, indeed, had happened to him. And, as much as she didn't want to, she was honor bound to sit and listen to him tell her about it.

Her phone buzzed. A text. "Excuse me," she said and reached for the device. Rouse did not react. She could not be sure he heard her. No matter. She recognized the texter immediately. Her seventeen-year-old son. They weren't supposed to use phones at school; kids younger than high school age weren't even allowed to carry them. Hard-and-fast rules of the district. Didn't Aaron know he was risking losing his phone permanently?

Car down. Don't know why. Can you get me to work?

She glanced over Rouse's shoulder to the clock on the opposite wall. Ten after two. She didn't realize it was that late. Time for Aaron's early release from school so he could go to his job at the game store. After Christmas, the school had granted its permission. Elizabeth didn't understand why, but apparently this was customary at Caddo High, even in 2014. Every day, dozens of teenagers skipped out of eighth period to stand behind cash registers and answer phones and flip burgers and park cars. An old legacy, she assumed, from when no one in the middling Arkansas town gave a thought to attending college. When a life of flipping burgers might have been exactly what they were being trained for. Aaron was definitely attending college, but he also wanted his $7.25 an hour. He must be standing in the school parking lot that moment, staring at his malfunctioning Y2K model

Buick Century—the oldest, dumbest, least sexy thing they could find for him—thinking about how he was going to get in trouble with his boss, a finicky man named Gregory. Gregory had hired Aaron quickly and recognized his rapport with the customers, but at the same time, Aaron reported, Gregory seemed to despise him.

"I apologize," she said to Rouse without actually looking up. "Really." She sent a reply to Aaron: *Can you wait a few?*

No!

I think you can.

Why?

You have to.

Gregory will kill me.

You exaggerate.

I don't.

"Problems at home?" Rouse said. His face seemed calmer now; the anger, or at least the public face of it, had subsided. In its place was the irony and the attitude of control from before. She wasn't sure she liked it any better.

"No, no problems. Just the stuff of life. My son's car is having issues."

He nodded distantly, as if he were thinking of something else. "So," he said then, "clarify this for me. You're all dressed up like a priest—"

"Because I am one."

"With your tidy black shirt and collar."

"That's what priests wear."

"But you're a woman."

"Obviously."

"But I can't call you 'Father.'"

"Call me 'Reverend.' Or just call me Elizabeth."

"Elizabeth?"

"My name. Elizabeth Riddle."

"And you have a son."

The discussion was set to leap into all new directions from which she could not see any good coming. First the man pretended he wanted to kill someone, and now he was about to berate her for assuming a place no God-fearing woman should want or ever deserve. She'd heard all that crap before. She heard it practically every week in Caddo. She didn't need to hear it again, not when her son's car had died.

"Look," she started, "I'm not sure what you're getting at, but—"

"When I was a kid, all the priests were men, and they didn't have wives. They weren't allowed to. I never liked any of them. In fact, I thought they were probably all perverted. I could not stand to be in their presence. When did this stuff change?"

She started to answer flippantly, and then it occurred to her that he had paid her a compliment—maybe an accidental one, but a compliment indeed. He used not to like priests. *When did that change?* he asked. Maybe he liked her?

She consciously adjusted her tone, made her voice grow soft. "You're not sitting in a Catholic church, Mr. Rouse, but an Episcopal one. I'm an Episcopal priest, not Catholic. This collar I'm wearing is not a Roman collar. It's an Anglican collar."

"Anglican collar? That's what they call it?" He acted as if this were the best joke anyone had ever played.

"We are Anglican, after all. Even if sometimes Canterbury doesn't like to think so."

He looked confused again. That last comment was a mistake. Unless this man followed the political battles of the Episcopal Church in the United States—no chance of that—it was a meaningless, distracting sentence.

"As I said, you're in an Episcopal church. Our trappings might look very Roman Catholic, but we are not."

She had thought this would clarify matters for him, but he kept looking at her like she was a lunatic person telling a hopeless story. One that he couldn't accept because it could potentially upend his life. "How about this," she said. It had begun to dawn on her that perhaps the man's real reason for coming was to find a new church home. Why else all his questions? "Let me get you something to glance at. You can look it over, and then we can talk about any questions you have. I've got to run and rescue my son at the high school, but when I get back we can go over the pamphlet. I'd be happy to."

He sat still and stone-faced, even as he watched her. She stood up, walked around the desk, and left him sitting there while she went to find the pamphlet. There was a whole stack of them in the narthex, on the table that faced the door of the sanctuary. As soon as she was out the doorway of her office she felt an immense and automatic sense of relief. She wasn't trapped. She'd found a way out. The feeling surprised her, because she hadn't thought she was trying to escape. She thought she was trying to get a pamphlet that she'd given to scores of people before. It was exactly what he needed to read: *Twenty Questions About the Episcopal Church*. A good, quick primer for those who knew virtually nothing about Anglicanism except that it started with Henry VIII and his need to get a divorce. The heels of her heavy priest's shoes clattered against the linoleum. She liked the sound. It sounded like control. She reached the table in the narthex, grabbed one pamphlet, and headed back, not in any particular hurry but not dawdling either. It felt good to be able to give the strange, troubled man something, but also good that she had an ironclad excuse to leave him for a while.

When she reached her office again, she was stunned to see it was empty. The man was gone. She hurried back into the lobby and out the front door. She looked at both ends of the little sidewalk in front of the church. No one. She looked at the parking lot. Not a single car she didn't recognize. There was her own. And the secretary's. And the bookkeeper's. There was the sexton's, who'd made a rare weekday visit to finish up some cleaning she couldn't get to the night before. Finally, there was the van belonging to the plumber who was around back surveying a bad drainage situation behind the Christian Education wing. But that was all; no other cars. With rising impatience, Elizabeth walked across the lot, in order to better survey Schott Street, which ran parallel to the church. Then she stopped herself. What was she doing? Hadn't she, just moments ago, wanted to escape from this man?

2

The little Pomeranian was tussling against the restraint of the leash—scrambling for a sniff here, a sniff there: a crusted half of a French fry, a spritely lemon-green weed, a dried mound of some other dog's tar-black poop—and Baine was about to lose patience. This wouldn't work unless the dog could stay calm and let him concentrate. He couldn't do it without the dog, of that he was certain. The last time he'd selected a school to observe, over a month ago, he'd taken every imaginable precaution. He had made sure to not actually touch his feet on playground grass but instead stand on a side street, one that could not be called suspiciously close but was close enough. Yet, despite the distance he deliberately put between himself and the children, a professionally nosy teacher had approached and asked if he needed assistance. Not a real ask, of course. The kind of I-have-my-eye-on-you statement that mall store managers are so adept at hurling at even the slightly conspicuous: "Can I *help* you, sir?"

Maybe at night the nosy teacher did work as a mall store manager. She would have been perfect for it: her forty-five-year-old's standard frosted dye job and a face as focused as a hatchet. He wasn't sure what color her eyes were because he had refused to meet them. And, of course, there was no answer he could give. No, he hadn't wanted her help. He would have despised her help, because it would not have been help that would have done him any good. Indeed, her help would have thwarted him. Perhaps he did need help—some specific person's help—but he wasn't sure where to find such a person. How would you place the ad, what would you say in it? *In need of expert kidnapper. Please send resume and contact information to the following address. Photo a must.* And how could you trust whoever answered? There was no honor among thieves. Baine knew that all too well.

More or less expelled by the nosy teacher, he had had to leave the school and walk back to his car, which he'd hidden away on a residential street about four blocks west. He'd been thinking ahead. He wasn't dumb. *Say what you want to about me; I'm not dumb.* If someone noticed him in an untoward way and he had to retreat, at least they would get no read on him through a make and model or a license plate. And if they actually followed him—he doubted anyone connected with a school had the time or patience for that—he would just keep walking. He would avoid the street where his car was parked until he could be sure no one was watching him.

It was after that surveillance mission that he'd decided on the dog. What better cover could one own? Not only did it provide him with a useful alias—kind and responsible pet owner; concerned citizen of the animal world—but it gave him a good reason to walk past a school anytime he wanted to. Who would care or even notice a man out walking his dog? It was like wearing camouflage. No, it was like wearing an invisibility suit. It made him blink off the radar of all those professionally concerned, hawkishly suspicious teaching professionals with their lousy hair, cruel eyes, and chubby hips. And whereas before he'd selected a school miles away from where he lived, he now realized there was no need to do so. It would be possible—no, it would be better—to choose the middle school that was within walking distance of where he lived. The more he was seen on the streets of his neighborhood with the dog, the more casual waves and adoring questions he received, the more harmless he seemed and invisible he became. Why, the dog might even attract the kids!

Baine had imagined dozens of children surging toward him as soon as he appeared on the street that bordered the playground. *Can I pet him? What's its name? What a cute puppy! Here, puppy! Here, peanut!* He'd gotten plenty of that already, in just one month of dog ownership, out on his neighborhood walks. Roving groups of kids, loose on the street once school ended, could not keep themselves from approaching Cocteau. In fact, if he'd wanted to, Baine could have acted already. He could have done what he was set to do. But he wasn't ready to act yet. He'd learned long ago that if you acted before you were ready, everything went to hell and you never got the chance back. There might be only one chance at doing anything. You had to plan for the chance, plan so thoroughly that mistakes were not possible.

Thus, for the sixth day in a row he'd walked Cocteau slowly, as if distracted, down the narrow stretch of Upman Street: that homely, unmarked expanse of blacktop that for seventy-five yards or so jutted right up against the grass of the playground of Virginia McKinley Middle School, before breaking away in a riotous curve to the left, where it proceeded dead straight for a quarter mile and then reached the intersection with Western Avenue, a newly remodeled four-lane thoroughfare that ran nearly the whole length of Caddo. Baine never went anywhere near that far. No, he plodded along Upman, head down, as if his thoughts were constricted around some holy purpose, as if he were unaware that the school and the playground even existed. Then he would stop as if he'd randomly chosen to do so, and he would allow Cocteau to do his business on the grass or merely sniff around: head low, nostrils flaring and constricting in quick palpitating movements, intent for buried treasure. Well, maybe there was. But that was not the treasure Baine was after.

While Cocteau sniffed and peed, Baine lifted his head introspectively and directed, as if thoroughly bored, his attention toward the children. He made sure not to look too frequently from one child to the next or to follow a child too long as she walked from one piece of play equipment to another. He was careful not to express interest or attention or purpose. His only purpose, his show was meant to suggest, was to let his dog pee. He always kept his head rigidly still, facing one direction, and within that set band of visibility he darted his eyes from face to face, skull to skull, knee to knee.

Reconnaissance work, he thought of it. Research. Fact finding. Baine was no spy, but he always prided himself on thinking that he could have been one; if he'd only applied to the CIA after college, if he'd only had the guts, instead of taking what was perhaps the most boring job in existence: as a data entry clerk in a local office of Southwestern Power, and only because it was not far from his parents' home in Bossier City. How pathetic and yet life-determining a start that had been for him, ending in a job as a manager at the regional office of Entergy in Caddo, Arkansas. He should have taken the spy exam instead. He would have passed with flying colors. He could be secretive. He could be clever. He was expert at disguising his true motivations. What else did a spy need?

But now Cocteau was getting out of hand, jerking the leash so badly that Baine was not able to hold his head straight. Someone was bound to notice him. Either a teacher on the playground—although he saw none of those at the moment—or someone idly glancing out the window of one of those homes directly behind him on Upman. Then he saw her: a skinny girl in a long blue coat, the kind of outfit her mother would not have wanted her to wear if she planned on charging around a playground and climbing a jungle gym. The kind of coat that looked like an imitation of the dressy winter coats that New York models wore, something like a pea coat but longer and softer, not so bulky. Hanging all the way past her knees, it clung to her almost like a gown. Certainly more so than the standard order hoodies, camo garb, and waist-hugging, puffed-out ski jackets the other kids wore. She looked like a Scandinavian princess. The dark blue of the coat accented her long, fire-blonde hair. Even from this distance he could see the upturned butt of her nose, the elongated neck, and the glinting coral blue of her young eyes. (Sixth grade? No, most certainly seventh.) The eyes were smiling as she yelled insults at this kid or that. They smiled even as insults were hurled back.

Perfect. She must be an open kind of girl, one who took contention as the normal stuff of life: the fun stuff of life. This girl wasn't one to run from any old stranger, as he knew the kids were all told to do today. She knew better. She knew that not all strangers were dangerous. Some were actually helpful. Some actually wanted what was best for you, even if what that meant was something other than what their parents meant. The scared, pitiful parents had no idea; the scared, pitiful parents, and their hired help—these stupid, monotonously suspicious teachers—were the problem. How come this wasn't obvious to everyone?

He ignored the dog and followed the girl with his eyes. She slipped through a bending rectangular hole in the jungle gym and dropped to the ground, bored apparently with the company of kids around her who looked at least a grade younger than she, if not two. She landed with ease, her knees bending just so to absorb the impact. *Athletic type.* Then she ran across a field of mulch—*lithe form, graceful and easy, even inside a coat*—to the tetherball court, where two students idled by the pole. One, a tall, light-brown-skinned girl with a narrow face and passing gray tint to her eyes, leaned her back against it and smiled at her friend with a keen, knowing look, as if she'd just admitted to reading the other's murkiest romantic secrets. Far from seeming bothered, the friend, a dark-skinned girl with a head of loose, crazy curls, reared back and laughed hysterically at whatever the first girl had said.

Neither seemed to realize that the blonde girl was nearby, wanting to start batting the ball, by herself if necessary. Suddenly, the narrow-faced girl reached over and began tickling her friend, which caused the friend's paroxysms of hysteria to grow almost painfully noisy. The blonde girl watched for only a few more moments, then yelled at the two of them. "Stop taking up space!" The laughing girl stopped laughing. The tickling girl stopped tickling. They both looked up at her, surprised and wary. "I'm trying to play with this," the blonde girl said. With shared, guarded looks, the other two muttered something to each other. Then the tickling girl shrugged and turned, and the pair of them slowly sulked off.

Baine didn't care to see where the girls went. Instead, he watched intently as the blonde girl positioned herself inside the tetherball court, raised the ball carefully in her left palm and then brought her right fist around like a flaring hammer and sent the ball in a shrieking-fast arc around the pole. With practiced agility she quickly repositioned herself so that she was in just the right place to meet the ball as it came around, to hit it on the backside and send it squirreling even faster around the pole. She did this once more before the ball had completely tied itself to the pole and could move no more. Wow, Baine thought. Such athleticism—and command of the playground too. Clearly those two girls idling around the pole did not feel it was within their rights to deny her a tetherball experience. Maybe someone else, but not her. "Stop taking up space!" she had said, and they'd felt compelled to move. *Stop taking up space, indeed.* He could say that to half the kids on this playground. And the kids' parents. If they listened, he would surely have an easier time approaching her.

Now the blonde girl spotted someone on the other end of the playground. She cupped her hands around her mouth. "MacKenzie," she shouted in a delirious pitch, as if shocked to see the other girl in that place at that time. Baine's heart almost stopped when, in attempting to reach her friend, the blonde girl started in his direction. She would come right by him. To run how far he couldn't know—she probably didn't either—but that didn't matter. All that mattered was that for a few spare seconds she would be near him. He would see her up close. Maybe she would spy him, something would register. They could share a communication.

Sure enough, the girl's stray gaze happened to meet his own. Her eyes shined darkly but shined, even on a cloudy day. Maybe they shined even more when it was cloudy. She stopped. Something about his looking at her brought her to a standstill. She stood wavering, not six feet from where he was, studying him with confusion, as if thinking she should be able to recognize him, as if maybe it was her fault that she could not. *Yes, dear, you know me*, he thought at her while his heart pounded. *You do. You do.*

"Hi, can I help you?" Baine heard from his left. He wheeled to see a tall, thin, darkly brunette woman with a calm, smiling aspect. She stood on the other side of the chain-link fence, regarding him out of steady brown eyes, as if her question were genuine. Maybe, he thought with surprise, it was.

"Hi. No. Just enjoying the neighborhood," he said. *Wrong*, he thought. *Wrong answer. The dog, remember?*

"Do you know Jeannine?" She motioned with her head to the girl, that smile even longer, even more placid.

Quickly, too quickly, he shook his head. "No, I don't." He was careful not to look at the girl. But he thought: *Jeannine. A grand name.*

The woman was silent for a moment, studying him: his hair, his nose, his chin, his eyes. Baine could not tell if she was coming to a summation about him, and this bothered him. Suddenly, she looked down at Cocteau. "I love little dogs," she said. "Yours is beautiful."

He nodded. "Thanks."

"What's her name?"

"Him."

"Sorry. Little dogs always look girly to me. What's his name?"

When he told her, she squinted, brows crossed, like it was the most baffling appellation in the universe. *Stupid, stupid woman. Intruder.* And now Jeannine was gone. He didn't know where, but she must be gone, and he never had a chance to say a word to her, because of this intrusive, idiot teacher-woman.

"That's an interesting name," she said and smiled again. *Which only means you don't understand it.* She turned her gaze back to the playground where she silently surveyed the children there, as if she were supposed to keep an eye on them, but of course she wasn't. She was keeping an eye on him. Her next question shocked him. "Is one of these yours?"

"Sorry?" His shoulders actually trembled.

"Do you have a child at the school? A boy or a girl?"

"No," he said. And then, he wasn't sure why, it wasn't as if he trusted her: "I don't have a child anymore."

"Anymore? Is that what you said?"

"Yes." He had to fight to contain his shoulders. Single syllables were better.

"I'm sorry to hear that. What happened? Is the child all right?"

Fool woman. Why would he have said that if the child was all right? Pissed at her, at the very fact of her, at her pretend kindness and her condescending assumptions, and most of all at her interruption, he decided to tell her the truth, to inflict her with it. "I had a daughter. She was abducted and murdered."

3

I have to squint to see the blackboard, but then I feel myself doing it so I stop before Miss Angel can see me. MacKenzie told me that if you have to squint to read it means you need glasses. I do not want glasses. Not that I wouldn't look good in them. I just don't think I want that: to be the girl who wears glasses. I don't have a problem with other girls who wear glasses. That's who they are. But it's never been me, and it's not a change I care for. I've had more than enough change already. I'd rather stick with what I have, thanks. Otherwise, I might have to invent a whole new life.

"Say it altogether now," Miss Angel says, pointing to a three-word sentence she wrote in black ink on the white board. For the last ten minutes she's been trying to get us to pronounce the different parts of this sentence. Now she wants us to say the whole thing. *Je suis etudiant.* "Go ahead and try: Juh sweeze etoodeeahn." We murmur along with her. Her eyebrows do something weird on her face. She seems to frown and smile at the same time.

I wonder how old Miss Angel is. She looks like a kid. Mrs. Mason has already told us that Miss Angel is a college student, one who studies education because she hopes to teach someday. But her main major, Mrs. Mason says, is French. "While we don't have regular foreign language classes at Virginia McKinley," Mrs. Mason said to us at the beginning of the semester, "Mrs. Nixon"—that would be our principal—"wants to experiment with a trial program that you all"—she spread her saggy arms apart—"get to enjoy. Miss Angel is going to visit with us one day a week and tell us a little something about French." Miss Angel is a funny name for a teacher. A funny name for anyone. Angels don't teach in middle school; at least not at Virginia McKinley. Most of our teachers seem paranoid and overstressed. They're all scared of the spring testing. They don't seem to love their jobs. They need to smile more.

Mrs. Mason isn't so bad. She's been here forever and isn't going anywhere else. She moves slow, talks slow, and doesn't have a lot to reveal about her private life—not like Miss Barclay, whose fiancé is killing people in Afghanistan, or Mrs. Caldwell, who is divorcing her husband after he was arrested for propositioning an undercover cop at some park in Morrilton. Apparently, it was a "sting" operation, which meant a bunch of police went undercover together—for several nights in a row—in an elaborate plan of action. In this case, to stop gay men from taking over that park every night. At least that's what MacKenzie says. *They meet there every night, and they touch each other's penises, except with different partners every time. People they don't even know.*

I don't care about the park or the gay men, but Mrs. Caldwell's troubles make for great news. Mrs. Mason is duller. Her son is in medical school; her daughter is married to a man who does something with computers. She has a granddaughter she loves. She has a dog that licks her face to wake her up every morning. She has a husband who works at the paper factory but keeps talking about how he wants to retire and fish and ride a big, safe motorcycle. Very boring stuff. I mean, I like Mrs. Mason—everyone does—you can't not like Mrs. Mason—but her life is boring. At least Miss Angel is something different once a week.

"No, no, no," Miss Angel says, "this is important. *Sweeze.* Okay? *Sweeze.* Like squeeze without the q. Say it."

We say, "Sweeze." Miss Angel smiles, all at once, happy and surprised. We can say any part of this sentence; just not all of it together. And this matters why? "Okay, now, *ehtoodeeahn.*" She says it again. We say, "Etoodeeahn." Miss Angel looks delirious.

"Okay, okay." She starts talking fast, like she just won a bet. "Does anybody remember why we say *sweeze* and not *swee* with this sentence?" She's certain we will know the answer. "Remember, I explained it to you last week? Does anybody remember last week?"

I can't, although maybe someone else can. It's difficult to commit any of these lessons to memory when they only come once a week, and there won't ever be a test. I feel sorry for Miss Angel, actually. Why are they making her stand up here and teach a bunch of seventh graders when she has her college classes to finish? She must have a lot of those left, because she looks so young. She doesn't look much older than my brother—he's a junior at the high school—or any of the kids he hangs out with. Of course, maybe it's because she's in the same room with thick-necked, slow-moving Mrs. Mason, who is really fat and has skin tags. I honestly like Mrs. Mason, but I also wonder sometimes if she is one of those people who have to ride the electric scooters when they go to Walmart.

Tommy Washam's hand goes up. That's surprising. But Miss Angel loves it. She perks up, lifts her head.

"I think," Tommy says, very slowly, "it has something to do with the 'e.'"

Miss Angel smiles. She's hopeful. "Which 'e'?"

Long pause. "The second one."

Miss Angel nearly jumps in place. She begins clapping her hands. "Wonderful, wonderful, wonderful. Very good. Excellent! What about that 'e'? I'm sorry, what's your name again?"

Tommy seems confounded by her question. He looks around the class like he's hoping one of us will answer for him. Is he bothered that she doesn't know his name, or is he confused because he knows he never gave it to her in the first place? So why would she ask for it "again"? I can tell that Miss Angel is just covering. She doesn't want to admit that she doesn't know Tommy's name, so she's pretending she momentarily forgot. She's assuming Tommy will believe her when she says he told her his name before. Because she's an adult. And the teacher. Clever, clever, Miss Angel!

"Tommy," Tommy finally says.

"Tommy what?'

"Washam."

"Washam?"

"Yes." He almost says it like a question. Poor Tommy. You can't help but like him; he's so goofy and kind. But I also feel bad for him: the weird hair pattern on the top of his head, his slow way of talking that makes it sound like he has a speech impediment, the ditzy way he acts. I'm proud of him for jumping in with an answer.

"Okay, Tommy," Miss Angel says. "Now what about that second 'e'? You mean the one here, at the beginning of *etudiant*. Right?" She points to the letter.

Tommy looks at it, thinks. He nods.

"And what kind of letter is 'e'?"

Now Tommy looks worried. His eyebrows bunch up; his nose curls. "A small one?"

Miss Angel is disappointed. "No. I mean, yes it's a small 'e.' But that's not what I mean. Besides that, what kind of letter is an 'e'?"

Tommy squints. I see Miss Angel realize that she has to stop relying on him for answers. Poor Tommy. "All right, everyone, anyone," Miss Angel says, "tell me. All the letters of the alphabet fall into two broad categories, right? What are those categories?"

Now I'm even more confused. Two categories? Where is Miss Angel going with this? Ugly letters and pretty letters? Mean letters and sweet letters? K, for instance, is definitely a mean—and ugly—letter. F, on the other way, always strikes me as sweet and broad, like summer.

"Ladies and gentlemen," Mrs. Mason says from her desk at the side of the room, obviously embarrassed, "you learned this in first grade." Mostly Mrs. Mason stays quiet when Miss Angel teaches us, but apparently this demonstration of our dumbness can't go unanswered. Mrs. Mason gives us a hint: "Consonants and . . ."

We shout the answer at once.

"Okay, okay, okay." Miss Angel is moving again, energized. "So 'e' is a vowel, right? *Etudiant* is a word that begins with a vowel! And what do we know about the ends of French words when the next word begins with a vowel?" Miss Angel really believes one of us will be able to supply the correct answer. She waits for several seconds, but it's useless. We don't understand. We don't know what she's talking about. Her face falls. "We talked about this last week." *Maybe you talked about it*, I think.

On the other side of the room, from a desk near the front, Imani Frazier raises her hand. She is brown-skinned, with a sweet face and a nice, strong nose. I've always liked Imani, even though we're not friends. Secretly, I've always wished I could be her. Imani is probably the smartest kid in class, although I don't know if anybody realizes it. I don't know if Mrs. Mason does.

"I think," Imani says, "that when a vowel starts a word you combine that word with the word before it."

Miss Angel rushes over to Imani, as if she might hug her. As if she might start to cry. "That's right! That's right! And we call that *liaison*, remember? It's very important! When a word ends on a constant sound—like 's'—and the next word begins with a vowel sound—like 'e'—you run those sounds together. Normally, in French the consonant sounds on the end of the word are not pronounced. But with liaison, they are! So in this case"—she goes back to the whiteboard—"we don't say 'Juh swee etoodeeahn,' but 'Juh sweeze etoodeeahn.' Right? You have to really drag out that *eeze* sound."

"That's fucked up," Kyle Thompson says. He sits right behind me. I'm not sure, but I think Miss Angel heard him. She kind of jumped when he said it. *You can't let him say that*, I think at her. *You have to crush him*. I so wish she would crush him. Or at least correct him. *Explain why it's not fucked up. Embarrass him*. I don't want a jerk like Kyle Thompson thinking he can run the class. That will only make these lessons take longer.

But Miss Angel doesn't crush him. More like she gives up. "Okay, let's go over some more basic stuff, not so tricky as liaison." She scribbles a list of words: *je*, *tu*, *il*, *elle*, *nous*, *vous*, *ils*, *elles*. They're all pronouns, she says. Then she asks us what each word means. This goes smoothly enough. But for some reason when she gets to *nous*, she drifts off on one of her tangents. I feel even more sorry for her then. Miss Angel knows so much French; she loves the French language so much; there is so much she wants to tell us about it; but the bottom line is our class doesn't care. It's hard to make seventh graders care. "*Nous* means 'we.' *Nous allons au parc*. 'We are going to the park.' Simple enough. What's interesting though is when you get to something called 'reciprocal' verbs, which tell us what we're doing with each other or to each other, and then you get a funny-sounding construction that I love: *nous nous*. Isn't that fun? Such as, *Nous nous retrouvons*. 'We are meeting each other.'"

Kyle grunts. "Don't," I say over my shoulder. "I mean it." He makes a disappointed sound, as if I'd just stabbed him.

"Jeannine," Mrs. Mason says, "is something wrong?"

Ouch. That's embarrassing. It's always shameful to be called out. "No, Mrs. Mason. I'm sorry." I look at Miss Angel. "I'm sorry," I say.

Miss Angel seems pleasantly shocked that anyone would apologize to her. "It's okay," she says. She smiles. Wow, when she stops being hysterical about French and just smiles, she seems like a regular person. An attractive person even. Someone you might like to know.

Time's up, and recess beckons. When we stand up to go out, I see Kyle staring at me. Hard. "Suck up," he says.

"Shut up," I say. "You're an idiot."

Kyle snares my upper arm. He pinches it. It feels like a wasp sting. I yank my arm out of his grasp. "You want to not go outside?" I say. "All I have to do is tell Mrs. Mason."

He sneers. "Yeah, right," he says, but he doesn't test it. He knows I'm serious.

"I think we need to discuss this outside," I say. "I don't want you getting me in trouble." Kyle grunts, which I hope means he's willing to talk to me. But as soon as we go through the double doors that open on to the playground, Kyle starts running toward the grassy stretch at the far end where kids play soccer. Probably he wants to find a sixth graders' game in order to break it up. Because that's just how Kyle is.

I shrug it off and start toward the climbing equipment. It's overrun with fifth graders. The little bugs. I look to see if any of my friends in other classes are out yet, but so far ours is the only seventh grade class. I'm moving slowly today; I'm not into my usual rhythm. I don't know if there were anybody watching me if they could tell, but I just feel slow. I guess I'm still thinking about French class, how sad the teacher is, how we're not really helping—but why should they expect us to help her when we don't have to, and when it's so hard for us to understand it? Not that I don't like Miss Angel. I just feel bad for her. And I keep thinking about how young she looks.

I give up on the jungle gym and try the tetherball court instead. Maybe if I just start hitting, someone will come over and want to play me. For some reason I really feel in the mood to hit today. But I can't because Janeka Johnson and Shaundra Baker are standing in the middle of the court, doing nothing but messing with each other. I don't have anything against either of them, but this is annoying. I tell them to move, and they do—but not without dawdling about it. I'm finally able to start hitting, but then I see that MacKenzie's class has come out. At last! I start to run to her, but then I see someone *is* watching me. A man. Not a teenager man or a college student man, but an actual man. He isn't just staring at the group of us but at me in particular, as if he has a message for me. Then I see that Assistant Principal Mauldin is standing next to him. She's looking at me too. What is it? What's wrong? Is something wrong? I start in their direction. I better ask him what he wants to tell me.

4

When Angel got back to her apartment, she collapsed on
the couch and just sagged. Arm over her face, mouth open
in an unexpressed moan, her closed eyes tormented by
silver images of how she must come across to a room full
of dumbfounded, resentful twelve-year-olds. This sucked.
This sucked. This whole thing sucked. If it weren't 11:30 in
the morning, and if she didn't have a class at 3:00, she would
have considered getting drunk. She was already considering
quitting college. Or changing majors. At the moment, it
seemed that the smartest thing she could possibly do was
get plastic surgery and escape to the west coast, where she
could spend the rest of her life living under an assumed
identity. No one would ever recognize her as the woman who
had tried to teach French to seventh graders. Tried to get
them excited about it.

How could she possibly be so bad at this? Even more
to the point, how could she have ever thought she would be
good at it? The whole time she was up there she heard herself
and watched herself: behaving like the worst kind of spaz

teacher, the kind the kids laughed at the moment her back was turned—and why shouldn't they? They couldn't give one right answer without her jumping up and down and shouting like they'd just cured cancer. God, she was such a dork. Why should anyone care about anything she said, especially when she didn't even see them but one hour a week?

Who thought this plan was a good idea in the first place? And how were they supposed to learn French? She knew the answers to these questions. The person who had thought it was a good idea was herself. Anxious for more teaching experience, worried about how the world of teaching middle schoolers had changed since she had walked among them, worried lest she be setting herself up for a failure of titanic proportions, Angel had shared these fears with her French advisor and teacher, Dr. Rene Hurd. Dr. Hurd had only nodded at the time, only barely, and with a clinical coldness in her eye, as if it was hard for her to fathom that anyone would care to teach anything to that age group, much less a foreign language.

"What do you have in mind?" Dr. Hurd had asked.

"I don't know. I don't know," Angel had sputtered, and in groping after an answer the idea of teaching school kids on a volunteer basis for an hour a week had slipped out. It had just been an idea, just an example of what she meant. She hadn't actually submitted it to Dr. Hurd as a formal proposal. And besides, Dr. Hurd would not be the one to supervise such a plan; that would have to be her minor advisor: Dr. Caroline Fitch, in the College of Education. Rene Hurd was all about getting her students to fluency status and then helping them find positions in the Francophone world. She wrote letters of recommendation for Fulbright grants and for graduate study and for jobs with multinational corporations with offices in

Paris and Brussels and Montreal. She did not concern herself with schoolchildren in Caddo, Arkansas.

"I'll see what I can do," Rene Hurd said and stared at Angel with a directness that told her Dr. Hurd was telling the truth. "Wait for a message from me." As it turned out, Rene Hurd was close friends, quite close, with Gloriana Nixon, principal of Virginia McKinley Middle School. Even more remarkable, Ms. Nixon had just been saying to her staff that she wished there was a way to introduce the children to a foreign language in an organized but non-threatening way. Which more or less meant a way that didn't put them at risk for missing state-required time for math or gym or reading. Also, a way that would not cost the school a dime.

Rene Hurd put forward Angel's idea exactly how she had formed it: an hour a week with one classroom of kids. No homework. Just teaching. An hour of French fun. A few days later, Rene Hurd met with Angel in her office and outlined the agreement reached between her and Ms. Nixon and Theresa Mason, one of the veteran teachers at Virginia McKinley: Wednesday mornings, 10:05-10:50, no textbooks, no quizzes, no homework, just an introduction to the bare essentials of a foreign language. As entertaining as possible, but no French films and no French websites. Angel had laughed at the latter stipulations. What did they think she was trying to do? Make them existentialists?

"They'd rather it be Spanish," was Rene Hurd's only reply. "For obvious reasons. But no one in Spanish approached them. I did."

Angel nodded slowly, and only then did it begin to occur to her the breadth of her new audience's ignorance of all things French.

"Maybe it's better this way, though," Rene Hurd said. "If you were teaching Spanish, they might be afraid you would bring in the roofer or the lawn guy for spicy show and tell."

Angel's mouth dropped open.

"I was being funny," Rene Hurd said.

"Oh," Angel said and tried to giggle.

After that, Angel hadn't had a single other conversation with Rene Hurd, at least not about teaching. She soldiered off every Wednesday morning determined to do more than just the basics—despite the agreement they'd reached with Principal Nixon; no, she would really show these kids the beauty of the French language: its musicality, its innate logic, its misunderstood flexibility. She was determined to turn at least one of those kids into a Francophile, to put the dream of majoring in French and traveling the world in their tiny Arkansawyer heads. The first class had gone very well, mainly because Angel had splurged on a supply of fresh croissants from Primordial Bakery. The kids smiled and ate and ate and smiled and life seemed perfectly French until Mrs. Mason informed her that under current guidelines teachers weren't allowed to bring food to class, unless such food was individually wrapped. "Just this once," Mrs. Mason said with a patient smile. "But no more."

"I'm sorry. Why didn't you tell me?" Angel sputtered.

"Because I wanted one of those croissants. They're killer." Mrs. Mason winked, picked the last one out of the bag and wobbled back to her desk. Everything after that had gone bad, worse than useless, had made Angel doubt her value as a human being. The kids were so clearly bored, so not paying attention. Strangely, when she stopped talking about the language itself and tried to entertain them with news of French pop stars and tennis players and fashion movements, their eyes only glazed over more. *What do you want?* she felt like screaming. *How can I get you to care?* She had imagined creating a roomful of France lovers and was closer to generating the opposite: kids for whom the worst possible vacation idea was anywhere within 4000 miles and a few *nous* of Paris.

She could only languish for so long on the couch. Her roommate would be back at any time—she should have been back already—and probably with her boyfriend Jess, he of the nose ring and ear tattoo and Tourette's-like grunts. He was extremely intelligent—a mathematics major—but also extremely uncomfortable around most people. She suspected the ring and tattoos were his way not of consciously looking better but of consciously driving onlookers away, so he would be spared even the slightest chance of having to talk with them.

Angel wasn't sure how Jess hooked up with her roommate—a thoroughly southern, heavy-lidded, big-shouldered, and old-looking girl named Shelby. They'd been dating for as long as she'd known Shelby—just over a year—and neither member of the pair was the sort to reminisce; or say much of anything, for that matter. Their evenings together consisted of staring wordlessly at Netflix documentaries for two hours and then retreating to Shelby's room for what sounded like brutal, even painful, sex. Weirdest of all is that following sex neither one ever went to the bathroom to wash up. That, for Angel, was completely unfathomable. Did they clean each other, like cats? Nor did she ever hear conversation or giggles or disagreements. Neither came out of the room for a postcoital glass of water or a cup of tea or a cold beer. (Well, neither one ever drank alcohol, actually.) It was as if the sex—started apparently with no warm-up conversation—was so brutal they knocked each other unconscious. This was only a guess, and Angel would never know. Because she certainly had no intention of opening the door to Shelby's bedroom to check on them. Talk about your horrors.

Maybe, she thought, she should talk to Dr. Hurd. She could talk to Dr. Fitch, but she knew that the woman—all excess warmth and toothy smiles and ringleted blonde permanent—would simply tell her to buck up and keep going, that she was probably reaching these kids in ways she didn't recognize, that the atmosphere in the classroom was bound to change any week, and that by the end of the semester she would be so glad she'd tried the experiment. Wrong on all counts. There seemed no life challenge that Dr. Caroline Fitch had not met and tackled with a grin, a wink, a laugh, and a new bra. On the other hand, Dr. Hurd—about the most phlegmatic instructor she'd ever known—would better understand her hurt and self-hatred and listlessness. Most of all, Dr. Hurd would understand the heart of Angel's pain: that she was failing the French language; that she was not acting as its fair representative; that this most mellifluous of human tongues—which from its sound alone should have ruined them for any other—was stirring nothing in their ears and in their hearts. They had rejected it. They had declared it stupid. They had decided it was beneath them. (Oh yes, she had heard that moronic boy's comment that French was "fucked up.") This was precisely the reverse of what foreign language instruction was supposed to accomplish.

She surged to the front door. Just as she pulled it open, she saw Shelby, one hand extended toward the knob. Behind her, two inches shorter, stood Jess, his eyes dim with shyness and resentment.

"Oh," Shelby said. "What are you doing here? Don't you have class?"

"A: I'm not here, I'm leaving; and B: I never have class at this time. You should know that by now."

Shelby's face froze; the skin about her eyes stiffened. "Not really," the girl said. "I have too much going on to memorize other people's schedules."

Angel thought she recognized a grin on Jess's face: some private satisfaction that came at her expense. When she tried to meet his eye, however, he looked away and even leaned a perceptible half-inch or so to his left, so that his head nearly disappeared behind Shelby's mountainous mess of disordered brown hair.

"I'm going out," Angel said and moved past them. "I don't know when I'll be back." It occurred to her that she had not brought any of the books or notes she would need for her 3:00 class: French Civilization, with Dr. Stephen Shea, chair of the Modern Languages department. She thought about going back to get them but decided against it. She wasn't sure she was up for hearing about French civilization today. She was having enough of a time with her own.

When she tapped on Rene Hurd's door, she heard nothing from inside. She checked the time on her cell phone—1:23—and the office hours posted on a little cork board attached to the wall. Maybe Dr. Hurd was still in class. No: classes at 9:00 and 11:00 on Wednesdays. Office hours from 1-2. Where was she? Angel knocked again, and again hearing nothing she lowered her head with a sigh. She spied on the floor an upside-down sticky note: golden yellow, its gluey edge brittled with dust. Angel picked it up, turned it over. She saw, penned in Dr. Hurd's careful cursive hand, *Office hours cancelled, Wednesday Feb. 19.* Defeated, Angel collapsed on the padded chair outside Hurd's door and began to sob.

She had a sense of two or three bodies passing nearby. Otherwise, time and sense were lost to her until she felt a hand pressing gently on the top of her head. Once, twice, then the pressure was gone. She opened her eyes to see Rene Hurd staring down at her: a quizzical frown on her face, a look almost of fear in her strict brown eyes. It occurred to Angel suddenly that the square-faced, no-nonsense, heavy-browed fifty-year-old might be beautiful. You might call her that. Someone might. The way some old Russian peasant woman—with her big nose and eagle eyes and a face scrawled with crossing patterns of wrinkles—might be called austerely handsome. Rene Hurd had a peasant's tough beauty, visible only in certain conditions, certainly not when she was teaching—for she was quite a demanding teacher—but when she looked at you with fear and sadness and befuddlement.

"Dr. Hurd," Angel said with astonishment. She wondered if this Rene Hurd was even real; perhaps she had conjured her out of simple longing. "What are you doing here?"

The woman's look changed to something more characteristic: intelligence with a pronounced undercurrent of irony. "Why shouldn't I be here?"

"Your note. It fell on the floor. It said you had left." Only after she'd gotten the words out did Angel realize that she was wrong; that's not what the note said.

"No, I never left," Hurd said.

"I thought you had."

"Do you want to come in?"

"Very much."

Hurd opened her door with a thick, bronze-colored university key, part of a small collection of keys bound by a simple metal ring that she held in one hand. In the other was a leather-bound portfolio case. Inside, she gestured Angel to the chair in front of her desk. She closed the door behind them.

After she sat behind her desk, Hurd said, "Why are you crying?"

Angel started to smile, some self-effacing, dismissive expression, but she couldn't pull it off. The smile only halfway insinuated itself before her eyes began to water and her lips tremble. "Because I'm terrible. I don't know what I'm doing."

Hurd studied her for a moment with visible concern. "This is in regards to the classes you need for graduation?"

Angel had to laugh. "No, no, no. My classes are fine. *My* classes." Hurd was visibly relieved—given that she was Angel's advisor and they had carefully drawn up a graduation plan several months ago—but also newly confused. "It's these kids. I'm making them hate French. I'm terrible at teaching it."

Hurd leaned back in her chair and smiled. She scratched the side of her cheek slowly with one hand. "Is that so?"

"I'm afraid it really is so. Really. It's like everything I do to try to get them to marvel at French only makes them hate it worse. I can't even bring in croissants because that's food, and food is restricted, so instead of the food-bringing girl I'm this manic French-loving monster-girl, who can't stop talking. I can't stop talking because I know when I stop talking there will be nothing but silence in the room—and I just can't take that."

"Why?"

"Because it's a rebuke. The worst. Like not just French isn't worth listening to, but I'm not worth listening to. I'm not worth helping out. I'm not worth trying to give an answer to."

Hurd nodded once.

"The thing is, I don't care if they give a completely wrong answer. I'd love a wrong answer. I just hate to see them sit there and stare at me, bored and angry."

Hurd turned her head slightly. "Would you like some coffee?"

"Coffee?"

Hurd pointed behind Angel. Angel remembered that in the back corner of her office was a coffee table and a black Gevalia machine. Angel shook her head.

"Kleenex?"

Angel smiled. "Do you have any?"

Hurd opened one of her drawers. "I thought I had some left over from allergy season last fall. Ah." She extracted a wrapped travel pack of tissues and handed them across the desk. "You can keep it."

Angel nodded, murmured thanks, and wondered what in the world she really had expected Dr. Hurd to do. She was just sitting here, whining, taking up the woman's Kleenex and her time. But even so, she had no better plan. She had nowhere else to go. She wiped her eyes. She blew her nose.

"You should take a linguistics course," Hurd said. Angel met her eye. Yes, apparently, this non sequitur was a serious comment.

"I don't understand."

"Have you?"

"No."

"You should."

"Why?"

"Because then you would understand their hatred."

"I understand it already."

"No, you only think you do. You're just the conduit, Angel. You're revealing to them what they didn't know about themselves—and still don't know, even if it utterly governs them."

"I don't understand."

"I know." Then Rene Hurd did something astonishing. She leaned across the desk and took Angel's hand. Angel almost yanked her hand back—a compulsive sudden recoiling such as one does before a cockroach—but stopped herself. She forced herself not to react to Rene Hurd's dry, scratchy touch. "No language in the world is any harder than another, any better or worse, any more or less difficult to learn—if you're a native speaker. The native speaker picks up his language effortlessly, no matter what the language is. Do you believe that?"

"Yes," Angel said slowly. She'd never thought of it, but it seemed true now that Dr. Hurd said so. Still, she wished the woman would let go of her hand.

"The reason for this is that the language we are born into helps to shape our brains. It literally carves tunnels into the brain. And the brain thus understands the world according to where the tunnels are and how long they are."

"You mean what language we learn determines how we think?"

"Yes. Exactly." Rene Hurd seemed pleasantly surprised. And then she finally released Angel's hand. "But it also means that, after a remarkably short span of time, every person's brain gets set up for the quick processing of one particular language. This is the efficiency of nature at work. Since most of us only need one language to survive, it makes sense for nature to privilege that one language, to serve its needs, to do everything it can to help us pick up and use that language as expertly as possible. Yes?"

"Sure."

"But what this means is that when you try to learn another language, with different grammatical constructions and pronunciations and word order and gender markers—all of that—you are literally handicapped by nature. Nature doesn't want you to learn that other language; it wants you to learn yours better."

The woman sat back, contented, brimming with a satisfaction that almost made her flush. Clearly, she'd said what she'd said and expected Angel to understand the implications. But Angel didn't.

"You're saying I should stop trying to teach the kids French because their brains won't let them learn it."

The satisfaction on Hurd's face immediately became something else. Angel saw a spot of red in those dark eyes. She saw hardening around her brow. "No, that's not what I'm trying to say. If I believe that why would I have the job I do? If you think it's hard to get middle schoolers interested in French, imagine how hard it is to do that for college students who have been walking around for another six or seven years with their brains calcifying around English." She calmed herself, leaned forward. Again, she took Angel's hand. "All I'm saying is that the resistance the children are giving you has nothing to do with you. It's only on account of their brain chemistry, and you can't be faulted for that."

While it was nice of Dr. Hurd to say this, and while it sounded perfectly reasonable, Angel also knew it was wrong. Or incomplete. Because she knew her problems also had something to do with her. She knew the kids didn't like her.

Her specifically. Worse than that: to them, she was a joke. She couldn't imagine that Dr. Hurd had ever been a joke to her students. No matter how much they hated French.

Dr. Hurd released Angel's hand a second time. Again, she leaned back. Angel felt dry now. Totally dry and very tired. And stupid. "Thanks, Dr. Hurd. That makes a lot of sense."

Hurd nodded.

"Maybe," Angel continued, "I just don't like children. Maybe secretly I despise them, and the kids are picking up on that."

Hurd chuckled; she shook her head. "I have absolutely no comment on that comment. I don't know if you despise children or not."

"I didn't think I did. But now I wonder. I really wonder." After all, Angel thought, how come she wanted no part of motherhood until she was thirty? (She'd said that over Christmas break to at least two friends.) How come she wasn't in a rush to get married? How come she didn't even care that she wasn't dating at the moment? Why had she told herself that not dating might be better right now while she was rushing to finish her degree? Was that really true? Didn't plenty of people who graduated on time have boyfriends and girlfriends? Maybe the real reason she wanted no boyfriend was that she wanted to avoid even the slightest possibility of becoming a mother, because maybe to her that would be the worst fate of all. God, is that how she felt? And what did that mean for how she saw her own mother?

Lost in ruminations, she did not realize Hurd had stood up and was coming around the desk. The doctor stopped, said something: "I think you need to just think about what I said. Don't worry about yourself. Just do the job. If it makes you feel any better, in this country almost no one likes French. Or

France. Or Frenchmen. We've all been conned by pro-British propaganda. We've inherited a prejudice that isn't even ours."

Angel looked up at her. "I don't know what to say about that."

Hurd smiled. Okay, Angel thought, she wants me to go. She's waiting for me to leave.

"Do you want me to call Gloriana and cancel the experiment?"

That was the last thing Angel thought she would say—and it annoyed her a little.

"No, not yet. For now, I'll keep going."

Hurd nodded. "I was hoping you'd say that."

In the silence that followed, Angel stood. She was shocked when Hurd—stiff, fifty-something Rene Hurd of the peasant type of beauty—hugged her. "See it through," Hurd whispered. "It's the only way it will get better. If you quit now, it will always be bad." She squeezed Angel once warmly and then let her go. Angel felt herself blushing—and scared—and giddy—and embarrassed—and grateful. She turned and moved quickly for the door.

"Let me know what happens," Hurd said behind her.

She supposed the responsible thing to do would be to walk back to her apartment and gather everything she needed for French Civilization—interrupting Shelby and Jess as required—but she just could not bring herself to do that. It had been too hard a day already. Sitting through another French class—this time from the student side, watching a veteran professor perform with ease—might only depress her. Besides, something, something else, needed doing. Something wasn't finished. Something needed completion, and that meant action by her. What the nagging something was, she couldn't be sure. But if she went to French Civ. she was certain she would miss it. What then?

Instead of homeward, she took a detour to the Psychology building because there was a Starbucks on the first floor and it made sense to pick herself up with coffee—or anything warm—while she waited for the revelation of what the something was she needed to do, to fix, to heal. *Yourself*, she thought. Well, yes, but she already knew that. She ordered the biggest mocha possible—the cup was twice the length of her hand—and took a remote seat in the corner of the shop, two seats away from the nearest person but with a view of the door. Perhaps what she was supposed to do would walk in and announce itself. It was almost exciting, this distraction—almost curative—certainly it got her outside of herself, which these days was always a relief. And the mocha, she decided, might actually be more useful than a whiskey. Warmer. More subtly exhilarating, whereas whiskey merely made her stupid. Useful for certain occasions, but not when she needed to make decisions.

It was not the busiest hour at Starbucks. For a chunk of the population, 2:00 classes were well underway; meanwhile, with the afternoon encroaching across campus, non-academic duties beckoned to everyone else. Even so, at least five people she knew wandered through. A girl from her dorm Freshmen year; a brusque and nasally guy in her Modern European Cinema class; a girl—a junior, one year behind Angel—from the French club; a guy who worked at the gym and who, when for a period last semester she had decided to be vigilant about exercise, had seemed to go out of his way to talk to her, so much so she might have thought he was hitting on her, except that she was certain in her gut he was gay; and her lab partner from last semester's biology class, the one general education requirement he had delayed taking until she couldn't delay it any longer.

For the entire semester, the girl, even though she was a sophomore, had acted like she didn't trust Angel. She had insisted on running their experiments her way. If not for her complete indifference, Angel would have been offended, but instead she decided to let the girl—with a tense low brow, brown-black eyes, and an agitated tick behind her tongue whenever she spoke—have her way. Angel's revenge came at semester grade time. She pulled out a B, a grade she was proud of. Whereas ticky, condescending Super Sophomore earned a C. Angel had never been competitive about grades, but this was the one time in her life when she relished the victory. She would not have even known about it except that the girl texted her as soon as grades were posted, shouting about the dishonest professor, threatening action, and demanding to know if Angel had also received a C. Angel had texted back, in the sweetest tone possible: *My grade is fair. Prof is fair. Like him. Got a B.* That was all that needed saying. Now she hid behind her huge cup of mocha until Super Sophomore left the shop. In fact, she hid from all these people, and fortunately none of them seemed to notice her. Okay, so they weren't it. None of them. Of that she was sure. And she did not want any distractions.

By 2:46 her mocha was all but gone, with the dregs growing cold. No revelation had occurred. There wasn't even anything meaningful in the lyrics of any of the songs that were playing. She felt thoroughly let down and still nagged at by something. When she heard a certain voice at the counter ordering a double Espresso Macchiato she knew she had to go. It was Jacob, her history major boyfriend from junior year.

He was the only person she knew who ever asked for a double Espresso anything. Besides, she knew his voice; she knew it like she knew her brother's: that warbling tone that seemed to be emitting a mere idea, a possibly cock-eyed premise for philosophical inspection, when in fact Jacob always felt absolutely sure about everything. Everything. His certainty astounded her. Where in the world did he get such a global sense of confidence? Had he spent his whole grade school and high school career among mentally handicapped kids, so that now he took it for granted that he was the only one who ever had a worthwhile answer to anything—from seasoning your food to sexual positions? It took her quite a while to understand this about Jacob, but when she finally did she realized she had to quit the relationship. She couldn't spend the rest of her life merely going along with whatever he said.

She had no time to deal with Jacob's certainty now. She had to find out what was nagging at her. If she stayed, he would see her. She couldn't hide from him. His eye was too quick and too demanding, his intelligence too restless. He had radar for when she was in a room. He would spot her and then sit with her and then ask her to explain herself, although those were not the words he would use; he would say something in his speculative warble that might sound innocuous—or even kind—to an unwitting passerby but really meant *explain yourself*.

She surged from her spot in the corner to the door: a direct, narrow line. She didn't hesitate, didn't look back. When she reached the big glass door she pushed it open. Not until it was almost closed, and she was moving along the sidewalk, did she hear a noise from inside that might have been Jacob. It didn't matter. She kept walking. In a few minutes, she reached the end of the academic part of campus.

She crossed Spratt Street and found herself in the parking lot of North University Village, the complex where she lived. She remembered Shelby and Jess. Would they be done yet? Done what exactly? It was hard to guess. She might walk into one of their barking, tortured sex sessions—or they might be doing homework.

She checked the time: 2:55. She could get her books and still make it to French Civ. No, she wasn't going to do that. Despite Jacob, despite Shelby, despite Jess, the nagging was still there. She hadn't fixed it yet. She saw her own car—a 2003 gray Impala that her dad had forced on her—only ten yards from where she was standing. She didn't remember parking it there. Then again, she was so dazed with humiliation after that class at Virginia McKinley that she didn't know what she was doing. Suddenly, her keys were in her hand. Had they been there all afternoon, even at Starbucks? She couldn't remember. Had she slipped them in the pocket of her jeans like a man would? She didn't remember doing that either.

Oh well. It seemed to be a signal. Maybe the one she was waiting for. She opened the driver's side door and slipped in behind the wheel. She turned the engine on. She had to admit she liked this car, as boring and as ugly as it was. Even though it was eleven years old. It made her feel safe. It made her feel loved. *Maybe*, she thought, *I should just take a nap in the front seat.* But, no, she was too juiced by the extra-large mocha for a nap. She put the car in D and drove out of the parking lot. At the first traffic light she turned left, putting her on Lindenhurst, and headed north. She hadn't turned with any conscious thought or intention, but it took only seconds for her to realize that she was driving toward Virginia McKinley Middle School.

Okay, she thought. *Okay. So that's what I'll do.*

A mile and a half and six traffic lights up Lindenhurst, there it was: on the left, a dopey, flat-roofed, red brick structure that looked like it might have been built eighty years ago. Actually, Angel remembered, it was. Since she'd begun teaching at McKinley she'd heard its history recounted with disappointment by more than one teacher and office staffer.

For most of its life McKinley had been an elementary school—it certainly looked like one—but with the surging population of Caddo, the town's school board had been forced to drastically reorganize the system two years earlier. Until funds could be secured for the big, shiny, respectable new building they had planned, McKinley had been temporarily converted into a building for fifth, sixth, and seventh graders. This came with a host of attendant problems that the teachers never let her forget. The classrooms were too small. They barely could contain the desks needed and, worse, they trapped the kids' atrocious, prepubescent smells. The bathroom fixtures were the wrong size, leading to disgusting messes. The computer lab was a joke, and the playground equipment had not been entirely replaced. Mostly, but not entirely. The old metal jungle gym and a wooden structure that looked like a fort remained.

Angel had asked the school's secretary if the board intended to replace the equipment all over again when McKinley was converted back to an elementary school. After all, what else could they do?

"Oh," the woman said, staring off distantly, as if the question had never occurred to her. "I don't think so."

"I mean," Angel had clarified, "did they maybe hold on to the old equipment, store it somewhere?"

"Oh no," the woman swore confidently, her eyes wide, her big head wagging back and forth. "That stuff they junked, thank God." Then she laughed.

Despite the griping, all at the school seemed resigned to toughing it out there until sanity prevailed and these big-boned, broad-shouldered, hairy-armpitted youngsters could be shipped off to where they really belonged. Presently, cars were parked every which way near the front of the school: on the righthand shoulder of Lindenhurst, along the side streets, and in a snaking line that went from Lindenhurst (coming the other way) through the half-circle in front of the school. Parents eager to pick up their kids. Parents who acted as if they needed to be there the second their child emerged from their classroom or else risk unspecified mental trauma. She'd always been a bus rider herself, back in middle school. Not that she enjoyed it. Not that she didn't envy the kids whose parents came in their Lincolns and Buicks and Toyotas to fetch her classmates. But at times, such as during traffic jams like this one, the fussy need to fetch one's child in a private car seemed excessive.

She pulled onto the shoulder and just watched. No point in trying to enter the school. It was about to let out. And, besides, what would she do? Who would she talk to? She watched as teachers on the front side of the building opened their classroom doors and released students to their parents standing on the grass. She saw the automatic, relieved smiles of the parents—*finally you're done*, the smiles said, *finally we're together again*; she saw the coy but appreciative looks on the faces of the kids, and she felt surprisingly moved. These were all such good people. Such good, ordinary people. Her eyes watered. She felt a pang of guilt.

And I am the one commissioned to teach their children.

But this pang didn't last long, not like in the morning. Because she also realized, like a revelation—so maybe this was it, this was the something she needed—that parents this good and this ordinary would forgive her. So too would their children. They would not expect too much from her; they would not expect what she couldn't deliver. They would be happy with what she could give their children, because it was more, after all, than nothing. And nothing was what foreign language instruction amounted to at Virginia McKinley Middle School. They would forgive her and be kind to her and tell her—even at the cost of lying—how much their children had learned from her. These good, ordinary people. She teared up at the thought of it, but these were happy tears for once. Healing tears. Tears that brought peace. Suddenly she began to chuckle. She realized how she could go on. She realized she would go on. And by the end of the semester, just like Rene Hurd suggested, she would feel better for having done so.

When the tears were finished and the new wash of peace almost worked itself through her, she looked again at the parents on the grass, fewer now. One man, she noticed, had a Pomeranian with him, on a leash. A very cute dog: orange and white. The man had not paid for the dog to be groomed or styled, so it had that naturally manic Pomeranian hair: shocked as a lead singer in an 80s metal band. Angel guessed that his son or daughter must really love that dog. The man stood rod straight, several yards back on the grass, not chatting with any of the other parents. The Pomeranian, meanwhile, aggressively sniffed the ground, especially the ground beneath a thick old oak, a few feet or so to the man's left. It occurred to her that the dog looked a little thin, even for a Pomeranian, even with its hair. She glanced again at the building. She saw which room it was the man was facing with his strict, set manner. Why, that was her classroom.

A girl emerged, one with extremely yellow-blonde hair, a long blue winter coat, and a quietly cocky expression on her face. She knew that girl, Angel realized. That girl was one of her students, although for the life of her she could not have said the girl's name. Memorizing names was impossible when you only saw the kids once a week. This girl was the smart one, the one who was always silent during class, but at the same time she seemed to be paying attention. Angel was sure the girl knew more than she was letting on. She sat in front of the rude kid. The one who said *fucked up*.

Now the girl eyed the man with the dog speculatively, as if not quite sure why he was there, as if this was not the normal protocol. *Maybe her dad's usually at work. Maybe this is the first time all year he has come to get her.* A last-minute emergency with the mom? A broken home, with parents sharing duties? Maybe it was as simple as that. Then Angel saw the girl smile smartly and say something to the man, as if she'd gotten the best of him. He smiled back. The first actual expression Angel had seen him offer. The girl said something else. Then the man turned and the two of them began to proceed across the grass, dog in tow. They hadn't hugged and they weren't holding hands or touching shoulders—in fact there was a good five inches between them—but they were still talking: heads down, quiet mutters.

Something about the man's features was different. Not alarming. Just different. But it was hard to tell with his head down and passing through the shade provided by the oak. Angel decided she had been wrong. The man might be stoic, and his behavior with his daughter awkward, but they'd been through this routine before. They were a father and a daughter who did not quite know what to say to each other or how, but together they were meant to be.

At a certain moment, before they'd walked too far, the man lifted his head and glanced Angel's way. Then she saw what was so unusual about him. The left side of his face was drenched in a deep red mark: from his eye socket, down his cheek, over his chin, and even partly down his neck. Probably a birthmark. Perhaps an industrial accident. An old army injury? Might he be getting some kind of disability pay, which made work unnecessary and him able to pick up his daughter?

Why was she speculating about this? She would never know the truth. It took a lot of inner strength for the girl not to react to this mark, to just accept it. But then again, that was what you did—right?—with your parents? They were your parents, for all their physical imperfections and personality defects and bad decisions and inexplicably stupid behaviors. They were your parents. They loved you. So, you accepted them.

5

He still wasn't sure if this would work. Standing on the grass outside her classroom door, Cocteau being the distracting, sniffing busybody he was supposed to, listening to but trying not to listen to the inane chitchat of the other parents— problems with a soccer coach, husbands called out of town to corporate events, gossip about Walmart's plans for a third store in Caddo, reactions to the last *American Idol* episode— Baine could feel his heart pound faster. He didn't want to be this nervous. It might disable him. It might cause him to make a mistake: to forget a necessary fact or to mix up details or to contradict the story he'd already established. He almost had her; he was sure of that. He'd almost convinced her— when he spoke to her briefly during recess—that he knew who she was, that he knew who her parents were; indeed, that he was friends with them. And he had given himself a new name: Jim Hutton. Jim because it was about as common and unnoticeable as you could get, and Hutton because it was the most harmless name his mind could find on short notice. Jim Hutton. Who would have anything to fear from a man named that? His own name—Lawrence Baine—had always struck him as fairly milquetoast, almost to the point of embarrassment, but Jim Hutton was even blander. Jim Hutton. Yes.

As they talked at recess he had seen the veil of doubt and suspicion begin to lift from her; what's more, he saw the pleasure in her at that lifting; the good feeling that comes when you know you can trust someone, you don't have to suspect them. You don't have to carry the burden of hate. He knew all about that burden. He knew how good it would feel for her to throw it off. He'd once thrown it off—only to have it put back again, more indelible than ever.

Now as he stood outside her classroom door on a sunny, late winter day, he felt a chill encroach his body. It wasn't because of the shade from the oak tree just behind him. No, it was the frigid sting of memory, stiffening him, bracing him, icing his spine. Baine, even now, could not believe he did not hesitate longer before saying yes to Murphy. He'd never liked Murphy after all. He didn't like his smell: some cross between a bucket of live worms, a new fart, and an inexpensive cigar. Deep and sharp at the same time. The man—maybe he was thirty-five, maybe younger; maybe much younger—wore mostly white t-shirts and strangely indifferent, inconsistent trousers: baggy gray sweats, coaches shorts, black wool slacks that looked like some old man's church clothes from the 1930s, torn wind pants that might have been plucked from someone's trash. The top of his head was almost bald, but what hair he had was black. Naturally so. He shaved some, but not often enough.

He went to church—Krystal's church, in fact: Agape Pentecostal—but Baine never understood why. Murphy almost never talked about it. And Baine knew that, unlike other churchgoers, the man didn't linger there all Sunday morning and afternoon. He left at 9:00 and returned home less than an hour later, slamming the door of his truck as if with relief. Why go at all? For years, this was simply another one of the mysteries of Murphy. There were so many it didn't seem worth asking him about.

Besides, in general Baine didn't like talking with Murphy. Murphy never met Baine's eye when he talked; instead, he stared off distantly, as if musing about a proposition too deep to utter. He lived on a disability check but was murky about the details: why he needed it, what had happened to initiate it. Baine didn't want to pry as long as his neighbor minded his own business and kept to his own space. He was also worried about what the truth might be when he found it.

In some ways, Murphy had been a good neighbor. Three times he'd lent Baine tools to work on his car and the pipes beneath his garbage disposal. Once he'd actually come over and looked under the sink himself, straining and barking, making a show of how much effort it was costing him but giving Baine useful advice for all of that. He'd clued Baine into neighborhood politics: whom to trust, whom to avoid, whom not to borrow from. In some cases, his opinions were on the mark; in others, deeply unjust, marred by some previous misunderstanding Murphy himself was probably the cause of. He'd brought Baine's trashcan back up the driveway a few times. He kept close watch on Baine's house once when Baine went away for two weeks; and Baine knew that he'd actually done it too, because Murphy was able to report exact car sightings and give exact hours; he could describe so well the different people who knocked on Baine's door that Baine knew exactly who they were.

But even so. Even so. He neither liked nor trusted Murphy. Something was wrong with the man. Something was ... not right. Krystal used to claim that Baine was too cynical and too prissy. That he understood neither her nor his neighbor nor Caddo nor the power of God's spirit. Well, about all that she was certainly proven right, especially the first. The fact that Baine refused to attend Agape Pentecostal was not what finally broke them apart, but it didn't help. And it certainly revealed why they were mismatched. If Baine had not been festering with loneliness when he noticed Krystal working in Lou's Diner one Saturday morning, her wide eyes containing a brightness that suggested she wouldn't rebuke him for a little bit of small talk, he was certain he wouldn't have uttered a word to her.

Krystal assured Baine that Murphy was a good person who'd had some bad things happen to him, just like a lot of people. And God, Krystal claimed, was helping to get him right. Baine, she said, just had to stop assuming the worst. Baine decided to take her word for it, even if he never saw the evidence himself. He'd never gone into Murphy's house and never wanted to. He was afraid for what he might find there. Piles of accumulated garbage with fulminating smells would be the least of it. Baine feared gay porn, or maybe violent straight porn. He feared dead animals and movie star pictures with angry messages scrawled all over them in black Sharpie; mean books with sections circled in testy green ink with notations in the margins: "Yes!" "That's what's wrong with America!" "If this were only possible to do by yourself!" No, he didn't want to go inside that dungeon. And Murphy never invited him.

But somehow—through the pressure of the moment, in the necessity of meeting Krystal where and when she said—he'd relented. He relented when Murphy came over, out of the blue, as if summoned—just when Baine was in the middle of a most pressing panic—and asked if he needed anything. He relented when he explained to Murphy his problem—that he couldn't not attend a critical meeting with his ex-girlfriend, and yet he could not bring his six-year-old daughter to that meeting—and Murphy had immediately offered to watch Paige. Not stay with her exactly, not really babysit her, just turn on the tv and check in on her a few times while he was gone. At that moment, Baine did not feel the usual revulsion, the normal paranoid suspicion he felt toward Murphy, but an actual abiding relief. Relief that he didn't have to doubt Murphy anymore. Relief that he could trust the man and that he could go to the meeting, and that everything would be made well. Relief that life would be easier then; Krystal could stop hounding him and insulting him and badgering him. Trust, he saw, was the only way to safety. To never trust people was to live a life than never got anywhere, because you failed to forge the connections necessary for you to proceed. He understood it all in the moment, and it felt almost blissful.

When she stepped out of the classroom and saw him, her expression froze in place like a monument. Then her lovely blue eyes moved, her mouth stretched wide as if in a wry question.

"I realize I'm not who you were expecting, but they asked me to."

"They?" the girl said.

"Well . . . you know." His heart was pounding worse than ever. He felt sure he would screw this crucial moment up: this earliest part of the gambit in which any wrong information would immediately cancel the tiny belief she might have felt. Maybe if he left some details blank she would fill those blanks in.

Jeannine blinked; her head bowed, as if reminded of a pain she was all too familiar with. "Why?" she finally said.

"An emergency."

He could see the comprehension in her eyes, the acknowledgement. Then the sadness. To Jeannine, an emergency was perfectly plausible. Maybe usual? What she said confirmed this: "Another one of Mom's situations."

"Sorry," Baine offered. "I know I'm no substitute." Pause. *Go for it. Go for it now.* "But at least I'm here."

The girl nodded, slowly. "What is it this time?"

"This time?"

"What's the emergency?"

"I don't actually know. She just said it was bad. To be honest, she sounded kind of embarrassed about it."

Small smile from Jeannine. *Whew.* "I bet she is," she said. Then: "How do you know Mom again?"

"Oh"—well, how did he?—"we met at a party originally." Safe bet. Everyone goes to parties, right? Everyone but him. He could tell from her neutral expression that she believed him. Her mother must be a social woman. "And then I started seeing her around town. We talked. She's an amazing lady." What daughter wouldn't want to hear that?

The girl grinned. Direct hit. "Yeah, that's what everybody says."

"Well, it's true." Baine smiled back: the broadest, faux-friendliest grin he could manufacture. Actually, not so "faux," really. He felt so happy he had guessed right that the smile came almost naturally. Just a little bit more, one detail more. "And it seems true of her daughter as well."

Now the girl laughed. "Oh, shut up," she said. "You don't even know me."

"Not yet, maybe. But we'll have a chance to get to know each other, before your mom shows up."

Tugging on the leash, Baine took a chance and turned toward the street. He took an easy first step, hoping that this casual move would bring on a normal reaction in her: She would follow him. So far, he'd been lucky that neither one of her parents—although it looked like the mom was the one with pick-up duty—had arrived on time. While he'd stood outside her classroom, he'd been furtively watching for someone who looked like an older version of her—a man or a woman—but Baine had seen no one. It was only this fact that gave him the confidence to continue. It would be extraordinarily stupid—to say nothing of dangerous—to approach the girl with one of her parents around. Yes, he'd had his stroke of luck; but there was no reason at all to believe his luck would hold. Luck rarely did. For him, it never did. Baine needed to get the girl away from this school, onto a side street, and then as far from here as possible, as soon as possible.

He felt Jeannine come even with his shoulder. "Does this mean you go to our church? I don't think I've seen you there."

"Uh, no. I don't go to your church."

"Most of Mom's friends are connected with the church. I would think one of them would get me. In fact, that's what happened last year. She asked the church secretary to pick me up."

"Do you like the church secretary?" A smooth question, he thought. He needed to get the conversation away from himself and what he didn't know. He needed to find out what she knew.

Jeannine shrugged. "Oh, you know, she's okay. She's a little weird, actually. Who isn't weird who works at a church?"

Baine wanted to ask her which church, but that would be an idiotic question: death to his cover.

"Oh, I don't know," he mumbled. "I think everyone's a little bit weird." Then he smiled again. It took a bit more work. He didn't check to see if she bought it. They crossed the street—Lindenhurst—and he pulled harder on the leash to make sure Cocteau didn't delay. He would probably have to ditch Cocteau eventually, but he hadn't made up his mind yet as to where. A dog and a kidnapped girl were too much to control at once, but he couldn't deny that he owed Cocteau. The dog had played his part well, even better than Baine had.

They hurried to make it safely across, and then they were. He'd done it. She was out of the immediate school zone. The street they found themselves on—Wilcox—was not particularly large, that was good, but neither was it a skinny, out-of-the-way one. Like most streets bordering Virginia McKinley, Wilcox featured one example after another of run-down, noticeably degraded single-story family dwellings, dating from the 1950s if not earlier. Most didn't look like they'd had any work done on them since that era. Some were brick. Some featured siding. Each had a small front lawn and a miniature backyard, many of which were filled with junked cars or junked bicycles or junked furniture or just junk. Baine passed houses like these so often in his walks with Cocteau that he didn't even see the junk anymore. But now, as he considered how this street looked through Jeannine's eyes, he saw it with painful clarity.

"Where are we going?" she asked, the first note of fear he'd heard from her all day.

"Your mom told me to take you to my house. She's going to meet us there. She said it wouldn't be long."

"Is one of these your house?" Even if he hadn't seen the way her nose pinched with disgust and the way her eyes perceptibly narrowed, he could have read the condescension in her voice.

"No," he answered, happy in fact that this was the truth. His house was not one of these, but his house was close by, only one block further up and two blocks over. More important, his house didn't look anything like these debased husks. The man who had owned his house before Baine bought it was one of those fussy, impeccable types. He'd left the place with virtually nothing to repair. "No, my house is much nicer. My house"—here he hesitated a millisecond before proceeding with the lie—"is on Lake Cedar."

"Lake Cedar? We have to go all the way out there? Why don't you just take me to Mom's office?"

Hmmm. The first complication. He knew she was smart—he could tell just by watching her play—and he knew that when you set out to kidnap a person, any person, complications should be expected. But even so it was disconcerting to have to fend them off so soon in the process.

"Your mother told me to drive you out to the lake. I think she wants to see my house, actually. I've talked to her about it, but she's never been inside."

"My mom doesn't care about lakes. I'm not sure she can even swim. We belong to the pool here in the summertime, and she never ever goes. She just drops me."

"Don't worry," he came back at her, "your mom has no intention of ever swimming in the lake. She just wants to see my house. And here's a secret: most of the people who live on the lake never swim in it either. They just want to look at it. They like the idea of having it. That doesn't mean they're going to do anything with it."

He saw her process this explanation. To his amazement, he also saw her accept it. It was true that he was taking her to the lake. Not because he owned a house there but because he'd rented one, for a month, just to be able to do what he was about to do. He did not want the girl in his actual house. That was too great a risk. Not that he was afraid she would be found there. He was afraid some suggestion of her would. He did not know what the law said about such matters: how much evidence was enough, how much evidence was just shy of enough. He imagined it mattered how good a lawyer you had and whether people liked you; whether they wanted to believe you could have done it. He didn't know if he was liked or not. He tried to wave and nod to people when he was out walking Cocteau. He hoped that amounted to something. But how much he couldn't be sure. And whether it was enough was a completely open question.

He had parked his car not far from where they were at that moment. Only a half block further up Wilcox and a half block to the south—in a different neighborhood from his own. He didn't even want her to see his house, even by accident, even just in driving past it, even if she would never know it was his house because he would say nothing about it. He wanted absolutely no association of her with the building in which he lived.

"Okay, almost there," he said when they'd reached the corner of Wilcox and Yerby.

"Almost where?" Her questioning look contained something new: a meanness. He had to be supremely careful now. Until he had her safely in his car, he had to be so careful.

"My car, silly girl. You didn't think we were going to walk all the way to Lake Cedar, did you?"

"No," she said slowly, with an embarrassed lilt that suggested that was exactly what she had thought.

As the crow flew, Lake Cedar was not all that far from Virginia McKinley: less than six miles. Yet to get there one left Caddo proper and anything associated with it: schools, libraries, fire stations, restaurants, a strip mall, aging but chummy neighborhoods like those around Wilcox Street, the cookie-cutter brick neighborhoods further out that were built in the last fifteen years. The road to the lake was paved but curving and fairly narrow, bordered on both sides by shade trees and the occasional farm. And while people lived on the lake—there was even a homeowners association—the houses were set at wide distances from one another and shrouded by trees. It was all but impossible for any homeowner to see inside another homeowner's house. Most never saw each other except for the monthly association meetings—and it was not at all unusual for a lazy, indifferent, antisocial owner, one who never went to the meetings, to live an invisible life.

When Baine had worked at Entergy both of his bosses had owned houses on Lake Cedar. Several times he'd been invited out, and not infrequently he accepted the invitations. He didn't really like either man, but he was not yet in a strong enough position in the company to risk offending them. As beautiful and secluded a spot as Lake Cedar was, both men did nothing but bitch about the conditions. One complained that only 5% of the homeowners did all the work "keeping this community together"; the other complained that the Homeowners Association was trying to treat the place like a "goddamn commune," with all their meetings, fees, regulations, notices. He hadn't moved out there to associate with people but to get away from them. As uncomfortable as those evenings had been for Baine, it was on account of them that he knew where to go to rent a house for a month.

When he turned onto Yerby and saw his little Rio parked near a mailbox about thirty yards away, he felt a wave of relief. It was going to happen. This was all really going to happen. He hadn't actually expected his car to be gone. Why should it be gone? People parked on these streets all the time—why would his car be gone? It wouldn't be, he knew that, but for some reason when he saw it again Baine felt delicious relief and a new certainty. He could pull this thing off. He was capable of it.

He yanked on Cocteau's leash to fight him away from the stop sign, the bottom of which he was sniffing, his nose as mobile as a squirrel's. "There it is," Baine sang. He was glad he had paid for the car wash and the interior cleaning. The car sparkled like it never did in real life. It sparkled as if it might be five months old instead of five years. He knew how convincing a clean car would be to the girl. Murphy's car had never been clean. Murphy's car was a garbage can on wheels. It was one of the things he most detested about the man—until he found a far darker reason to detest him.

"That yours?" the girl said, as if she couldn't believe it.

"Yes. Why?"

"It's cute."

The humming that had started in his mind when he saw his car became an opera.

"Thank you. Surprised?"

She shrugged. He knew she couldn't say out loud why she had been surprised. Best not to press her now. Maybe later. Indeed, later. He'd make her say it.

"I think I know someone else who has one of these. But hers is black."

"I don't like black. Too depressing, don't you think?"

She shrugged. "Black's okay."

"Too scary."

She looked at him strictly, then laughed. "Maybe if you're three years old."

Baine blushed. Okay, so that tactic—pretending to be so wimpy as to be harmless—wasn't working. Besides, he didn't need to play it anymore. As soon as she was inside the car, the game could be over. One worry: the closer they came to the vehicle, the slower Jeannine walked. No, not now. *She can't start having doubts now.*

"Tell me," he said to distract her, "who is this person with the black Rio?"

"A friend's mom." Short, curt words.

"Who's the friend?"

"MacKenzie." She seemed to be purposefully not looking at him. The car wasn't more than twelve yards away.

"Do you go to MacKenzie's house a lot? For playdates?"

"*Playdates?*" She stopped. "You do realize I'm in seventh grade, right? I'm going to the junior high next year."

Not sure how to respond, he nodded. He needed to get her walking again. Twelve yards.

"I don't go on 'playdates,'" she added for good measure.

"What do you do?"

"You mean with MacKenzie?"

"Yes."

"We just hang out. God!" She turned from him as if anyone so misguided was no longer worthy of her. She turned back: "What did Mom tell you about me, anyway?"

Now that put him on the spot. To stall, he looked back and down at Cocteau. The dog was stopped too, no longer sniffing, just staring at him as if waiting for his answer.

"She said you were very smart, Jeannine. She said nobody can fool you. She said she admires how you take control and don't let anyone give you guff."

As he spoke he saw the change in the girl's eyes: the relenting. More than that: the emotion. The gratitude. "Did Mom really say that about me?" she said.

"Yes."

"She said she admires me?"

"Absolutely. I wouldn't lie to you."

"Wow," she said and just stood there, lingering. "She sees more than I thought. I didn't think she even liked me."

"She's your mother. She has to like you. I mean, you know, she—" Baine was surprised to hear his voice catch. But it did. It caught on the thick wad that had balled itself like some new muscle in his throat. "She loves you. She wants the best things for you."

The girl was nodding now: distractedly, as if half hearing his words, and not really listening to them. Her fire-blonde hair went up and down. "But she's always so busy. She spends more time with people in our church than she does with me."

Jeannine's mother was sounding like a religious fanatic. Of a different sort maybe than crazy, charismatic-leaning Krystal, but one nonetheless. That was at least the third time the girl had mentioned church. Baine wondered how this complicated matters, or if it did at all.

"She loves you," Baine said. "After all, that's why she sent me to get you." He smiled at her, and she returned the expression. Then she smiled again. Bingo. *Game over.*

They started walking again. He'd left the car unlocked, so he didn't need to fish around for his keys. Instead, he quickly pulled Cocteau inside, shut the rear door, and then went around to open her door.

"Madam," he said and lowered his head.

"Ooooh," she cooed. "So formal. I like it."

The singing inside him returned. He practically skipped around to his door. When he was firmly inside, behind the wheel, his seatbelt on and hers, the key in the ignition and the engine humming, he did one last thing. On the door handle beside him were the up and down controls for the windows but something else too: a little square, black button with a red X crossed across its front. He pushed the button and immediately heard the *thunk* of all four doors locking instantly. And they could not be unlocked from any other place in the car besides that button. "All right then," he said to her, barely able to keep the excitement from his voice, "now we're safe."

I like his car: a cute little thing. The kind that you think should just jump ahead as soon as you start it. And it's so clean inside. There's even an air freshener hanging from the rear-view mirror. The freshener is square with a peach-colored middle. I don't know what the scent is supposed to be, but it smells a little like watermelons. Watermelons with a breeze blowing across them. With the neatness and the air freshener, Jim's car makes Mom's look and smell like a picnic table in comparison: the kind where people leave behind their paper plates with leftovers crusted on them, and the ants have taken over.

Quickly, he gets us on the road to the lake. This is my chance to really look at him. Back at school, he was almost ticking, walking on eggs. Like he was afraid of me. His half-red face seemed a little creepy, definitely surprising, but it also is the kind of thing that can make you feel sorry for a person. The nervousness was actually worse. But once we are together in the car with our seat belts on, and his dog settled in the back, and Caddo passing by, Jim's shoulders relax. And his cheeks and even his elbows. *Maybe*, I think, *he's just someone who likes to drive.* Mom always drives like she is battling her car, trying to bend it to her will, a battle she always loses because there are more ways for cars to fight back than there are ways for Mom to control them. She never gets comfortable behind a wheel. Like she thinks at any moment she'll be exposed as a fraud and her license taken away. Jim, on the other hand, seems not only at peace with his car but tied to it, skin to skin.

"Mom likes your house, huh?" I say, as gently as I can.

He looks surprised. "Well . . . no . . . she's curious about my house. She's never actually been. That's why she's coming out later."

This seems strange. It has since the first time he told me. After all, Mom has never said anything to me about wishing she could live on the lake or wanting to see the inside of other people's houses. Mom is kind of blind to things like houses, even her own. She's said, more times than I can count, that her only requirement for a dream house is that everything works. Other than that, she doesn't care. Because she has too many other cares at work—she has everybody's cares at work. That's what being the rector of a church means: You're the mother hen to everyone else's problems, even if that means not being the mother to your own kids' problems. I guess that's the tradeoff you make to stay in the good graces of all those hundreds of people, to make sure they don't fire you. Most people have one boss. My mom has dozens.

And the divorce didn't help. I'm not saying she had much of a choice. Well, no, actually, she did. I always thought that Dad's getting involved with that woman from the restaurant was kind of a signal to Mom that working 65 hours a week, being home for dinner maybe one time out of five, had consequences. Physical consequences. I think she could have avoided the divorce if she really wanted to, but she didn't. That's the fact. Deep down, I think she was happy to see Dad go. To be done with the responsibility of him.

And boy did he go. Dad didn't just leave Caddo—which he always said he hated—but the whole state of Arkansas. He went all the way to Florida. Lots more restaurant options there, he said, and most of his family. That really hurt. *We're his family.* But I think he finally really just wanted to get away from Mom. I think he couldn't stand to be within an inch of her, after the divorce deal, which didn't go well for him. But even so, even so, this means he's living far apart from me and Aaron. And instead of working at a bistro, he's now got a job at a place called Señor Billy's! Yes, with an exclamation point in the name. I mean, really.

It doesn't make any sense. He claims that when he can get together the money, he is going to put up another fight for us. A better fight. And then we can all three be together all the time—and someplace better than Caddo. But I don't really think that will happen. And even if it does, it means Mom is the one left out in the cold instead of him. So how is that better? Sometimes, I think the whole point of Dad's leaving Caddo was just to give a big FU to Mom's FU of insisting on the divorce. If he couldn't keep us at his place—wherever that turned out to be—then he was going to make it as hard as possible on her to keep us. Funny how two peace-loving, Jesus-talking people can act so mean to each other. But they do. And Aaron and I are the ones who get stuck.

"Where did you say you met Mom?" I ask. Jim seems nice enough and pretty normal—despite his half-red face—but I just can't see how he and Mom have become such good friends if he isn't associated with the church.

"Oh," Jim starts and stops. "You know . . ." His mouth hangs open, but something is blocking his words. I see his eyes moving. He is watching the road, but at the same time he seems to be looking at something a hundred miles away. Then he gets unstuck. "There was that party I told you about. And then I just started seeing her, here and there. I can't remember exactly where. Kroger probably. That's where I see everyone. I do remember that she asked me to come to her office when I had the time. After that, I had to call her once or twice about some business stuff, and the boss asked me to go to her office again to represent the company in an official capacity. We talked some more. Talked about you."

I wait. I think he will say more, maybe something about me, but he doesn't. The dog pokes its nose at us between the seats. I guess it isn't so settled back there as it seems. Or maybe it is just one of those antsy little dogs. Are any little dogs not antsy? Our dog Bridie is anything but antsy, but she's a Setter, and she's eleven years old. All of a sudden, Jim's dog jumps through the seat onto his lap. Jim startles—he hadn't seen the dog stick his nose through—and he almost loses control of the car. Still, you might think that he might think it's cute: having a dog want to jump in your lap. But he gets angry. With one hard shove, he pushes the dog away: at me, in fact. It lands square in my lap and decides to settle again, at least for the moment. I'm shocked how light it is. Yes, of course it's small, but it has that crazy long hair sticking every which way that makes it seem bigger than just a tiny dog. And it is a dog, after all. But it feels as light on my lap as a cat. I run my hand over its head. The dog pulls away and twists, in order to smell me. It keeps smelling. I don't know what it smells. Ham and butter sandwich? It starts licking my fingers. I laugh. Its tongue tickles.

"What's its name?" I ask as I wipe my hand on my jeans.

"He. It's a he," Jim corrects. "He's a he."

"Okay, what's *his* name?" I am already getting the feeling Jim can be a little petty. I wonder why Mom even likes him. *Oh my God*, I think, *I hope she doesn't like him in that way. No, please.* That would be way too soon. I am so not ready for that. Dad just moved away in December. Please, God. I don't want my mom dating anybody, especially not a man with a half-red face.

"His name is Cocteau," Jim says.

"Cock toe? Cool name. Weird, but cool."

He smiles and seems surprised. "Thanks."

"Except chickens don't have toes. They have like claws, right?"

His face darkens. Like I said something offensive. "No," he says, with emphasis. "Not 'cock.' Cocteau. All one word. It's a man's name." He spells it for me.

"Oh, sorry. Which man?"

"Never mind," he says.

We drive for a little bit in silence, rights and lefts through the local streets. I keep my hand on Cocteau's back while he constantly moves and resettles, moves and resettles. He can't decide if he wants to look out the window, smell me, or sleep.

"Anyway," Jim says. He looks calmer—his voice normal again. "That's how we really got to know each other: business." I forgot I asked him that question, but his answer makes me remember. And the other questions too. I look at him.

"What kind of business stuff?"

He doesn't answer right away. Then he says, "Huh?"

"What business stuff?"

"What was my business?"

"Okay, you can answer that question instead."

"I worked for Entergy, the Caddo office."

"The power company sent you to meet my mom in her office?"

"Yes." He looks a bit pale now. I mean pale on his right side. Of course, not on the other. He said "worked" not "work." I'll have to ask him about that. But I have other questions to ask first.

"That's weird. I didn't think the power company went inside people's offices."

Now he laughs, kind of a crazy, sweaty cackle. "How else are we going to fix stuff?"

"The power lines?"

He laughs again and shakes his head, as if I am making a joke, but I'm not. He doesn't actually answer. We have passed through all the subdivisions near school and are on Route 47 now. We go through a traffic light at the intersection with North Lindenhurst and pass a laundromat on our right and a Shell station and strip mall on our left. I looked at the sign above the place at the very end of the strip mall: Wally's Catfish Hole. It occurs to me that I've never eaten at Wally's Catfish Hole. I've also never been inside any of the stores in that strip mall. It makes me sad to think that, and I don't know why. It's not like I've wanted to eat there before, and it's not like I won't have a chance to later on. Heck, after Mom picks me up I can just ask her if we can eat at Wally's Catfish Hole. But for some reason, I don't think I'll be able to do that, not anytime soon. Maybe never, I think, and I start feeling sadder.

I remember that the turn for the road that will take us to the lake should come soon. And there it is. I see the green road sign as we turn: Lake Cedar Road. Of course. Duh. I'd forgotten that was the name. Lake Cedar Road is a long, curvy, two-lane thing that takes you into the country—and to the lake, of course. Eventually, you start to see it on your right. I have been to Lake Cedar maybe twice. Maybe three times. I don't know how close we are at the moment, but at least we are on the way; we're getting closer. Mom too, I hope.

"Okay," I say, "because you're Mom's friend I can ask you this. I wouldn't, except that you're Mom's friend."

His eyes get small, and I see the Adam's apple move in his throat. "Yeah?" he says, except it doesn't come out that way, not like a word, but like some dry dull sound.

"How come half your face is red?"

I see his cheeks relax. Good. Before, I worried he might get pissed off when I asked the question, but instead he smiles. He smiles like he is so glad I've asked this. "You want to know the truth?" he says.

"Of course. You think I want you to lie to me?" What a dumb question: *Did I want the truth?* Sometimes grown men and women think in the strangest ways. I have the feeling that him even asking this means that he wishes he could lie to me, as if that is a legitimate option.

"No. No, I don't think that," he says. He pauses. He breathes in. He cracks a quick embarrassed smile, like he just farted. But he didn't. I decide right then that maybe Jim is a lot stranger than I thought. I mean, a lot stranger. Probably a lot stranger than Mom thinks too. "Truth is," he says, "I got hurt in a fight."

"A fight? You?"

"Yes," he says quietly, like it is a horrible thing to admit.

"Did he attack you or did you attack him?"

"How do you know it was a he?" Bad smile. Bad, fake smile. I can see it from a mile away.

"I know it was a he. Don't be an asshole."

75

He blushes. His pale side catches up just a bit with his red side.

"Okay, it was a he. And the truth is I attacked him."

"Seriously?"

"Yes."

"Wow."

"What?" He seems amused.

"You don't look like that type at all."

Big broad smile. Apparently, it's the best thing I can say. This makes me think he'd been bullied a bunch when he was my age. Else, why be so proud of attacking someone?

"Well," he says, "I had a reason." He stares fiercely at the road. We go through another curve, and then another. We hit a straight patch. To our right is a midsized field full of brown cows. I keep my hand on Cocteau's back and watch them. I wish we could get to this so-special house, so I could get out of the cramped car. The watermelon smell is actually starting to get to me.

"Are you going to tell me the reason?" I finally say.

He hesitates, but only a second. "He hurt somebody I loved. Somebody I really loved." Still, he isn't looking at me. "And that's all you need to know."

You mean all you're willing to say.

"Excuse me for saying this"—I can tell he is starting to lose patience with this conversation; hopefully not all his patience, not yet—"but I've seen plenty of fights at school, and I've never seen anyone come away from a fight with a half-red face."

He still doesn't look at me. In fact, those eyes of his narrow even more. This I don't understand because I'm not accusing him of anything. I just want to know.

"The other guy kept hydrochloric acid around." He says it without any tone, any feeling at all. "He pushed me into it. Facedown."

"Really?"

"Yes, really." Now he sounds mad. Maybe furious. Too bad. I still want to know more.

"That must have hurt."

He looks at me: once, tentatively. "What do *you* think?" he says. He says it with such a sneer, such blatant hatred,

"I'm sorry," I say.

My words hang in the air for a second, like droplets that need to land, and are about to land, but no one can guess where. Then he lets out a long breath through his nose, and the atmosphere in the car clears. The hatred is gone.

"It's okay," he finally says. "You didn't do it. He did."

"So," I say—very carefully now—"that must have made it hard. I mean to attack him. Or catch him. Whatever you wanted to do."

Before I'm even done talking he is nodding: up and down, up and down. "Yep," he says. Another pause. An impossibly long one. Then: "That pretty much ended it."

"He got away?"

More nodding. Hard and sad. "Yes, he did. He got away."

We turn off Lake Cedar Road into a long, paved driveway that takes us past a cute yellow cottage on the right—it sits right there on Lake Cedar Road—then dips severely and goes back a ways, past a whole string of trees reaching out to each other. We arrive at a black wrought iron gate. Jim reaches up and touches a little control mechanism hooked to his sun visor. The door part of the gate swings back.

"Nice," I say. Jim doesn't say anything. He proceeds to the right and parks his car inside a massive garage. I mean, it's massive. It might be as big as Mom's whole house. Probably five of Jim's little cars could park in it. We leave the garage through a side door and then follow the driveway around to the front of the house. It's awfully fancy. Very wide and very deep, with bushes that have been trimmed just so and on the lawn little bronze-colored statues here and there. There's one of a boy holding a pail. There's another of a woman in a dress reading a book. There's one of a teenager who looks like he's laughing. The teenager guy looks a little like Aaron—the same mopey, straight hair—except Aaron never laughs. On both sides of the front door are long glass panels about a foot wide. As Jim fuddles to find his keys I take a peek at what I can see through the panels. Wow. A huge open center space. And very nice furniture. Way nicer than Mom's. Nice floor. All wood. Nice rugs. On the far side of the house is a huge flat-screen television attached to a wall. I see a back door too: a sliding glass door with the curtain pulled back. It looks like there's a pool behind the house.

Inside, Jim gives me a tour, and I see it's as nice as I thought: seven big rooms—plus two bathrooms—with stuff that looks like it has just been delivered from some catalogue store: leather sofas, the monster tv (as well as smaller ones in two of the bedrooms), new computers everywhere. One of the bedrooms has a king-size bed; the other two bedrooms have smaller beds, but they're still big. I guess that makes them queens. Best thing of all is what I can see right outside the back door. There is a pool there—covered, of course—and past the pool a rear lawn that goes on for almost the length of a football field until it reaches the lake. It looks to me like every single blade of grass has been manicured by leprechauns. And it's so green you'd think it was summer outside.

"Dang," I say, when we return to the center area. "You weren't kidding about this place."

"Don't you want to take off your coat and stay a while?" He smiles.

I shrug. "I guess. If you think it will be a while."

"It might." He smiles again: harder. I unbutton my blue coat and take it off slowly. I feel my fingers deliberately taking their time at forcing each button out of the hole. I don't know why I'm going so slow; it's just what I want to do. When I've got the jacket off, I hand it to Jim, who's standing there, waiting calmly. Immediately he starts for the bedrooms again. Both he and my coat disappear out of sight.

The center room—while it's an enormous space—still has some definite areas to it. The part closest to the door is the fanciest, with the most furniture. I guess that's the sit-and-talk part of the room. This leads back to the kitchen. The kitchen is about the size of Mom's garage and has shiny black marble counters (at least they look marble) about twice as broad as hers. As I said, there's a hallway that begins just past the edge of the kitchen, running along the backside of the house. That takes you to the bedrooms and the bathrooms. Next to the kitchen is a big, heavy, rectangular table—so I guess that makes it the dining room—and then just over from where the table sits is another sofa: a rectangular sectional thing. It faces the back wall, where the flat screen is mounted. That's how wide this part of the house is. The back wall stretches the whole length of the kitchen; then there's the huge sliding glass door; then there's still room to hang the biggest flat screen tv I've ever seen. Funny how Jim doesn't put his tv in the center room, but I guess this way whoever is in the kitchen gets to watch.

Jim returns from the bedroom and for a moment just stands there, not saying much, just smiling. Cocteau, meanwhile, is going nuts, running from room to room, sniffing and jerking and climbing furniture, like it's his first time there, like he is on vacation.

"Told you it was nice out here," Jim says. "Now you know why your mom wants to see."

I nod, but I'm not really listening. "Are you rich or something?"

He chuckles. "I don't know if I'd go that far." Each second he looks and acts more like the guy who picked me up at school because Mom couldn't make it and not like the mad guy I saw in the car.

"Well, this is the richest house I've ever been in."

"Possibly," he says. I swear he pushes up on his toes he is so proud.

"No. Not possibly. It is."

Cocteau starts making more of a nuisance of himself. "I'm going to put him in his room," Jim says. He grabs the dog and lifts him like a loaf of bread. Jim walks down the hallway and disappears. I hear him open a door and push the dog in. He shuts the door quickly before Cocteau has a chance to react.

"Will he be okay in there?"

Jim waves. "That's where his food and water are. He'll be happy. But you know how it is with dogs. They get excited when new people are around."

"I guess," I say, and go straight across the living room to the sliding glass door and try to open it. Nothing.

"Hey, don't," Jim says.

I look at the mechanism. There has to be a switch—or a latch rather. These kinds of doors always have a latch that you push down and then the door unlocks. You can pull it open. But I keep looking and don't see any latch.

"Hey!" Jim shouts. His face is a tangle and his hair sweaty. "We are not going to open this door, all right? We are not going to do this."

I don't understand. What would make him so angry about a door? At first I'm so shocked, I only nod numbly and look away. Mom will get here soon. As in any second. I don't want to be in this house anymore. But when he stops yelling, when he is no longer breathing on me but only glaring—studying me, testing me with his eerie green-gray eyes, trying to see if I've gotten the message—I can't help but ask a question.

"What's so bad about the patio?"

Then he hits me. With his whole right hand, straight across my cheek. I almost topple over, I am so surprised. And my face is in flames. I start to cry. Big gobs of wetness fill my eyes. Then they spill over. I don't want to cry—I don't like to cry—but I can't help it.

"You don't know who might be out here, Jeannine," Jim says. "You don't know who might be watching. You don't know what kinds of dangers there are. You're too young. That's the thing. You're too young to understand them."

I know better than to ask any more questions, but that doesn't stop them coming into my head. *What's the point of having a beautiful backyard if no one's allowed to walk on it? Does this mean you don't let your guests swim in the summertime? Isn't it cruel to have this huge sliding glass door with the curtain pulled back, so you can see everything all the way down to the lake, and then tell people it's off limits? What kind of person acts that way?* My face is still on fire and I can't stop blinking away the tears.

"You can't go outside," Jim says. He turns from me then and finds the cord for the curtain and begins yanking on it hard: hand over hand. The curtain comes across the door, closing off the view. And that makes me feel almost as sad as him hitting me. It's like he's hitting me again.

"To make sure we understand each other," Jim says, "we're just going to cover the door. That way you won't be tempted."

I nod. I wonder if he expects me to thank him.

"Sorry I did that," I say and move to the couch in the corner of the room. As much as my face, and my pride, still hurts, I have to admit that when I sit on the couch it feels wonderful. Like someone is hugging me. Then I stand up. Jim is looking at me. I don't know how he feels about this: sitting on the couch. I think maybe this will get me another slap.

"No, it's okay. Sit. Sit. I want you to sit there. Relax. Sit. Watch television."

Now I'm not sure I want to sit, but I do anyway.

"Let me get you something to eat," he says. "I've laid in everything kids like: chips, crackers, Doritos, popcorn, gummy candies, soda pop. I've got it all. What's your pleasure?"

He is smiling again, but I have no idea what that means anymore. I don't see how a person can smile at another person right after he hits that other person in the face. How do your emotions do that? Besides, there is something scary about the smile now. It's not the same as his other smiles, in the car. Or even when he told me to take my coat off. Now it's like he's trying to sell me something. I don't like the way this smile goes with his acid burn mark.

"I don't think I'm hungry," I say. I sit down. "But thank you."

"Oh, come on. You might as well eat. I've laid it all in. I come prepared." The smile again.

"What do you mean prepared?"

He shrugs. "For you."

"But you said Mom only told you this afternoon to pick me up."

He blushes so bad I swear the good half of his face looks as red as the bad half. I see something in his eyes. Not anger. Not anger. Something like being trapped. But then he changes his face around, really fast.

"She did. She did," he says. "I mean I like to have kids come over. I'm always prepared for them. I keep prepared. I think I mentioned that to your mom when she called me today."

But he didn't say that he prepared for kids. He said he prepared for me. I can still feel the sting of his slap, so I decide not to question him about it.

"What will it be?" he says, the salesman's smile back and even wider.

"Doritos," I say. I am not even the slightest bit hungry. But I know I have to force something down. Jim is pretty much demanding that I eat. "Mom's coming soon, right?"

7

She took a quick glance at Aaron's engine to see if anything obvious stood out; not surprisingly it looked just like an engine was supposed to look. She had no idea, without any glaring evidence, what to poke at or push in. She had Aaron turn the key a couple times. It revved and then died. Revved and died. As if it couldn't hold on to the eruption that the spark plug and the gasoline had provided, like its hands were fumbling with the fire. *That's a fine poetic simile*, she thought, *but it doesn't go a single step toward figuring out what's wrong with the damn car.*

Sometimes she wished Max still lived with them. This was the sort of problem you could put your husband in charge of. Thing is, Max, for all his theological eloquence and artistry in the kitchen, and hard-won firsthand farm knowledge, was almost as dumb as she when it came to automobiles. Back when they were in seminary together in Austin—before he quit to enter culinary school—he'd changed her oil for her. Several times, actually. He came to her rescue once when her tire blew out on 183 and she'd nearly lurched into the next lane before bringing the car safely to a stop on the shoulder. She'd called him, and he'd come, and he changed the damaged wheel in only twenty minutes, even with traffic screaming at them from a couple feet away. When they lived in Beaumont, her first job out of seminary, Max was forced one winter to give her a jump-start each morning for several weeks running until he got sick of it and just took her car into the shop for a new battery.

These were acts of selflessness, and implicit indications of his love for her, that she had deeply valued—even now, even after all that had soured and turned rotten between them, she had to admit that he had been quite the gallant back then—but at the same time they represented the limit of Max's vehicular knowledge. These were the things he knew how to do: change oil, change a flat tire, jump-start an engine. A very small list—she was coming to understand—given all that could go wrong with a car. She wished Aaron's engine had made no sound at all. Or only that clicking noise she remembered from her own car. If these were the symptoms, a jump-start might have fixed things, and a jump-start—because she'd paid attention when Max had done it—was something she could probably pull off. But instead, Aaron's engine just groaned and coughed and stopped. Like a person who had tried to pull himself off a sick bed but only got a quarter way up before he collapsed back to the pillow.

She wondered if this meant the Buick was dead. Maybe so. But what then? Would Max be willing to chip in half the cost of a new one? Probably not. Certainly not right away. He would accuse her of overreacting. He would say she should explore other avenues first: like taking the damn thing to a mechanic. He would insist that even to put in a new engine was cheaper than buying a car. He would ask why he should contribute to a stupid mistake on her part. She could tell him, of course, that if he had been here, if he hadn't fled like a coward to Florida—where nearly his whole extended family lived—if he'd simply stayed in the same town with his children, she would have consulted with him and perhaps chosen the course he was recommending. In the present situation, she was simply trying to do the best she could, and thus she needed his support. She could say that to him. And those would be truthful statements. But she knew exactly how he would reply: *If you wanted my support you shouldn't have insisted on divorcing me. You should have listened when I said we could try counseling. You could have acted a little less like I warranted excommunication. And having excommunicated me, what possible right can you claim to tell me where I should and should not go?*

She could just hear him say those things, in just that tone of voice: whiny and righteous and insistent all at once. And maybe right, too. Maybe. Maybe she had been hasty. Maybe she'd been motivated a bit too much by vengeance rather than justice. But she'd feared and anticipated Max's cheating on her for so long—for almost a year she'd been in daily terror of it—that when it actually happened, some door closed in her mind. Some kind of explosion went off. Reconciliation, to say nothing of mercy, became impossible. She went mildly insane for a period, unable to reason. She didn't feel good about that, especially when a couple in church came to her to discuss their own marital problems, their own need to forgive each other. She felt embarrassed, actually. A lot embarrassed. On the other hand, Max's move to Florida was meant to humiliate her; it was meant as a declaration to the world, and especially to everyone in Caddo who had felt so close to them for so long, that his once dear, idealistic wife had made it impossible for him to stay on. She'd become that big of a bitch.

Elizabeth could not forgive him such small-minded pettiness, not when it was damaging their children. And she also knew—and maybe this peeved her more than anything—that if she had been a male priest whose wife had been cheating on him with a coworker, no one would have complained about his divorcing her. *Throw the hussy out.* She knew three or four older parishioners who would have used those words exactly. *Throw the hussy out.* Yes, she'd divorced Max, but she hadn't thrown him anywhere. He'd packed his own bags, loaded up his own Corolla, and with a smug, serious, defiant look waved a curt one-motion goodbye, gotten into the car, and galloped off to exactly where he wanted.

"Can't you just drive me?" Aaron said, looking at his phone to check the time.

"You called him, right?"

Aaron rolled his eyes. The expression reminded her not so much of a typically exasperated teenager as it did of Max. The same impatience. The same condescension. The same certainty she was always wrong. *Hey*, she felt like screaming so many times at her husband, *I'm the one who finished seminary. I'm not the one who quit.* "Yes. I already told you that," Aaron said. "That was like the first thing you asked me."

It was? She couldn't remember. She had no recollection of ever inquiring about it. Then again, she was forgetting all sorts of things these days. Probably because—as a single parent—she had so much more to remember.

"All right," she agreed. "We'll leave it. After I get Jeannine, I've got to go back to the office. But I'll call a tow truck this afternoon and get them to take it somewhere. I'm not sure where. Maybe someone in the office will know."

Aaron only nodded and kept his mouth pursed, as if he was holding back a secret. *Probably*, she thought, *he doesn't care about any of my plans. He just wants to get to work.* Traffic was especially bad on the way up Western—the busy street that led to the Caddo Mall, where Aaron's employer, an outfit called Game Brands, was situated. As they approached the mall, they discovered the reason for the stalled traffic: a fender bender near the exit for I-40, too many cars needing to go in too many directions, with too many other cars in their way. Well, Elizabeth figured, no point in doing anything crazy. Her son was already late anyway. Aaron was getting more and more exasperated, though. So much so that he was literally huffing by the time they pulled into the mall parking lot. Before she even came to a full stop by the front door of Game Brands, he had the door open and was stepping out of the car.

Standing on the curb, he turned back and said one thing, "You do realize you are way late to get Jeannine."

She was? Elizabeth found her clock. Oh my God. 3:27. 3:27. Her daughter had been standing outside her classroom at Virginia McKinley Middle School for seventeen minutes. By the time Elizabeth got back down Western Street and arrived at school it might be 3:45—or even later. She'd never been that late. Never. In fact, ever since Max left she'd tried to be more on time. She knew they resented the fact that he was gone. She knew they partly blamed her for that—which was exactly what Max had hoped. Well, his plan had worked. They did blame her. And now she was late. Way way late. If it got as late as 3:45 the office began telephoning parents and threatening action: calls to police; Saturday school; long, uncomfortable, midday meetings with Principal Nixon; fees for babysitting by teachers forced to wait with unpicked-up kids.

She wasn't even out of the mall parking lot when she began dialing. She would cut to the chase, call them before they called her. Plus, she hoped someone could reassure Jeannine. It rang only twice before a woman answered. It didn't sound like Principal Nixon. That was good. Elizabeth was not sure she liked Principal Nixon, and she'd had the distinct feeling, on the few occasions she'd had conversations with the woman, that Principal Nixon did not like her or at least the idea of her: the female priest. Principal Nixon, she suspected, was a Southern Baptist. Maybe worse. Maybe Disciples of Christ.

"Hi," Elizabeth started, trying to squeeze as much apology as she could into her voice, as much as she could while simultaneously negotiating the parking lot of the largest mall in Caddo. "I'm Jeannine Riddle's mother. Elizabeth Riddle?" She paused for the woman to reply but heard not even a squeak of recognition. "I have been severely delayed in picking up Jeannine, due to an emergency with my son. Aaron. Jeannine's brother." Of course her son was Jeannine's brother. She wondered why she'd felt the need to say this, unless she suspected this actually was Principal Nixon, and she needed to clarify that being a female priest did not also make one immoral. But was sleeping with two different men even immoral necessarily? What if Aaron's father had died, and then she met Jeannine's father, and he was the most wonderful man in creation and . . . Of course, in that case, Aaron would still be Jeannine's half brother, so no, under no circumstances would she need to explain . . . *Shut up. Shut up, Elizabeth.* "Anyway, I've finally taken care of Aaron's situation, and I'm on my way now. I should be there in no more than ten minutes. Can you—please—tell Jeannine I'm coming? I'm sure she must be terribly worried." Worried or pissed off.

"Umm . . . sure. I guess I can take care of that. I'll go out front and, uh, see who's left out there." The woman slowed her acquiescence the longer the sentence progressed. Finally, she stopped altogether and reversed course. "But if you're on the way, and you can get here before 3:45, it's not really necessary. At least one teacher should still be around, waiting with the kids."

"I know. It's not that. I just don't want Jeannine to worry."

Long pause. Sigh. An eloquent expulsion of air, as if through the nose. Maybe this was Principal Nixon, after all. In fact, Elizabeth was sure of it.

"All right. I'll see what I can do. Just hold on."

"Thank you," Elizabeth breathed. *Bitch.* She'd turned on to Western to head back to the center of town. She drove as fast as she could, but this was rush hour in Caddo, dominated not by the 4:30-5:30 end of the office day but the uniform, across-the district 3:10 end of the school day. So many parents hurrying to so many different parts of the city to pick up their kids, or, having picked them up, hurrying to take them somewhere else: clothes shopping, Sonic, a spouse's office, music lessons, karate lessons, dance lessons, a dentist appointment, maybe even home. So many buses filled to the gills with those unlucky, frowned-upon kids whose parents couldn't afford to pick them up; so many vans for after-school programs, their brightly lacquered sides advertising cute, homey, harmless, even fun-sounding names—*Little Sprouts After-School Play Place*; *See-Us-Grow Daycare*; *Miss Jennifer's Most Awesome Children's Center Ever*—when everyone knew the last thing any real live kid wanted after being stuck for seven hours in a building with other kids was to be shuttled to another building and made to "play" there with more of these same kids. And this was Western: the most congested, most stop-lighted street in the whole city. The one necessary street that took you anywhere you needed to go and thus always had cars on it. Going fast on Western at this time of day was a physical impossibility.

She was trying to change to the left-hand lane—even as she was approaching a stop light about to turn red—when the woman's voice came back on the phone: different sounding, tentatively worried, perhaps even defensive.

"Mrs. Riddle, I don't see your daughter out there. Are you sure someone else didn't get her? Your husband, or another family member?"

Elizabeth went morbidly cold, all the way to the ends of her toes. This was the very worst thing Principal Nixon could have said to her. Way worse than, *If a man cheats on a woman it must be because she's not doing her best to keep him.* (Which she'd heard on Sunday morning television a couple weeks earlier.) Worse than, *I'm not against women working; I'm against mothers working.* (Which she'd overheard from another parent, a woman, outside Jeannine's school.) Worse than, *It doesn't feel the same when I get the Eucharist from you as opposed to a male priest.* (Which she'd actually heard from one of her own parishioners.) This was nightmare stuff. And for a simple reason: With Max gone to Florida there was no "other family member" who could pick up Jeannine. There was no one. Only her.

"No. No, I was definitely supposed to pick her up today. And her father . . . he's out of town this week." Her mind was coursing brutally through possibilities: some banal, some terrible. She'd talked a friend into taking her home. She'd gone back into the school to use the restroom. She'd tried to walk home herself, to teach her mother a lesson on promptness. Max decided to remove her to Florida.

"Okay," the woman said, "I'm sure there's a simple explanation. I know that miscommunication happens all the time." She sounded like she was trying to convince herself as much as Elizabeth, and this made Elizabeth all the madder. Principal Nixon wasn't supposed to deny danger; she was supposed to take care of it.

"There's no miscommunication. I pick up Jeannine. That's what I do. Every single day. There's no other plan, no other backup possibility. We didn't talk about doing anything different today when I dropped her off. She should be out there safely waiting for me." That *should* and that *safely* were not accidental word choices. She was putting Principal Nixon on notice. *If anything happened to my daughter—in fact, if I don't see you jumping into action right now and doing everything humanly possible to find out exactly what did happen to my daughter—there will be a price to pay. A steep, steep price. A seriously steep price.*

"Mrs. Riddle, we will find her. Are you sure you didn't—"

"I'm completely sure. And I'm terribly worried now, I don't mind saying. I'm freaking out, to be honest. I will be there in minutes, and my daughter better be waiting for me. Go find her, Ms. Nixon. Go!"

She punched END before the principal had a chance to reply. Elizabeth had said what needed saying. She didn't want to talk anymore. She wanted to get there. She wanted to fight through the traffic. She wanted to rescue her daughter. She couldn't do any of that talking to this woman.

When eight minutes later she pulled into the driveway that curved past the front door of the school, she yanked her car to a stop and jumped out. Nixon was speaking with loud gestures to one of the teachers: a thin, dark-eyed, olive-skinned young woman who seemed to have car duty quite often. Somehow, Elizabeth knew, it wasn't the young woman's fault. Whatever happened—whatever she would find out had taken place—it wasn't this woman's fault. She blamed Principal Nixon. It was Nixon and the policies she enforced or chose not to enforce that let what happened happen. Whatever that was.

"Have you found her?" Elizabeth shouted as soon as she was out of the car. "Jeannine Riddle?"

Nixon regarded her with something that could only be described as fear: naked, real fear. If she hadn't been so dizzily anxious about Jeannine, Elizabeth would have savored the woman's expression. Now it only made her mad. The young teacher, meanwhile, merely scowled. Obviously, she had no idea what to think.

Principal Nixon looked at Elizabeth from beneath her tower of frosted gold hair, from behind eccentric, loopy black glasses, and shook her head slowly. Elizabeth wished she knew the woman's first name, just so she could wield it like an axe. She'd heard the name before, but just couldn't bring it up in the crisis of the moment.

"No? No? What are you doing? Are you even trying to find my daughter?"

Now the principal turned haughty. She permitted herself to be offended, as if the loss here were her own, not Elizabeth's. "Of course we are."

"Yes, and what does that mean exactly? Have you called the police?"

Elizabeth could see that it took Principal Nixon all her strength not to roll her eyes. "You can't call the police because a child has been missing for twenty-five minutes. They won't even listen to you."

"Do you know that for a fact? Or are you just saying that so I'll leave you alone?" Elizabeth knew her tone wasn't helping, her expression wasn't helping; her innate hatred for this well-connected local woman was keeping her and Principal Nixon from forming a partnership, which was the only thing that might bring about the discovery of the whereabouts of her daughter. But she couldn't help herself. Her anger was real. It was automatic. It was the same as terror. Because, in fact, she was terrified.

"I know that for a fact," Principal Nixon said coldly.

"And that's because you're so experienced at losing kids?"

Elizabeth saw the outrage in the woman's white eyes. They went wider and whiter; the hard kernels of brown at their center went browner. To her credit, the principal did not bark back. "I know," she tried, "that this is very disturbing for you—"

"Oh, you've figured that out, huh? What a smart woman you are."

"—But I don't think exchanging insults is going to help us find Jeannine."

Elizabeth's eyes watered; her anger suddenly tasted like sour milk in her mouth. The next moment, her head went woozy and her vision darkened, as if with a sudden blood rush.

"Mrs. Riddle," the young teacher broke in. "As soon as you called, Ms. Nixon and I started asking whoever was still around"—Elizabeth realized, for the first time since she arrived at the school, that there were still kids waiting to be picked up, five of them; and thirty yards away, two teachers were standing by their cars talking to each other in low tones; the head janitor, meanwhile, emerged from inside, carrying a large yellow plastic trash can; he walked toward the right side of the building, where the dumpsters were hidden away behind a brick façade—"and no one can recall seeing Jeannine getting into a car."

"Has anyone seen her at all, doing anything?"

"Not yet," the teacher said. Then: "I'm sorry."

It was impossible—and yet terrifying—for Elizabeth to think that Jeannine could just be led away by a perfect stranger. Her daughter was too smart for that. Way too smart. Even more, she had spunk. Jeannine was not the kind to feel pressured or hurried by anyone. She had to believe—*she had to believe*—that her daughter had not voluntarily put herself into a strange man's car. And if she'd been forcibly abducted someone would have noticed. Someone would have said something. Might she have just walked away by herself?

In the moment, this seemed actually possible, and the idea warmed Elizabeth's heart. Both her daughter and son were so unhappy that their father lived 900 miles away; both of them blamed her even as they tried to act like they didn't blame her. Was it so hard to believe that Jeannine, on realizing how late Elizabeth would be, had decided on payback? But to where would she have walked? Home? A friend's? Nowhere in particular?

There were several snagging points to these ideas, however, and Elizabeth couldn't chase them from her mind: 1) As late as she had been, she had been almost as late before—several times before—especially last semester. While not happy about it, Jeannine had never seemed overly angry, just annoyed. 2) Their house was three miles from school. How many seventh graders will walk three miles just to make a point? Jeannine would not. 3) A couple of Jeannine's friends lived close to Virginia McKinley, but she couldn't see her daughter just heading to their homes without an invitation—and wouldn't the friend's mom or dad have called her to say so? 4) Jeannine was too purposeful, too project driven, too task oriented to just start walking with no place in sight or in mind. *Unless her project is to make me crazy with fear—in which case she succeeded.* She wondered if she should walk around the neighborhood shouting to bushes and backyards and garages: *You got me. You can come out now, Jeannine. You really got me good.*

"I have a call in to Jenna White," the principal said. "She's the teacher who was helping the bus riders when school let out. I wasn't able to get a hold of her, the first time." Nixon hesitated, lifted her voice a measure. "I also have a call in to Amanda Mauldin." Then, as if not confident Elizabeth was versant in even the basic facts about the school: "She's my Assistant Principal."

"I know that," Elizabeth declared in a tone Principal Nixon could not misinterpret.

"But she left work early today, to start on her way to Knoxville. There's a wedding over there. In any case, she didn't answer. And I'm about to call Mrs. White again," the principal said. "She was out here earlier with the kids but then she left, and Heather took over." She gestured toward the young teacher. "I've called her twice already and left messages. I might as well try again."

Elizabeth nodded, numbly. Okay, okay. She had to admit that sounded reasonable. "What about Mrs. Mason? Isn't she the one who controls the door to her classroom? I mean she's the only one who can open the door that Jeannine comes out of, right?"

Nixon nodded stiffly. Elizabeth wondered if she'd hit on something. Did somebody let her daughter out when they weren't supposed to?

"I've already talked with Mrs. Mason. She's on her way back, right now, to talk with you—with us. She's very upset."

She doesn't get to be upset, Elizabeth thought. *She gets to be guilty. If she is.*

"Apparently, when she was releasing the walkers to their parents two boys started a commotion in the back of the room. She let Jeannine out quickly and then hurried to stop the fight. She said she thought she saw you there, waiting for her."

"She couldn't have seen me. I was on Western Street driving my son to his job at the mall."

The principal nodded. "She thought she saw you."

Elizabeth's anger was back. "Now wait a minute. These teachers are responsible for the kids they let out that door. That's always been my understanding. That's what I've been told. I was told that unless they see a parent and make eye contact with that parent, they don't let a kid out. In fact, they keep the door locked. They let the kids out one-by-one and lock it each time, after each one leaves."

"That's exactly right," Nixon said, with the preening gloss of authority recognized.

"No, it's not! That's not right! Mrs. Mason sent my daughter out that door without making eye contact with me. Because I wasn't there! And now no one knows where my daughter is. Does that sound 'exactly right' to you?"

Principal Nixon stared at her coolly—boy, did this woman know how to maintain her composure; no wonder the kids saw her as an ice witch—and then let out a carefully modulated, professorial sigh. "Mrs. Mason is very upset. I've told you that. She's on her way back here. She should be here any second. And then we can talk to her and make some plan of action. Meanwhile, I need to call Mrs. White again. Or would you rather I not?"

Disgusted, Elizabeth waved her away. Of course she should call Mrs. White. Of course. For God sake. But that wasn't fair. She was making a legitimate point about how Mrs. Mason failed in her duty—a failure that might be directly related to Jeannine's disappearance—and Principal Nixon had shrewdly twisted the conversation away from the idea of guilt and brought it back around to action. Fine. Fine. For now, they would talk about action. They should. But sooner or later, Elizabeth was going to come back to the question of guilt. And none of these people—none of them—were going to get off easy.

Her head burned as she watched Principal Nixon, in her officious turquoise jacket, dark pantyhose, and not-so-low heels stalk back to the front door, her absurd hair sparking the air like a giant zippo lighter. The woman looked like a peacock. Hell, she was a peacock.

"I'm really sorry about this," the young teacher said. Then: "She's doing all she can."

"No, she's not," Elizabeth shot back. "I've been here ten minutes and she hasn't even apologized to me for losing my daughter. No one has, except for you. And you had nothing to do with it."

The teacher studied her a moment with those sad, dark eyes. Then she shrugged and looked away at the same time. Elizabeth was mortally afraid that was what this all would add up to: shrugs and a refusal to even issue a simple *I'm sorry*. She heard a car turn erratically into the lot. She wheeled around and saw a champagne-colored Mazda, with a bulky woman behind the wheel, brake to a stop only a few yards from where she was standing.

Mrs. Mason emerged from the car crying and hobbling. "Elizabeth," Mrs. Mason said. "What's happened? Is Jeannine all right?" Elizabeth could appreciate how upset Mrs. Mason was, but she couldn't help but think that she should be asking these exact questions to the teacher. Elizabeth wasn't the one in charge of opening the classroom door.

"No," Elizabeth said and stood in place. Mrs. Mason's voice sounded like she expected Elizabeth to hug her—or maybe she wanted to hug Elizabeth—but Elizabeth didn't want hugs; she wanted answers. "I'm worried that she's very much not all right. I have no idea where she is. I don't know. So far, no one here does either."

"Weren't you here earlier?" Mrs. Mason said. Then again: "Weren't you?" As if she actually thought she could rewrite reality to her convenience. Elizabeth put an end to that.

"I was never here. Not until ten minutes ago. Jeannine's brother had a car emergency, and I had to drive him to his job, and I just got here now." She paused for only a millisecond. "Who did you release Jeannine to? Who was out here?"

All of Mrs. Mason's hurt seemed to gather in her eyes at once and she began to howl. "I don't know. I don't know. I'm so sorry. I was letting the kids out, and then it was Jeannine's turn and then two boys were fighting, so I had to stop them. I swear I saw you out there. I saw Melissa Singleton, and I saw Lauren Roop, and I saw Patrick Langley, and I swear I saw you there too. You were with them, like you always are. So, I quick let Jeannine out and then . . . I locked the door again . . . because I had to stop those boys. They'd been fighting so long. It was bad."

Of all the disturbing elements of this account, one of the most disturbing was that a teacher could take a decisive, life-altering action based not on what she saw but only what she expected to see. Equally disturbing was that apparently keeping two stupid boys from squabbling was more important than the safe release of her daughter. It was clear which teacherly duty took precedence in the heat of the moment.

Guilt, Elizabeth thought.

Guilt.

Then she had an idea. Why hadn't she done this first thing? She texted Aaron: *Have you heard from J?* She stared at her phone, begging it to give her an answer. And not just an answer but the right answer.

"Who are you—" Mrs. Mason started.

"Shut up," Elizabeth said. "You've done enough." She didn't care or notice how Mrs. Mason reacted. She stared fixedly at her phone. In no time at all, Aaron replied: "What do you mean?"

Has she contacted you, maybe from home? Or a friend's house?

No. Why would she contact me?

Are you sure you didn't miss a call, from anybody?

I'm sure.

Really sure?

No calls since you dropped me off. No texts.

Can you check? Please?

A second later: *Checked. No calls no texts no messages.*

Her head went light—bad light, too light—but she forced herself not to break down.

If she contacts you call me immediately. Immediately!

OK. Why?

Just do it.

Is she missing?

Elizabeth stared at the question for seconds before she thumbed a reply that was both honest and thoroughly disingenuous: *I don't know.*

She heard new footsteps behind her. Wheeling again, phone in hand, she saw Principal Nixon: her step stiffer than before, her face more closed and tauter. Her eyes were trying to hide something—or decide something. Perhaps hide while she managed to decide. Regardless, they were not the eyes of someone about to say, *We've found your daughter.* Principal Nixon did not seem relieved or pleased or hopeful on seeing Karen Mason standing next to Elizabeth. If anything, she looked like someone for whom hopefulness was decidedly fading but could not say so.

"I still can't reach Jenna White," she said. "I can't guess where she might be."

"You left a message?"

"Of course."

"What about the other parents? She"—she couldn't bring herself to say Mrs. Mason's name—"says that Noah Singleton's mom was here when she let Jeannine out. And Ava Roop's mom and Ethan Langley's dad."

Principal Nixon lowered her head: a solemn nod. "Yes, I know. I tried them all as soon as Karen told me. Patrick Langley and Lauren Roop can't remember if Jeannine left with anyone. They were paying too much attention to their own children to notice." Elizabeth hated them for this, and she was jealous of them: to have a child you could focus on, just as on any other day. But she knew in a different set of circumstances she could easily have been the oblivious one, caring only and entirely for her daughter, not knowing what was out of place, who should not have been there. She shook her head. So far, she reminded herself, no one could say if anybody had been here who should not have been. No one could say that her daughter hadn't acted entirely on her own.

"They apologized," Principal Nixon said carefully. "And they asked me to extend their sympathies."

Their relief, you mean. They're glad it didn't happen to them.

"And Melissa Singleton," Nixon continued, "did not answer her phone."

"Her phone? You only tried one number?"

Principal Nixon hesitated. She bestowed the condescending, patient look of those who are unjustly tried—and by an inferior. "I tried every number we had."

"What's wrong with these people? How can they just not be around? How can they not be at their phones? Don't they care?" It felt to Elizabeth as if the entire class, the entire school was closing her off, joining hands while she and her daughter were forced to the outside of the ring.

"I know how frustrating this is, Mrs. Riddle. But realize this may be perfectly regular. On a normal day I have no idea what these people do, what their schedules are. Once they pick up their children they're not required to report to us their whereabouts."

"Of course not!" she shouted. She was trembling now and her head was burning and her eyes were watery again. All of her joints—elbows, knees, ankles, hips, shoulder blades—felt like they might become unglued at any moment. No, not unglued. Explode. "Of course no one reports to you. But I can expect them to answer their damn phones!" She started crying, right where she stood. She couldn't see anymore. She couldn't stand. She wanted to run to the end of town and back, shouting Jeannine's name—or shrivel up and die. She lost all sense of herself and of time and of location. She didn't regain it until she realized she was sitting on the cold black pavement outside the front door of Virginia McKinley Middle School. She was missing one shoe. Someone's arm was around her shoulder, and bureaucratic chatter went on above. Her daughter was still missing, and she needed to go find her, since none of these people could. But first—the terrible thought said in her head—first she would have to call her ex-husband.

He was trying hard to control his temper—and his anxiety. He wanted to avoid the big giveaway, to delay as long as possible the moment when he saw that she knew and he would thus have to act   or risk her escaping. The blow-up over the patio door had come close. She seemed different for several minutes after: refusing the Doritos, then barely nibbling when he forced them on her, asking him precariously about her mother, staying silent and only staring at the wall. When he turned on the television for her, however, she seemed to relax. She seemed to smile at the shows she watched: teen comedies both.

The first was a preposterous ensemble vehicle in which twelve or so kids—who all looked liked they'd just escaped from junior high—wandered around a desert island unsupervised. How they got there was anyone's guess—this must have been established earlier in the episode or earlier in the series—and where the adults lived was never explained. None of the young people—except one fearfully skinny, wide-mouthed blonde boy who kept erupting in panic attacks that the audience was supposed to laugh at—seemed particularly bothered by their fate. In fact, the only thing that happened to them was that they kept running into bemused island natives with face paint and skirts made of leaves. It was difficult for Baine to watch anything so stupid, so he didn't. Baine considered himself a man of a certain seriousness. He didn't waste his time on frivolous things. But if the show calmed the girl, so much the better. The calmer she was, the easier the murder would be.

The island show was followed by another comedy, this one set at a high school. It starred a girl with vibrant, flame-red hair—so red it was almost orange—so red it must surely be dyed, or a wig—who slunk around in low-hanging jeans and made noticeably unfunny comments to her noticeably ugly friends: a roly-poly boy; a pimply boy with exaggerated glasses and a stick for a nose; and a girl with short, frizzy brown hair that fell about her upturned face like an Affenpinscher's. The show might actually have been more ludicrous than the island one. It depressed Baine to think that this was what passed for popular entertainment. It must be causing kids' brains to erode. This conviction only confirmed an idea he'd begun to toy with, even before he led Jeannine away from her school: Maybe what he intended to do to her was the best thing for her. Better than growing up in a world in which shows like these were made and consumed. A world in which those who watched such shows eventually took power and made decisions. He simply could not fathom such a world, such a future. He had watched almost no television since his daughter died, except for local news. He watched local news because he appreciated its grim reportage: fires, drug murders, rapes, school failures, bankruptcies, bridge projects over budget. Local news confirmed his view of the world: that everything was out to kill everything else. And God didn't care. Or maybe God approved.

In the weeks leading up to what happened, things had spun decisively out of control for Krystal. She lost her job when Lou's Diner couldn't survive the bad economy; then she lost the court case to determine the fate of Paige; then she proceeded to lose many of her friends, because she refused to stop talking about injustice. About the corrupt local courts. And about the need for more God in our government. She was close to going off the deep end, actually, a tendency she'd always exhibited but used to control through work and parenthood and friends and Baine. If only Krystal would think in terms of trust—he reflected as he left his daughter to Murphy's protection—life would have gone so much smoother for her, and for them. If Krystal had not been so combative, and so disdainful of him—even before they split—they could have worked out a mutually beneficial legal arrangement.

But since she had fought him and doubted him and despised him at every turn, he had decided to keep Paige for himself. That meant the court case and Krystal's subsequent, embarrassing defeat, almost unprecedented in Caddo custody decisions. He could understand how a defeat like that might unhinge her—he knew that he could not have taken it well—but to react as she did, to flip out even worse, to harass him even more adamantly, to call him at work and show up at his house and leave signs on his front yard (*Lawrence Baine Stole My Daughter!*). All that did was reassure Baine he'd done the right thing.

It was hard to believe now that he'd ever actually mused about the possibility of marrying Krystal, but he had: early on, in the eighth or ninth month of their relationship. More in his mind than his heart, though, because within a year of their beginning to date Baine realized that he could never truly settle down with Krystal Hodges. She was as open and vigorous as her first impression suggested—a buxom, extroverted woman whose outward energy and permed brown hair made a nice balance against Baine's inwardness and buttoned-up comportment —but she was also a fanatic about her church and disdainful of most every other, to say nothing of the owner of the fiercest, fastest-rising temper he'd ever seen in anyone, man or woman.

She wasn't just warm but overwarm, and Baine felt himself equally sunned and burned by her, both drawn to her presence and eager to hide from it. One morning, eleven months after they'd started dating, two months after she'd moved in with him, and eight hours after the conclusion of what might have been their most venomous argument yet, Baine woke to realize that to allow the relationship to go on even a single day more was to risk locking his head in a saw-toothed trap. Besides, it was unfair to Krystal to let her imagine a permanent future when none existed. It was that same day, however, that Krystal found out she was pregnant. After that discovery, breaking up with her did not seem convenient or even possible—not yet.

Not until Paige was almost five, by which time he and Krystal had mostly stopped talking to each other—except for arrangements about picking up Paige from kindergarten, or arguments about what they were feeding her or about how it looked to the good folk at Agape Pentecostal that he never attended—did matters come to a head. At the conclusion of their 374th discussion about whether or not to marry, Krystal simply stood up and announced that she was leaving forever, as if she'd just thought of the idea that moment. "If you want me to stay and live here with you and sleep in your bed, you've got to marry me. Period." She glared at him, a hand on her hip, her brown eyes alight with the optimism of her power play. Clearly, she thought this would work.

"Do what you have to do," Baine responded, for once returning Krystal's angry stare, "but I don't think we should be married. I'm not going to do that."

As bothered as Baine was by the absurd shows Jeannine was watching, he was bothered far more—completely snagged really—on the question of what to do with her; exactly what to do with her. After all, Baine had meticulously planned the girl's capture and her exile in this isolated lakeside home; he had laid the groundwork weeks ago when he started walking Cocteau every day, twice a day, in sight of the school; he had made sure to rent this house long enough that if something went wrong on capture day he could disappear for a week or two, even three, and then return to try again, the lake house still his to use, the original outline of the plan still feasible. What he had not planned so meticulously was how he would kill her. That he would do so, of course. But would he slit her throat, choke her, or drown her? He didn't know. He didn't much care for any of those solutions. He did not want to see, or need to see, her suffer overlong. The quicker the method the better. Other than that, it was more a matter of 1) what he was most comfortable with, and 2) what made most sense in the immediacy of the moment. And on both counts, he couldn't tell how to proceed.

He didn't like the idea of knives. Choking would take too much effort and seemed too brutal and, besides, he was afraid that somehow she would be able to fight him off. Drowning her would be the same as choking her, only doing it underwater. Shooting her was out of the question, as he didn't have a gun. He'd never even fired one. As for trusting "the immediacy of the moment," this meant he literally could not and should not plan ahead. He had to wait for a sudden insight that could only arrive when there was only one way left to proceed. And things hadn't gotten that far yet, so all Baine could do was push more chips at her, turn on the tv, and keep pretending that her mother would arrive any minute.

It was not, however, as if he came to this murder completely unprepared. For a drowning, if he chose that, there was the substantial Lake Cedar sitting just beyond the edge of his backyard. All he need do was wait until the sunlight disappeared, which, at this time of year, wouldn't be that much longer. Then he could act under the cover of darkness. For knives, there were plenty of sharp ones in the well-furnished kitchen. For suffocation, every bedroom offered an abundance of firm pillows. He'd tested many of them out the evening before, pleasantly surprised to find that they felt not like the crippled, worn-down wrecks that graced most household beds but the heavier, meatier kind you got in upscale hotel chains. And in addition to those advantages there was the length of fibrous rope, a bulbous round of duct tape, and a box of extra-large trash bags he'd bought at Walmart days ago, the same day he'd purchased the Doritos and the popcorn and the other snacks, and stored in one of the kitchen cabinets.

Knowing these potentials weapons lay only footsteps away calmed Baine, assured him that when the time came he would choose the appropriate option, because he'd given himself so many options to choose from. He'd almost secured a gun too. When he'd gone to buy the snacks and rope and duct tape and trash bags it had occurred to him to check out the gun counter. He'd walked almost all the way there before he changed his mind. He didn't want somebody to remember—in the days after the girl's dead body was discovered—that an odd, anxious-looking man had recently been asking about guns, asking in such a way that it was clear he did not know the first thing about them. Those were the kinds of people, Baine knew, who stayed in one's memory.

Baine was okay with taking guns off the table. He was pretty certain he would have eventually chosen one of the other methods anyway, with or without a firearm at the ready. The question remained, however: Which method *should* he choose? As he happened to be standing in the kitchen, he examined, for what must have been the fourth or fifth time that week, the knife set established in its elegant bamboo block on the counter: a Henckels collection that included not one but two 8-inch-long knives with comfortable handles and fat blades. One knife had a straight edge, the other was more jagged, with notches entered into the tempered metal; Baine was certain either could kill the girl when the time came—if, in fact, he made the decision to do it with a knife. The idea of blood still bothered him. Not just for its innate grossness but because he would have to worry about where it was shed and whether it left behind the evidence of a stain. Hard to kill someone without blood getting involved, he thought. *Unless I've decided to strangle her.*

Is that what he'd decided?

It occurred to him all of a sudden, as if the idea had been placed into his ear by an outside intelligence, that it wasn't a good idea to study the knives while in full view of her. What if she saw him? He spun around and caught the distinct impression that Jeannine had just moved her head and shoulders. But when he looked hard at her, when he really saw her, she was just staring fixedly at the idiot television show. She even laughed: loudly and abruptly—like she couldn't control herself—when all the main character had done was make a face. Baine was disappointed. Maybe he wouldn't mind killing her, after all. Maybe she didn't deserve to live. Maybe he should just grab the knife with the notched blade and go at her now—get it over with.

No. No, he wouldn't do that. The action had to be more precise than a whimsical lunge. He had to be absolutely sure it would work, that she couldn't escape. Because he could not fail in this attempt and have her escape and have her lead the police to him. That could not happen. Not even God could be so unfair as to let that happen. But he no longer trusted Fairness to treat him right. And certainly not God.

The show was winding down: credits rolling over clips from the episode while the trashy theme song played. Crashing guitars, a throbbing bass, a girl's voice singing nonsense lyrics; Baine supposed it was the voice of the actress who played the lead: *When we get home, back to the other side, oh all the way home, back to our side, our side.* Except those last words were dragged out pop style—*ouurrr siiiiide*—and finished off with a meat-chopping chord.

When the last of the credits flicked by, and the show switched to commercial, Jeannine turned her head numbly, like a person coming out of hypnosis.

"You like that show?" he said.

She shrugged, a tiny motion. "It's okay."

"Is this what you normally watch?"

"I watch it sometimes."

"You certainly seemed amused."

She stared at him without expression. Baine felt the seconds tick by one by one and disappear, like lemmings off a cliff. She lifted the remote, pointed it, and hit the mute button.

"Is my mom coming now?" she said.

"To be honest, Jeannine, I can't tell you exactly when she will be here." The girl blinked, possibly with fear—not a good sign—but Baine couldn't be sure. More than ever, his head was full of questions about her. He'd been so sure at first; he felt the plan going right, all the way right, as if it were divinely ordained. But now he felt clouds in his head and read doubts in her expressions. His heart was beating too fast. He had no way of gauging whether she was an actress or not; whether she was a fake or not; how much she knew. "Your mom is a very busy woman. She didn't say it would take her long, but she didn't give me an exact time either."

The girl blinked again. "But she would come for me before it got dark?"

"Oh yes," Baine said quickly. "I'm sure of that."

She nodded. Maybe Baine saw belief. Maybe.

"You do have a phone, right?" she asked.

"Of course," Baine said, "a landline though. Not a cell." Baine knew enough to know that having a cell phone on you while carrying out a kidnapping was about the dumbest thing a person could do. Then he realized he was in danger. He couldn't remember where the house phone was. If he looked to find it, it would be a dead giveaway.

Jeannine put the bowl of Doritos on the table in front of her and stood up. "And she has your number?"

"I think so."

"If not she could look in the church directory—oh, but you said you're not a member of our church."

"No, I'm not."

Shake of the head. "That just seems so strange."

Again, Baine noticed, this insistence on church as the focus of their discussion. He knew from living in Caddo for as long as he had that for some people church occupied the whole of their lives, at least what was left after work and sleep. Krystal often went to Agape Pentecostal for special midweek services in addition to the full, Sunday morning fare. But the Baptists were even worse: church as teenage hangout; church as basketball practice; church as ladies' sewing circle; church as singles mixer; church as Boy Scout troop; church as night school. Church open and occupied nearly 24/7. Jeannine's family must be one of those.

Baine could not imagine anything more foreign or more depressing. He'd grown up Catholic in North Louisiana, and what he'd noticed about his own parents and virtually everyone else in the church was that while they gave little bits of themselves at regular intervals—money, time, energy—most of the week they stayed as far away from church as they could. It was like paying a toll. You gave the required amount and the gate opened for you. No one—no one—paid more than the minimum required amount. That would have been stupid. And he couldn't remember any complaints from pastors about financial problems, or about essential parish tasks that were not getting done. On the whole, the pastors always seemed satisfied: fat, content, self-assured. The congregation was so large, Baine supposed, that the little regular contributions from all those many people added up to a comfortable amount.

For a time, while he was working at Entergy, he had wondered if he should join a church, only because it seemed to be the thing to do in Caddo. He was tired of being asked where he worshipped; he was tired of having to explain he was a former Catholic and then seeing the question-asker's eyes light up like they'd won the lottery as they begin to pressure him to visit their own (usually Baptist) congregation. Then he had to invent pretexts for why he could not go on a certain given Sunday; and then come up later with other pretexts, at least until the person got the message and stopped pressuring him. Krystal had pressured him at first, but finally she gave up too—at least gave up the explicit part—when he yelled at her to get off his back about God. He could tell that even after that she still wanted him to go with her; she just knew she couldn't say so, and she was congratulating herself on her supreme discipline. After all, there was only the small matter of his soul at stake, his soul that, according to the dictates of Agape Pentecostal at least, was on a highway to hell. Or maybe even the autobahn.

Only two weeks before Murphy had stolen Paige, one of Baine's bosses at work told him that he knew of a church and a lady minister he might like. It was in Caddo, not far from where Baine lived. It was called St. Thomas's, which sure sounded like a Catholic church to him, so Baine at first resisted. This boss claimed to have heard that they didn't spin any bullshit at St. Thomas's, that this lady minister went out of her way to talk to anyone. Okay, so that did not sound like a Catholic Church. Baine was curious, but he didn't follow up. He cherished his free weekends with his daughter, and he did not need God.

In truth, sometimes he was thankful Krystal was out of the house and their lives on Sunday mornings. He would prepare a kind of pancake Paige liked: with apple sauce and raisins in the batter, and cinnamon and butter on top. They would find something on television to watch, hard as that was on Sunday mornings—inevitably they resorted to repeats of *SpongeBob* or demised series like *Ben 10* or *The Fairly OddParents*—lounge listlessly on their couch, her body leaning into his, his arm around her shoulders. After an hour or more, worried that the television rays, to say nothing of the stupidity of the cartoons, were eviscerating his daughter's sensitive mind, Baine would sit up straight, forcing Paige off him and on to her feet.

"Come on," he'd say, "let's walk." Paige would always groan "Why?" her big eyes rolling, her six-year-old's whine lancing Baine's heart; but she never refused to come along. He knew she liked these trips as much as he did. In the spring they might saunter down to the school playground to see if anyone else from the neighborhood was there, and if Paige could use any of the equipment. In the fall, they would walk to the nearest convenience store, seven blocks away, where Baine would reward Paige with a cup of store-made hot chocolate or a fat shrink-wrapped Hostess cupcake filled with every kind of obscene, delicious food chemical. In the winter, he might ask Paige to hold a bag for him while he raked dead leaves or they might run a pretend sprint race to quicken their blood and keep the cold at bay. He didn't keep Paige out for that long, but when they returned she would be pleasantly exhausted, ready for a nap. In fact, if things worked out perfectly, Paige would be sound asleep when Krystal's old Malibu pulled into the driveway, its cranky, clacking noise distinguishable from every other in the neighborhood.

His Sunday mornings alone with Paige were among the most peaceful hours ever passed in their house. Then what happened, happened. And Baine reacted as he reacted and made the decision he did. More or less made the decision. In a way, he felt it was forced on him by circumstance and police incompetence and his cosmically expanding anger, which might never, it seemed, run up against a barrier and bounce back. An anger that made it impossible for him to get along a second more, to carry out the least little duty. Before he could follow through with his plan, however, he wanted to talk to somebody, to determine how someone else would see it. Would they understand the sense of the plan the way he did? Would it make sense to them as it did to him?

After spying Jeannine at the school earlier that day, on the cusp of carrying out his long-considered action, he had gone to find that lady minister. He was shocked to see that she wore a black shirt and a white collar, just like every Catholic priest he'd ever known. He didn't want to see a Catholic priest, but he started talking anyway, just to see what she said, to find out exactly what kind of priest she was. Did Catholics ordain women now? He gave himself the name Rouse and sat in her office and tried to explain to her what he intended to do. But she didn't believe him, and this angered him, and then she began to explain she was Episcopal, that he was in an Episcopal church—which meant nothing to him, really—and then she began checking her cell phone repeatedly. She claimed it was on account of her son, but Baine had his doubts.

He began to get nervous that something else was going on. Had she secretly alerted the police? Was she in communication with them as she sat there and so coolly explained the difference between an Anglican and a Roman collar? Were they on their way? Baine didn't know, but he didn't see the point in sticking around to find out. So, when she walked away to hunt out a pamphlet he ditched her. She seemed like a reasonable woman, and if he hadn't had a child to abduct and murder, he might have stayed and chatted. He would have told her the whole story of his pain, the terrible loss of his daughter; the maddening injustice of Murphy's escape; the betrayal by Krystal and then her death, with which she had eluded just punishment; the hopelessness of living in a world in which those things were possible. He would have poured out his broken heart to her—and told her why God should share the blame—but he couldn't risk the police. And he was going to do what he was going to do, anyway. No matter what she said.

It occurred to him now that the lady minister, this Elizabeth person—he thought that was what she had called herself—lived a very different kind of churchly existence from all the Baptist husbands and wives he'd known at Entergy. Church must mean, more than anything else, an absolute business to the woman. Because she didn't just hang out in the building but was responsible for everything that happened there. Anytime anybody needed prayers or a room to let or booklets or pamphlets. Anytime anybody got sick or near dying. Busy, busy, busy—solely with church matters, church people, church budgets, church equipment.

His thoughts stopped. His mouth opened. Judas Priest, how could he have been so stupid? *How had he been so stupid?* He looked at Jeannine and could almost smell the doubt budding in her. Okay, so he'd been stupid, but now he had something he could use. He had something that would really truly help him, that would make his plan completely possible, perhaps even easy. If he was right, that is. But he was sure he was right.

"You could just call my mom on her cell," the girl said. "Do you have that number?" She looked at him squarely.

"No, she didn't give it to me," Baine said.

"I could give it to you."

The girl was studying him even harder now, examining his eyes, his face, his hands, the kitchen behind him. He saw her glance toward the front door.

"No, no need. She's so busy at St. Thomas's, I wouldn't want to add any more complications to her day. I already told you that."

Jeannine turned her head back quick; her eyes were wide and shocked. Her thin little mouth opened and stayed that way a moment. He wasn't sure if he was looking at alarm or fear or pure befuddlement, but then he saw something else, some distinct separate vintage, bleed into her expression and relax her features: relief. The girl closed her mouth. She sat back down on the sofa.

"So, you did go to see her in her office," she said.

"Of course. Would I lie about that?" Baine laughed to show a breezy lack of concern. He had thought it was something he should force out, but when it came it came easily and naturally. Indeed, he even felt happy. It wasn't a lie, after all.

Jeannine looked again at the television, but she didn't seem to be really looking at it. Then she brought her head back. "I can just tell you her phone number, and you can call her."

"No, no, no," Baine said, palms up, insisting on this. "Stop asking. I am not going to bother your very busy Episcopal priest mother. After all, the whole point in bringing you here is so she can take as much time as she needs. If I call her it will only delay her further; plus, it would seem like I'm bugging her. Right?"

The girl held his gaze for a moment. Then she nodded.

"Look, it's past five," Baine said. "And I'm thinking I should start fixing some dinner. I'll eat, and you probably should too, in case your mom is really delayed. Although I don't think she will be."

"I'm still not hungry," Jeannine said.

"Oh, you're just out of sorts because you're not at home. Relax. Maybe eating will clear up your nerves."

"I don't think it's nerves," she said.

Baine decided to ignore the comment. It didn't matter. He knew who her mother was. He had this girl in his pocket. He figured that eating might make her warm and sluggish and all juicy-bloody inside, and that would only make it easier to catch her and do what he needed to. "How about I fix some spaghetti?"

She didn't reply. He started looking for a pot to boil water in and fortunately it only took his opening two kitchen cabinet doors to locate the thing. In addition to the snacks and rope and duct tape he'd bought days earlier, he'd laid in a small supply of foodstuffs. Among the food items were two boxes of spaghetti and a couple jars of sauce. He realized, though, that he should have bought some good bread from the bakery, instead of the spongy Wonder Bread he'd thoughtlessly pulled from the shelf. Bread that would sop up the leftover spaghetti sauce and set the girl's heart at ease. Who doesn't feel better, calmer at the sight of good bread? Oh well. Spongy Wonder Bread would have to suffice. He filled the pot with water and turned on the stovetop. He hunted through an overhead cabinet for the spaghetti he'd purchased. Not there. Strange. He was sure that was where he had put it. He tried the next cabinet. Then the next. Bingo.

"My dad likes to make spaghetti," the girl said suddenly. "But I guess you know that since you know him."

"I know your mom a lot better, but yeah, we talk about your dad sometimes."

He poured salt in the pot of water and opened the box of spaghetti, set it down. Now he needed to remember which cabinet he'd put the sauce in.

"He really likes his job at the paper factory," Jeannine said. "Weird. It sounds boring to me."

Golden, Baine thought. This was great information. She just thrust it at him without even having to ask. The only paper factory in Caddo was Kimberly Clark's, one of the town's biggest employers. And now he knew that Jeannine's father worked there.

"That's why he can't ever pick me up. I mean, at school. You know I was so surprised when you said 'they' couldn't get me today. That's because my dad never gets me. He can't. If he ever leaves the factory during his shift he gets in huge trouble."

"Well, factories have to be strict. They're under tight deadlines. Kimberly Clark especially, I imagine. That's one big outfit."

"Right," she started again, slowly. "So, Mom told you that my dad works at Kimberly Clark?"

"Indeed, indeed," Baine chirped. He tried another cabinet. Where was that sauce?

"I don't see why he likes working there," the girl said. "I mean, if he's never allowed to get away, even to pick me up."

Why hadn't he simply put the sauce in the same place as the spaghetti? He tried to remember what he was thinking the other day when he returned from Walmart with the four plastic bags of goods. He wondered if he'd forgotten it altogether. He couldn't be that out of it, could he? To forget the spaghetti sauce? For God's sake, why? No. No, he remembered the jar and the label. It was yellow and red and green, cartoony colors; a famous national brand. He thought he should get a brand; not just Walmart's Great Value. He thought a well-known national brand might satisfy the kid better—whoever she was. He remembered putting the jar in his cart. He remembered setting it on the conveyor belt at the register. He remembered the yellow and red and green label heading toward the cashier.

"You know what they say," he muttered, trying to keep up his happy tone, "one man's ceiling is another man's floor. Everybody likes something different."

The girl didn't answer. He looked through another cabinet. Most of them were completely empty. Then he noticed the silence. How thick a silence it was. He looked back. The girl was staring at him more fiercely than ever. Well, no, not fiercely. Not, that is, with anger, but with penetration. Baine didn't know what this meant. Maybe that was just her look.

"I guess you talk to my mom a lot, since she's told you about Dad and the paper factory."

"Oh, sure. We talk about that. We talk about everything. I love your mom."

She nodded once: carefully, strictly. "And she probably told you about Dad's new motorcycle."

Baine threw his head back and made a noise that was meant to be a throaty laugh. Now that did come out as forced. "Oh yes, that motorcycle," he said. Then he remembered where he'd put the sauce: in the refrigerator. *Thank God.* The water was boiling, so he cracked the spaghetti in half and dropped both halves into the water. He turned the temperature on the burner from HIGH to LOW. He fetched the bottle of sauce and found a smaller pot to use to heat it.

"They have arguments about it every night at the dinner table," Jeannine said. "My dad loves it. He doesn't want to ride anything else. My mom says she's worried that he might get hurt; plus, it cost too much."

Baine could not imagine a priest arguing about motor-cycles with anybody, but then again until today he could not imagine a priest who was a woman and who had two children. With some effort, he opened the jar of sauce and dumped it wholly into the small pot. He turned the burner on LOW. If all went according to plan, the spaghetti would be done cooking and the sauce heated through at about the same time. Then they would eat. Then the real excitement could start. Finally.

"What do you think?" the girl said.

Baine was concentrating on the meal. He hadn't really heard the last sentence she spoke. "About what?"

"About these discussions between my dad and my mom about his new motorcycle."

"Oh, I don't know," Baine said and shrugged. "Maybe she should just let the poor guy have his baby. Every man needs a baby, you know."

"Is that what you told her?"

"More or less."

"That she should let my dad keep his motorcycle?"

"Yep."

All the life seemed to go out of her then. Her eyes were no longer fierce or penetrating or studious or even neutral. He saw an overwhelming sadness enter her. Her blue eyes dewed with water and turned a foggy liquid-gray, resonant with fear and loss and hopelessness.

"But you know, it's your mom's house too. And if she really thinks the motorcycle is a mistake, she's got a right to say so."

The girl's eyes stayed welled with sadness, her hands clenched together between her knees, her shoulders drooped and her head tilted down: like someone who just lost their best friend or their best dog or their best toy.

The girl is nuts, Baine thought. *Just feed her and get this over with.*

I have to make myself eat. Otherwise he will figure it out. He will know that I know. This man, whoever he is—not *Jim Hutton*—is obviously messed up, but he's also not stupid. He got me away from school and into his car, got me all the way to this lake house and then slapped me before it dawned on me what was happening. That takes some smarts. Also, a really really bad heart. I need to act like I believe his lies, that I am happy to be here, that I don't fear him.

"It's good, right?" he says, his mouth curling up in a smirking half-smile. It could be a whole smile, but that stain on the left side of his face kind of blanks out his expression, so I only see one half of his mouth turn upward. At first, seeing the face, I'd felt sorry for him. Really sorry. Even more when he told me about the man who had pushed him down into the acid. *This is just the kind of man my mom would befriend,* I thought. Just the kind of person she would try to save. But this guy is beyond saving. He is a monster who looks like a monster because he is a monster. He shoves into his mouth a huge forkful of spaghetti greased with watery red sauce.

"Yum, yum," he says, like I am a toddler in a highchair and he has to convince me.

I stab at it, bring the end of the fork to my lips. "This is good," I say. No, it's terrible. "What kind of sauce did you get?"

"It's famous!" he shouts, still smiling. "It's one of the most popular brands. I can't really tell the difference between them, though. Spaghetti sauce all tastes the same to me."

I try to smile as if I agree, even though I don't. Not even close. I think about what Dad would say: *If you think all _____ (insert any kind of food here: tacos, pizza, chicken kabobs, steak subs, lasagna, spaghetti sauce) tastes the same, you haven't tasted the real thing.* He is right, almost always. And almost always he can prove he's right by making the "real thing" for us. I know enough to know that whatever Jim put on this spaghetti is crap: greasy, bodiless liquid with flecks of tasteless onions, stubble of something green, and a few rubbery mushrooms. I can almost hear one of Dad's "If you think you've eaten" comments.

There are worse things, I realized, than your dad cheating on your mom. Like having the dad who you love, who you used to see a lot more than your mom, live all the way on the other side of the country. And now it has gotten worse still, and I have been stolen by a creep who makes bad spaghetti and wants to hurt me, and I don't think Dad can possibly know, even if Mom knows, and I don't see how she can, and, in any case, I know I may never see him again. If Jim doesn't try to rape me—or even if he does—it's not likely he will let me live. Isn't that what happens to girls who are abducted? The men rape them and then … well, they don't ever let them live to tell about it, do they? Their bodies—their corpses—are found months later, buried in some obscure place, sometimes mutilated. I feel the same blistering rush of misery as I did a few minutes before, and I feel myself starting to shake and then to cry, so I raise my water glass to cover my face, and I drink a huge drink of water. By the time I lower the glass, I have the tears under control. But Jim is staring at me like he's worried.

"Something wrong?"

"No, a piece got stuck in my throat."

"Too bad." A smile again: one that's meant to look sympathetic but is deeply, deeply creepy. Creepier than the last one.

I pretend to chew a bit more on Jim's terrible spaghetti when an even worse idea hits me, and I feel a chill along my forearms and behind my ears. My head gets cloudy and I have to put the fork down. Maybe the reason he knew Mom would not be there to pick me up was that he had dealt with her already. Why not, after all? If he could kidnap me, and hurt me, what would keep him from doing the same to Mom? No wonder he could stand there and talk to me outside school. He knew no one was coming who could stop him.

I almost throw up, right onto my plate. Sadness—I mean bad sadness—has always done terrible things to my stomach. Some kids can't eat when they are sad. But I'm even worse. I want to throw up. It makes me think, *What's the point?* It makes me think, *Why not just let him do what he wants with me?* My father is almost a thousand miles away, my mother likely dead, and my brother—oh my God, can this man have done something to Aaron too? Is it possible he has a vendetta against our whole family? Is he someone from Mom and Dad's past? Or maybe he has gotten rid of Mom and Aaron only in order to isolate me, keep me here in this big, empty house without a chance of rescue. Because maybe nobody who matters will even know that I am gone.

"You're still not eating," Jim says. "I don't understand. Kids are hungry after school. You haven't eaten a thing since we came here."

I can't meet his eyes. I really can't. I can't bear seeing that face. Maybe he was the one with the hydrochloric acid. Maybe he was the one who tried to hurt someone with it. "I know. I'm sorry. Some days I just don't feel hungry."

I can feel him staring at me angrily, but I still cannot look at him. What if I see in his eyes that he knows that I know? Or what if, for the first time, he sees in my eyes that I do?

"I don't believe you," he says. "I think you're always hungry. Because that's the way kids are. That's how my daughter was."

I look up. "Your daughter? You have a daughter?"

"I had a daughter. Had." Yes, I see anger.

"What happened?"

He looks at me, hard-faced, then shakes his head. "It's not important." Then: "I don't want to talk about it."

"Sounds like you do."

"No. I said I don't, and I don't. What I want is for you to eat." He pauses. "Because that's what your mom is expecting."

"I thought you said you didn't know when she was coming."

Got him. I see him swallow, open his mouth, close it, start nodding in some retarded person's motion. "That's true," he finally says, "but I told her I would keep you as long as necessary. I told her not to worry about the time, because I could give you dinner. I didn't mind giving you dinner. I told her I was happy to do that. If she ends up getting here late, another hour or two, she's going to expect that you have food in your stomach and that she won't have to get home and immediately start cooking for you."

Despite the fact that it's total bullshit, what he says makes sense. Mom hates to cook, and that's exactly what she has to do if I don't take dinner at a friend's house. But Jim is no friend of my mother's—and I know for a fact he is lying. I wonder if now is the time to make my break. How long will it take me to get to the front door, and how hard will it be to stay a step ahead of him? And once out the door, where will I go? I take a big bite of spaghetti and chew. It is so terrible—so very very terrible—and getting cold now, too—I almost puke it up. But I hold the noodles in my stomach by swallowing two big gulps from my water glass. I reach for the bread: boring, sliced-up, white sandwich bread that Jim has taken straight from the bag and dropped on a plate. Jim slaps my hand.

"No. You eat more spaghetti first. I don't want you filling up on bread."

I almost laugh at him. I almost have the guts. I want to say, "What? So I'll have a full stomach when I die?" This man is so strange. Why is he feeding me? What does food have to do with anything?

As if to prove to me how good the meal is, how all it takes is a bit of appreciation, Jim picks the pasta scoop out of the bowl and, with great showy motions, like he is putting on a magic act, proceeds to put three gigantic scoopfuls on his plate. He gives me that creepy smile and starts eating again. He shoves the gross concoction into his mouth: forkful after forkful. Just watching him makes me want to be sick. When he's eaten every last bit of it, he takes a drink of water and then grabs a slice of bread. He moves the piece of bread around the plate, picking up the thin red liquid left behind. Then, in three sharp bites he finishes off the piece. Another drink of water: this one longer. He doesn't just set the glass down but bangs in on the table, like a period on a sentence. Like a judge on a tv show.

"There," he says. "That's how it's done. I just ate a whole plateful, on top of my earlier plateful. You can't tell me you can't eat even the least little bit."

"I can't," I say. Because I can't.

He leans back in his seat and stares up at the ceiling. I hear him exhale wearily, like everything in the world is conspiring against him. He leans so far back he is pushing the front legs of the chair off the floor; he is tilting it backwards. And staring, staring, mesmerized by something up there. I'm about to look to see what it is, but then he looks back at me, and for the first time I see true murder in his eyes. I mean an actual red color: of menace, of bad ideas, of frustration, of being absolutely sick of me and the whole friendly-guy act.

"Okay," I say. "I'll eat." I pick up the spaghetti and stuff more of it inside me. It doesn't matter that it is terrible. I can't even taste it now. It is just something I'm doing to stay alive. Jim sighs and stands up. He pushes his chair back with the back. What is happening? What is happening? My forehead gets hot. I eat as much as I can, as fast as I can; I make sounds as if I am enjoying it.

Jim walks around the table so that he is standing right next to me, just to my right. Looming over me. Then he speaks: "I have to go to the bathroom. When I get back here, I want to see that you've eaten that whole plateful. Do you understand?"

I nod.

"Say it," he says.

I just manage to get the mouthful down my throat. "I understand," I say.

"Promise me you will."

"I promise."

I glance up at him. He is nodding slowly. The red is still in his eyes, but not as bold.

"And here," he says. He gives me two more scoops. My plate is virtually sagging beneath the load. "I want you to eat all of that. There can't be a single strand of spaghetti left when I get back from the bathroom." Pause. "Or you are in big trouble."

"Okay," I say quietly.

"I made that for you, girl," he says.

I figure this is not the time to point out that he hasn't made anything. Three factories have: the one that made the spaghetti, the one that made the sauce, and the one that made the bread. All he's done is put the three things together.

"I know," I say. "Thank you. Very much."

I'm not looking at him anymore, but I know he is staring at me: scrutinizing, judging, trying to guess. Trying to decide. Another sigh: smaller, shorter. Then he turns on his heel and heads back, deeper into the house. He goes around the kitchen counter and then down the hallway back there, where the bedroom is that he stashed Cocteau in.

Immediately, without even thinking about it, because I know there is no time to think, I start for the front door. I don't run—that would be too much noise. But I will run as soon as I am outside. I will run to the nearest house: the one at the end of Jim's long driveway, up there by Lake Cedar Road. I will bang on their door. I will beg them to take me inside. And if there is no one home, I will just run into the road, waving my arms. I will make somebody stop. I will jump into the car, no matter whose it is.

I take a second to peer through the long glass window next to the door: to see where I am going, to set my mind on it. I see the black metal gate we came through in Jim's car earlier. It's about half a soccer field away. I don't know where the button to unlock it is. It must have a button that unlocks it. But I don't have time to look. I'll just have to climb it. I will climb it. I'm used to climbing. More than Jim is. If I make it to the gate, I might be home free. I might be done with him. If I make it to the gate, and over, I can probably make it all the way up the driveway before Jim catches me.

I turn the lock on the front door. I throw the door back and feel the February air. It stings me with cold, much colder than I expect, what with only my t-shirt and jeans on. But I don't care. Then, all at once, I hear Jim's noisy, pounding feet surging along the wooden panels of the floor, desperate to get back to me. "No!" he shouts. "No, no, no! No, no, no!"

I run. I don't look back. I run. I see the black metal gate in front of me. I aim for it. In my mind, I begin to plan for it. What I will do. Where I will put right leg down, how hard I will push off, where my left foot will go, where my hands will grab, how quickly my legs will have to move to help me up and over. I'll just have to. That's all there is. I'll just have to.

I hear a growl from behind me and Jim's feet coming over the concrete. He is getting closer, too close. Any other time, any other occasion, I would have looked behind me, but not now. I am too scared. I am running for my life. Fear is propelling me like a torpedo.

"Got you!"

My hair is on fire. My head is on fire. I scream. I've been yanked to a stop by my hair. I am being pulled backwards by my hair. Jim's hand is in my hair and he is holding on, like with a monster's claw, and he is dragging me by it. He is punishing me. It feels like being electrocuted on my head, every second for seconds on end. I tear up. I am screaming and tearing, not even making words. That's how bad it hurts.

"Girl," he says. "Stupid girl," he says. "Stupid, stupid, stupid little girl."

My heels hit the bump at the front doorway as I go over it backwards and I stumble, and for a moment it hurts even worse, even more suddenly. Then he loses hold, and I hit the floor inside the house. For a moment I think I can try to escape again, but he grabs me by the collar of my t-shirt and hauls me until I am halfway up, and then he begins hauling me backwards toward the dining room. I squeal and twist and flail, but he keeps his grip. Jim is stronger than he looks. He keeps his grip, and then I feel the tile of the kitchen floor beneath my sneakers, and then I feel a knife—wide, long, heavy—at my throat, and I feel him begin to saw my skin.

10

She didn't know what to do next. She had no experience with what to do. Elizabeth had spent an hour and fifteen minutes driving back and forth along the streets of Caddo. Mostly she focused on the neighborhoods near Virginia McKinley, but she also traversed—several times eventually—the route Jeannine would have taken if she had actually tried to walk home. In fact, she drove all the way into her neighborhood, to her house. She went into her house—three separate times—and called Jeannine's name. She searched the entire abode, even went into the small, trim backyard and called. Nothing. No sign of Jeannine anywhere nearby in Caddo. Finally, she accepted that Jeannine must not have tried to walk home or to any place far from the school, but she didn't know what that meant. She didn't want to think about what it meant.

She drove back to Virginia McKinley after the third check of her house and saw Principal Nixon standing outside the building, talking to a policeman. Oh God, Elizabeth thought.

God, oh god. It never occurred to her to pray. She turned off her car and ran.

"What?" she called. "What?"

For a second, Principal Nixon seemed surprised to see her. The woman squinted, adjusted her vision, as if Elizabeth were a mirage that could be dismissed by the slightest change in perspective. Then Nixon opened her eyes wide again and spoke. "We found out something."

"What?"

"Mrs. Riddle, this is Officer Byron Johnson."

Elizabeth refused to even look at him. "What did you find out?!"

The principal hesitated so long that Elizabeth wondered if she would have to beat an answer out of the woman. Then Nixon said, "I still have not heard from Jenna White or Amanda Mauldin. Mrs. Mason, like you, has been out driving the neighborhood. But I just now called her back."

"Why?" Elizabeth was almost 100% certain that she would not like the answer to this question, but she had to ask it anyway.

A single, lingering pause. Then: "Melissa Singleton returned my call. She saw your daughter walking across the front lawn here with a man in a green coat."

"What man?"

"She doesn't know. She didn't recognize him, but she says she did not think anything of it, because your daughter seemed perfectly comfortable with him."

"Was it Max?" Elizabeth could not believe this. Even though the possibility had crossed her mind earlier, she finally could not accept that her ex-husband would travel all the way from Tampa to kidnap her daughter. No matter how angry Max was with her—and by God he was angry—she couldn't fathom that he would do that. For two different reasons, both of which got to the nature of her ex-husband: 1) For all his obvious failures as a spouse she couldn't deny Max was a loving father. He would not do anything so frightening to Jeannine as to kidnap her and force her to travel all the way to Tampa to live in a state that was foreign to her and among relatives she barely even knew; 2) The very reason Max had left Caddo in the first place was to make Elizabeth pay as dearly as possible for pushing him away. To make Elizabeth realize exactly what it meant not to have him around from day to day, even if that meant giving up seeing his son and daughter with any kind of regularity, this after being thoroughly enmeshed with their lives for seventeen years: birthdays, recitals, soccer games, report cards, parent-teacher conferences, Sunday afternoon board games at home. (He had, actually, been that steady and that devoted.) In short, he was willing to hurt himself—and badly—if it meant he hurt Elizabeth more in the process. Max could be exactly as thin-skinned as that, just that much of an asshole, at least toward her. And he wasn't about to shift course this soon; not yet. Elizabeth knew precisely what he was waiting for: for her to beg him to come back. Not until he received such a summons could she realistically expect him to return to Caddo.

But, even so, no matter how unrealistic a hope it was, how she wished now it might be true. Because if the man in the green coat was Max, that meant Jeannine was still alive. She had texted Max earlier—finally she didn't have the courage to call—but then she turned off her phone, because she also didn't have the courage to endure his astonishment and his outrage. But maybe he hadn't tried to contact her at all. Because maybe Jeannine was with him.

No. She was only kidding herself. As much as it would bring the sweetest relief to think that Max was responsible for Jeannine's disappearance, she knew that wasn't true. She had been right the first time. Max couldn't have done it.

Principal Nixon lowered her eyes. "I'm sorry, Mrs. Riddle. Melissa knows what your husband looks like. She says it wasn't him."

"He's my ex-husband," Elizabeth spat at her.

Principal Nixon blinked and then said nothing more.

"Okay, I'm sorry, so what did the man look like?"

"That's just what I was explaining to Officer Johnson"— Nixon gestured once more to the man—"when you drove up." Elizabeth, when she finally deigned to look at him, saw a stocky African-American man, with an extremely close haircut, so close as to nearly be bald, and a good square jaw; she noticed that he was looking at her with concern. "Melissa said she just saw them for a second, and then looked away. Jeannine seemed so comfortable with this person that she didn't think to study him. All she could say, more or less, was that he wasn't your husband. Ex-husband." A quick half-apologetic smile.

"That's all she could say?"

"More or less."

"What's the more?"

"The more?"

"If that's not exactly, precisely all that she said, what else did she say?" Elizabeth was starting to wonder if Principal Nixon was mentally challenged. Why did she have to explain every little thing to this woman? Surely no person could be so cruel as to toy with a mother whose daughter had been kidnapped. It must be that she was stupid.

"All she said was that he had dark hair. And a green coat. That's all she saw."

"Tall? Short?"

"Medium."

"Fat? Skinny?"

"Medium."

"Did she get into a car with the man?"

"Mrs. Singleton can't say."

"Did she really see this man or not?"

"She did. She just didn't study him."

"Ma'am," Office Johnson broke in, "if I may?" He raised an expressive left hand in the air, as if to catch Principal Nixon's words before they might make it to an ear. "Mrs. Riddle, it's not unusual for eyewitness testimony to be sketchy. If people don't know something is important, they don't pay attention to it. If they're not told to pay attention to it, they don't. That's why a lot of eyewitness testimony is just bad. Or wrong. What we want is to get more—a lot more—eyewitnesses, listen to what they have to say, and start putting together similarities in their accounts. You do that, eventually you get something. The more people you hear from, the more likely you are to get something accurate. If you only hear from one person, you're not likely to get much at all. You might get nothing. Or what you get is wrong."

This all made sense. Too much sense. But it was so damn unfair. A girl walked away from a middle school in the center of the afternoon, and only one person saw?

"What we have to do is keep trying to find eyewitnesses," Officer Johnson said.

"Is that what you're doing?" Elizabeth asked the principal.

Nixon lowered her head oddly, very oddly, and bent from the shoulder. Then Elizabeth realized what she was doing: a mock bow. "That's what I'm doing now," the principal said. "I'll try Jenna White one more time. Then I'll call every other parent in seventh grade."

"Everyone, call everyone," Johnson said. "You never know who might know something. You might be shocked who knows something."

"But if I might never know, how will I know whom to call?"

Elizabeth had to admit that it was a fair question.

"Just call," Johnson said. "Call anyone and everyone. It almost doesn't matter. Put out an APB. Start a phone tree. Tell every parent to call five people in their neighborhood. Eventually somebody they call will know something. And that person, whoever that person is, needs to call us." He pressed a hand against his chest. "And this all needs to happen quickly, because if the girl has been abducted we are in a race against the clock."

He looked at Elizabeth guiltily, aware of what he had just admitted.

"It's okay," Elizabeth said softly. "That all sounds reasonable. Do you want me to start calling too?"

"No, ma'am," he said. "Not yet. Let her do that. Right now, there are some things I need to know about your daughter— and about you."

When she got home, after answering all of Johnson's questions and then driving the streets of Caddo for another forty-five minutes, she heard the house phone ringing. She ran to pick it up until she heard the automatic voice on the machine read out the name of the caller. It was Max. She stopped. She stood there, about to pick up the phone, except that she didn't. She couldn't. She didn't know what to say to him, how to explain herself. Max would blame her—only her—for whatever happened. She couldn't stand to hear his blame right now. She blamed herself badly enough. Just when the ringing stopped and the voicemail message started, Elizabeth heard Max hang up without leaving a message. It was just as well. Then she saw a number flashing on the machine: 13. Thirteen new calls. Good lord, she thought, when had that happened, and what did it mean?

Turning her cell phone off had been a cowardly act. She knew this, but she couldn't help herself. Max could be so righteous—even when he was in the wrong, especially when he was in the wrong. He'd slept with a nineteen-year-old waitress, after all. No, "slept" was too gentle a verb for what they'd done. He'd propped her up against a wall of the kitchen at Marino's Italian Bistro and banged her until he'd achieved whatever it was he needed from the action. He claimed it only happened once, but even if that was true it still happened. He'd violated their vows. And yet afterwards, as they talked about it, and as they fought about the divorce, you would have thought she was the one who'd cornered the waitress; you'd have thought she was the guilty party. The divorce proceedings became for a time, especially when they were deciding the fate of Aaron and Jeannine, nothing more than an attack upon Elizabeth's character. She was a bad wife. A bad mother. Too busy, almost never at home. Hopeless at keeping house; useless in the kitchen; barely present in their lives. Not even available to drive her children to school in the morning. Not even available for that!

The attacks were fundamentally not true, but they were true enough that she cried every day for weeks. It came to the point that she cried just at seeing her husband or his lawyer. When she finally stopped crying was when she watched his

Corolla leave her driveway and start on its way to another state. Then her sadness became what it probably should have been all along: fury. Not just at his cheating but at his reaction to the cheating, his reaction to the divorce proceedings and the custody discussions. Most of all, at his vengeful decision to leave the state and his family behind.

For a week, she burned with a pure holy anger at him. And then it went away, and she was left with the messy factual present: having to raise two kids by herself because she'd insisted that she couldn't stay married to a man who screwed a waitress while she was at home falling asleep over a book on homiletics. What she felt more than anything—at least before Jeannine had gone lost—was tired. Tired and frayed and listless and worried. Wondering if she was a fraud as a priest, she who had demonstrated so little forgiveness. Wondering if, in fact, she might be as guilty as Max and his lawyer had suggested. And then she'd had to text him to say that she'd lost his daughter. And then one other damning fact asserted itself. She was weak. Too weak to keep her phone on to read Max's reply.

But these calls—thirteen of them!—she needed to hear; they might contain something, maybe even a lead. Officer Johnson had told her to go home and wait by the phone, wait for developments. He would call her directly as soon as they found out anything, he said. Anything. If, in the meantime, she thought of something that might help the investigation—the police were calling it an investigation now, ever since notice came that Jeannine had walked away with a stranger—she should call them. Officer Johnson had given her a business card that listed his office phone number. On the back of the card he penned his private cell number. Call me if anything occurs to you, he emphasized. And try to rest. And try not to worry. *Try not to worry.* She had liked him—liked him very much—until he said that. *Try not to worry.* Was he crazy or heartless? Or just a fool? She didn't know. She walked away without answering. How could one respond to such a ridiculous suggestion?

She felt a cold, wet sensation against her hand. She startled and then saw that it was just Bridie, their English setter. Wondering where she'd been. Wondering where her dinner was. Wondering where the rest of the family had got to.

Elizabeth groaned. "Not now, Bridie. For crissakes." How could the dog expect to be fed and stroked when Jeannine was missing? Again, Bridie stuck her nose against her hand. Elizabeth sighed. "All right, but this has to be fast. Don't you get that? Can't you tell?" She practically ran to the laundry room, grabbed a scoopful of dry food and brought it to the kitchen. She threw it resentfully into Bridie's dish and then left the scoop on the kitchen counter. She went back to the living room and pushed the button on the phone to hear her messages.

The first message was from that morning: a carpet cleaner reminding her of a bill. The second message was from earlier in the afternoon: an automated call from the high school notifying parents about a course preference form that was coming home with their sons and daughters that day. Surely, Elizabeth thought, not all thirteen calls could be unrelated to Jeannine. The third call was from Max: a hang-up. And the fourth. And the fifth. She heard the machine tell her when the calls came through, starting about two hours earlier, soon after she'd texted him. He would have tried her cell: immediately and repeatedly. Texts, phone calls, more texts. Having no luck there he would have called her at home. Probably he had gone back and forth between cell and home, determined to keep dialing until someone somewhere picked up. Probably if she turned on her cell this minute she would hear it ringing with a call from him. She left it off.

The calls changed when they got to the sixth one. She noticed the time of it: 6:04, over a half hour ago. "Elizabeth," she heard a woman say, "this is Karla"—the secretary at church—"I just saw the report. Oh my God, please call me if you want to. If there's anything I can do."

Report?

The seventh, eighth, and ninth calls—coming only a minute after Karla's and within seconds of each other—were from St. Thomas's parishioners who also mentioned seeing a "report" and offered their help. The tenth call was from Max: a hang-up. The eleventh call was from the curate. He sounded stunned, beaten, out of hope, as if his best friend had died. His voice floundered through a brief, almost senseless message. "I just heard . . . from Karla . . . I can try to help . . . tell me, Elizabeth, how I can help . . . you must feel terrible." He sounded so distraught she actually felt bad for him, for his apparent pain, and for a millisecond wondered why he thought she should be feeling so bad herself. Then of course she remembered. The twelfth call was not a hang-up, not technically, but again it was Max. "Jesus, Liz!" he shouted. That was all. Then the call cut off. Whatever, Elizabeth thought. She was not going to worry about Max and his anger right now. She was not going to question whether she had been justified in turning off her cell. She was not going to tell herself that if she had intended never to talk to him again she shouldn't have texted him. Those were concerns for another day and hour. Right now, she needed to know what this "report" was. What did it mean? What did it say?

The last message was from another parishioner: Nettie Gamble. Nettie worked at the hospital as an administrator. Elizabeth had spent many hours with her a year ago when, within a time span of three weeks, Nettie's mother died, her younger sister was diagnosed with breast cancer, her son was arrested for trying to sell vicodin to his high school classmates, and her husband announced he was moving to Albuquerque to reunite with an old grade school flame, the girl who had always been his "one true love," but who he had assumed was gone from his life forever. A "girl," Nettie was quick to point out, that her husband had never once mentioned during the entire course of their courtship and marriage.

"That's one pothole I wish he had warned me about," Nettie had said, turning a rueful smile as she said it. Elizabeth had been amazed at Nettie's strength, amazed even more that what happened to her drove her not away from church but more fully into it. And eventually Nettie became one of her best, most reliable, most selfless friends. There was no one alive, really, whom she preferred to spend time with than Nettie. Now she was scared that it was Nettie on the message, scared what that meant, scared for what her friend might say. "Liz," Nettie said, "I'm here. I'm here, I'm here. I just heard about it on the television news. I'm here, baby." That was all she said. Then she hung up.

The television? What television? Elizabeth hurried to the set in her living room and turned it on. She looked at the clock. 6:54. Damn. Too late. She flipped through all four of the local television stations: CBS, NBC, ABC, Fox. The first three had all moved on to national programming; the latter was airing a special about Arkansas Razorbacks basketball. Local news was over. At least until 10:00. She'd missed it: all four programs. What had they said? And who said it? How did they find out? When she'd driven away from school for the last time that day, no news van was parked at the school. She saw no evidence that they had become a "story." Who told them? What did they say? And why, if something was going on, hadn't she heard from Officer Johnson?

The phone rang. She heard the machine read out the identity of the caller. Max again. She knew she owed it to him to pick up and talk. He was Jeannine's father. That was why she had texted him. But before she could make a decision, the machine picked up and Max once again refused to speak. She looked through her purse, it was still on her shoulder, she realized—still on her shoulder—and found the business card with the cell number Johnson had written down for her. She had to call him. But then the home phone rang again, and the call was coming from the Caddo Police Department.

"What is it?" she said. "Please tell me."

Johnson hesitated only a second before speaking. "Mrs. Riddle, I think you might want to come down to the station."

"Why?" Her heart was beating faster than it ever had in her life. In her mind, she kept hearing the terrible words he was going to say. She kept hearing them in her mind, even if he didn't actually say them.

"There's somebody you need to talk to."

"Who? Why?"

"I don't want to get into it over the phone. Can you just come?"

"Have you found Jeannine?"

Hesitation. "No, ma'am. We still don't know where she is."

She sighed soundlessly. *That means she's not dead. They can't tell me she's dead. They can't tell me that.*

"But I think if you come down here and talk to this person, you might be able to help us locate her."

She was off the phone and heading for the door before Johnson even finished his sentence.

11

Angel was almost done with her catch-up work in French Civilization: a chapter in the textbook on the history of French culinary arts, and two websites she needed to annotate. As soon as she'd returned from her trip to Virginia McKinley she'd felt inspired to reconnect with all the different aspects of her life, including homework, so she'd texted a friend in class to find out if she'd missed any assignments. Finished now with the French Civ. homework, she needed to turn her attention to French Literature 2 and *La Peau de Chagrin*, the Balzac novel she was supposed to have finished for yesterday's class. She checked her cell for the hour: 5:50. For the first time all day she felt hungry. In fact, she felt ravenous. *That's what happens when you don't eat. When you spend the whole day worrying.*

She looked in the refrigerator, but she was not surprised to see that it was empty. She hadn't gone grocery shopping in days, and neither had Shelby. Except for stray containers of mustard, ketchup, and mayonnaise, and a few bottles of Sam's Choice water, the only edible product in the refrigerator was some caked-up mass of brown with onion and mushroom stowed in a Styrofoam carton. A restaurant waiter had scribbled some identifying note with a Sharpie, but Angel couldn't read it. Even if the contents of the carton had looked appetizing she would have kept her hands off. Shelby might be a distant, self-involved roommate, but she went ballistic over two things: hair in the sink and her food being stolen. (As far as Angel could remember she'd never stolen a single bit of Shelby's food, but she'd been loudly, nearly crazily, accused at least half a dozen times since the start of the school year.)

Fortunately, the Tiger Café—an eatery operated by the campus food service, and specializing in your classic American greasy spoon—was open to 9:00 most nights and not at all far from her apartment. While she hated to admit it, nothing pleased her studying palate more than a drippy, egg-topped cheeseburger or a bag of fried chicken tenders. There was something about having to do homework that necessitated the ingestion of fried food. Good-for-you food never gave her the strength to endure four and five hour bouts of studying. Bad food packed more energy, an accidental gift from all the nitrites and additives and sodium and growth hormones. She wasn't going to deny it, despite how it violated core tenets of the French culinary arts. It was fact.

The square, brightly lit café—featuring flat-screen televisions on three of its four walls—occupied about a quarter of the bottom floor of the biology building. It was manned at this hour mostly by student workers who shuttled orders back and forth between the counter and the grill behind them, where two long-experienced food service fry cooks hammered out an array of Americana on a long, spitting grill. Everyone knew and loved Edgar and William. Edgar, a doe-eyed man with a tired face and a cautious smile, was in charge; whereas William, a toothy, exuberantly friendly guy moved from the refrigerator to the grill to the deep fryer and back again with complete ease and a constant whistle to accompany some song that blared from an old school boom box he kept on the floor. As far as Angel could tell, William only ever listened to the local classic rock station: all CCR and Eagles and Rolling Stones, all the time.

On a whim, Angel opted for the Reuben sandwich with a side of onion rings, two tastes which she knew did not go together—but that was what made her, on this evening, with this amount of homework left to do, want to get them. She paid and then searched for the farthest, most unoccupied table, which happened to be against the back wall. When she sat, she noticed that the television was set to the local 6:00 news. She was about to go ask one of the student workers if she could switch the channel when a photograph appeared over the left shoulder of the anchorwoman. She recognized the face in the photograph. Then she realized why she recognized it. "Oh my God," she said out loud. The sound was off, but in the closed caption box she spied the words, WALKING AWAY WITH AN UNIDENTIFIED MAN WHO DOES NOT APPEAR TO BE RELATED TO HER. CADDO POLICE ARE STILL TRYING TO ASSEMBLE A DETAILED DESCRIPTION OF THE MAN. THEY SAY RIDDLE'S DISAPPEARANCE IS TROUBLING BUT THAT IT IS TOO EARLY TO KNOW FOR CERTAIN IF FOUL PLAY IS INVOLVED.

The picture over the shoulder of the anchorwoman changed to one of the outside of a school. For a moment, Angel thought it might be Virginia McKinley, but then she realized it didn't look like Virginia McKinley at all. She read the closed caption box. MORE NEWS FROM CENTRAL ARKANSAS SCHOOLS ... PARENTS AT CARL SMEDLEY JUNIOR HIGH SCHOOL IN NORTH LITTLE ROCK ARE GATHERING TONIGHT TO PROTEST CUTS IN THE SCHOOL'S TRACK AND FIELD BUDGET.

Wait a minute, Angel thought. *That's all?* A girl walked off with a man not related to her, and then it was on to a track and field budget? She knew this girl. That was the girl. The smart one who understood but didn't say so. The one that didn't talk but who Angel wished would. The one she saw coming out of the classroom that afternoon. *Oh, shit.* Angel had seen the "unidentified man." The man standing on the grass outside the classroom; that must have been the man they were talking about. Or at least it could have been. It could have been that the man was her father, and he took her home, and then she walked off with someone else, but Angel doubted it. God, that must have been the man. No wonder he was standing so stiffly, so strangely. As if on alert. He was probably terrified of being caught in the act. And that explained the odd, surprised look the girl gave him when she saw him. But she'd smiled too. The girl had smiled at the man, so they must have met before. She must have had a reason to trust him, despite his disfigured face. Wait. The disfigured face. *The disfigured face.*

The police were still waiting for a detailed description?

She was dialing 911 before she was halfway to the café door. It did not surprise her that it took several moments for the woman who answered to understand what she was saying or that it took at least a minute longer for the woman to connect her to the officer she should be talking to. It didn't surprise her at all that after she said what she said to the officer he asked her to come down to the station. She was already at her car. She was going to drive there anyway.

She talked first to an officer behind a thick, bulletproof window. It may or may not have been the same woman as on the phone. She frowned with noticeable suspicion and told Angel to take a seat. Angel was too agitated to take a seat, so she merely stepped back and watched as the woman dawdled for a few moments, then dialed a number on her phone and spoke into the receiver. "There's a girl here who says you told her to come down." Whatever the other officer said in reply, no change registered on the woman's face. Her cheeks remained utterly flat, her chin straight. Her eyes ticked to Angel. They were hollow and ruddy brown. "He's coming," she said tonelessly. *Thanks*, Angel thought, *for being in such a hurry to save a girl's life.*

Moments later, a heavy metal door swung open behind Angel. An officer stepped out: a stocky, dark-skinned man, with a close-shaved head, and a model's jaw. He smiled at her. "You're Angel?"

Back to planet Earth. "Yes," she said with relief. "You're Officer Johnson?"

He nodded. "Byron Johnson. Thank you for coming in."

He waved her through the metal door, which clanged solidly behind them when it shut, then led her down a dingy, brown-hued corridor with faltering fluorescent lighting to a certain office on the right. She saw a desk with a chair behind it and two in front, a phone, a computer, a plant, a file cabinet.

"Sit down," he said and motioned to a seat. She had the sudden, crazy fear that maybe he had tricked her into coming so he could arrest her. After all, when the desperation to act becomes too great ... She remembered her own desperation that morning, how it had thoroughly screwed her mind into a weepy knuckle.

"All right," Johnson said, taking his place behind the desk, "explain it to me again. You said you saw Jeannine Riddle walk away from school with somebody." He turned toward his computer and readied his fingers over the keyboard.

"Yes."

"You were inside or outside?"

"Outside. In my car."

"How far from her?"

"Oh, several yards. I was parked on the shoulder of Lindenhurst. The northbound side."

Johnson typed notes as she talked; she was surprised at how effortlessly his fingers moved: as fast as any secretary's. "And you are sure it was her?"

"Yes."

"How can you be sure?"

"She's in my French class." Odd look from Johnson. "She's one of my students."

He bowed his head, a long but not completely certain motion. His head came up. He turned away from the computer and stared at her. "So, you're a teacher at Virginia McKinley?"

"Sort of."

His face almost formed a scowl, but then, as if from an act of will, resisted and became something else, something closer to confusion. "If you're a teacher, how come you weren't inside the building?"

"I wasn't teaching then. I only teach one day a week, in the morning."

He turned again and typed a short note. He came back. "And you don't mind if I call Gloriana Nixon to make sure this is all true?"

151

"Of course not."

The answer seemed to satisfy him. "Do you have a child at the school?"

Angel blushed. "No. Uh-uh." Really? Angel knew she was no stark, raving beauty, but neither did she think she looked like a thirty-five-year-old.

Johnson, without embarrassment, tried again. "A younger sister or brother?"

"No," she said slowly. She paused. She tried to make sense of what he was saying, but there was a block in her mind: a lever that had not been pushed down to link words with outcome. "I don't understand why you're asking me these things."

"I don't understand why you were parked near the school at 3:00 in the afternoon if you weren't there to pick up anyone."

Now the lever came down. He did suspect her. He actually, really did. She tried to explain to Johnson about the bad class she'd had, about being bothered all afternoon, about needing to take a drive and ending up in front of Virginia McKinley. She couldn't tell if she'd convinced him, but he did let her continue with her account. Finally, he typed some more notes into his computer.

"All right, you said Jeannine left with a man."

"Yes, definitely."

"Describe him."

She offered as much detail as she could about the color of his hair, his height, his build, his walk. The way he murmured to Jeannine and laughed with her. Eventually, though, she came up against the limits of her memory. When she could no longer be sure if the image in her head was a recollection or a fiction, she stopped describing. Johnson, meanwhile, kept nodding and typing furiously as she talked. When she mentioned the man had a dog and she could even identify the species—Pomeranian—Johnson smiled like she'd given him a box of chocolates. When she described the man's half-red face, Johnson's head popped up, eyes alive and thinking, as if he were a scientist with a new plan for reaching Mars.

"That's very good information. Thank you," he said when she was done.

She shrugged. It was a little bit of information. As she talked, what she realized was how much better attention she should have paid. How much more she could have told him then. She kicked herself for just assuming that what she'd seen was normal—for talking herself into this idea, when something in her gut had reacted from the first moment she saw the red-faced man.

"Somebody, somewhere," Johnson said, "should be able to recognize the kidnapper based on this description. Possibly because of the dog."

"Kidnapper? That's what you're calling him?"

He paused. His eyes ticked. "That's what I'm calling him. You can call him whatever you want."

"No, I think that's right."

"I'm going to need you to stay here a while."

"Of course."

"Before you even got here, I put a call in to someone we know who can use your information to draw a picture for public release. Now that I can see it's good information, I'd like you to talk with him directly, to look at his picture as he draws it."

"Sure."

"We'll release it as soon as you approve, but it won't get any traction until the 10:00 news shows come on. I wish we could have had it for 6:00."

"I didn't even know until I saw the repor—"

He waved his hand. *I'm not trying to blame you; I'm just saying.* "He should be here soon. While he's working on that, I'm going to call Gloriana Nixon and a couple others who work over there to see if your description rings a bell." Angel nodded. "But first, I want you to talk to someone else. I'm thinking that maybe between what you know and what she knows we might be able to figure out who this man is. And maybe where he is."

"And the girl," Angel said.

Something moved in Johnson's eye, something both hard and fractured. Something pestering, but also honest. "Well … yes," he said. "The question is whether or not she's still alive."

12

When she entered the warren of Byron Johnson's office Elizabeth saw a girl sitting in one of the two chairs on the other side of Johnson's desk: no one she knew. She was pale and frightfully thin, with bent shoulders and a beaten aspect, as if she were waiting out every day, enduring them, just dying to get to some invisible finish line. She was about average pretty, but she had intelligent, introspective brown eyes and an impressively cascading head of curling dark hair. It gave her a distinctive aspect she might otherwise lack. Elizabeth felt the girl examining her with concern and curiosity, as if trying to gauge how much Elizabeth knew.

But what did the girl know? Why was she there? During the whole manic drive to the station she'd been trying out a dozen scenarios in her head as to what to expect. For half a mile she had herself convinced that she would walk into the police station to find Jeannine sitting there: whole and undamaged and smiling and ready to go home. But then she realized that Byron Johnson would not be so cruel as to keep from her that they'd found her daughter. Then for another half-mile she'd become terrified that they'd located the kidnapper but not Jeannine. Perhaps she was being called in to identify the man. But that didn't seem right either. How could she identify someone she'd never seen? Finally, she told herself to spin other possibilities, and she had, but none of these were of a pale, bent, big-haired, anxious-looking young woman whom, for the life of her, Elizabeth could not place.

"I don't know you," she said to the girl.

The girl smiled sadly and said, "I don't know you either, but he told me who you were." She gestured to Johnson.

"Who is she?" Elizabeth asked. If Officer Johnson told her this girl was the suspected kidnapper Elizabeth would reach over and strangle her. Immediately. It would not matter that it cost her her job, her position, her identity. She wouldn't care. She'd rather commit murder.

"Mrs. Riddle, this is Angel York. She teaches part-time at Virginia McKinley."

Elizabeth whirled on the girl. "How come I've never seen you there?"

"I only teach on Wednesday mornings."

"Why?"

"Because that's the plan. I'm really a student at the university. I'm majoring in French."

Now Elizabeth remembered. "You're the one who comes in and tries to teach the kids how to pronounce words."

"Yes," the girl said, guiltily.

She looked at Johnson. "And what does she have to do with all this?"

Johnson gave her a hard look. Elizabeth knew why. She was taking out her tension and her desperation on the girl. Johnson wanted her to stop. He gestured for Elizabeth to take the other seat. Elizabeth didn't want to. She wanted the girl to say whatever she was supposed to—fast—so that could then tear through the streets in a police car: bound for her daughter. Her still-living daughter. Obviously, that wasn't what Johnson had in mind.

"Miss York saw your daughter walk away from Virginia McKinley with a man," the officer said as soon as Elizabeth was seated.

"What man?" Elizabeth asked. She was suddenly leaning toward the girl, chest and shoulders out. Elizabeth noted the fear in the girl's eyes.

"I don't know who he is. I just saw him standing outside the classroom, on the grass, with his dog."

"Dog?"

"He had a Pomeranian. Do you know what they look like?"

Of course she knew what Pomeranians looked like, but before she could even throw this out, the girl jutted ahead; she spouted facts, like a caught shoplifter worried about getting whipped. "He was standing very stiff, like he didn't want to talk with anyone. Then your daughter came out of the door and spoke to him. I saw her smile. Then they talked some more. Eventually he turned and started walking towards the street, and she walked with him."

"She did this voluntarily?"

The girl blinked. "I think so."

"Was she still smiling?"

The girl looked up at the ceiling, as if trying to examine the inside of her mind with her eyes. "I don't think so, but she was talking to him."

"He wasn't like holding her or anything? Dragging her along?"

"Not at all. They were just walking together."

"Was the dog with them?"

"Of course."

"Was he touching her?"

"Your daughter?"

"Yes, was the man touching my daughter?"

"I don't think so."

"You don't think so?"

"Well—no—I'm pretty sure no."

"You're *pretty sure*?"

"Mrs. Riddle," Johnson interrupted. "As I said this afternoon, it's normal for witness recollections to be sketchy."

"All right, all right, all right." She raised her hand. "All right."

"And actually, what Miss York has told me is fairly definitive."

"I said all right."

It was just the strangest thing Elizabeth had ever heard. It was like out of a nightmare. Or a movie. Why would Jeannine have walked off with someone she didn't know? Had it been planned in advance? Had she been in communication with this man? And who was he, anyway? Who was this dog? They didn't know anyone with a Pomeranian. Was this, as occurred to her earlier, the ultimate payback against Elizabeth for letting their family dissolve? She almost—almost—could believe it. Sitting there, listening to the girl's bizarre tale, she could almost believe it. Jeannine had to know that walking off with a stranger was the single most stupid thing she could ever do—and it was also the most terrifying for her mother.

"And you don't know who the man is?" she asked the girl.

"I've never seen him before. But I'm not at the school when they dismiss. I don't know what any of the parents look like."

Elizabeth felt herself get choked with unreasonable, petulant anger. She saw that the girl saw it. "I mean," the girl corrected herself, "I don't know who any of the adults are that normally hang around the school at dismissal. I couldn't tell if he was on the up-and-up or not. I just didn't know."

"So, you just assumed he was."

The girl looked at the floor. "Yes."

"Clearly the wrong assumption."

It was. It so was.

"Elizabeth," Byron Johnson broke in, "Mrs. Riddle, I think we need to let Angel talk. I want her to describe the man to you to see if it rings any bells. We're really on the clock with this one. Every minute counts."

"Of course," Elizabeth said, genuinely embarrassed. "I'm sorry. Of course. Please go on. I'm sorry."

The girl raised her head, and there was a certain kind of glint in her eye, as if she wasn't sure she wanted to help anymore.

"Please," Elizabeth said.

"Half his face was red," the girl said at once. "Like from about where his eyebrow was, all the way down to his chin and a little bit on his neck."

Elizabeth went cold.

"He had brown hair. A little bit of a bald spot on the back, just a tiny one. And the hair above his forehead was a little thin."

All she could do now was stare at her shoes and let the girl's description pummel her.

"I'm guessing he was maybe thirty, thirty-five, but I'm not good at that kind of thing."

"She's convinced he had no gray yet," Johnson said. "With the thinning hair, mid- thirties sounds right. Forty at most. What else, Miss York?"

"He was kind of average height, but his shoulders and his waist and his thighs were a little thick. I mean, he was wearing a coat—a dark-green coat, almost army color but darker than that—but that's how it seemed. He wasn't obese or anything. I don't think you'd even say he was fat. He just didn't look like he took care of himself."

Elizabeth nodded once, a small motion. She was still staring at her shoes. The room was silent, waiting for her.

"Does this man sound like anyone you know?" Johnson said.

When Elizabeth finally raised her head, she felt the streaks that the tears made on her face. So many. She hadn't realized there were so many. She couldn't see Johnson. Her vision was utterly blurred. "I met him today in my office. He said he wanted to kill someone. But I didn't believe him."

Things were happening. While she sat in Johnson's office and grew increasingly hysterical, almost not able to breathe, she was at the same time aware of people coming in and out of the room: talking, discussing, planning. Someone, some man, came in and said he needed to talk with the girl, talk about what the kidnapper looked like. They went to another room to work. Elizabeth didn't understand. They already knew what the man looked like. *We know what he looks like*, she wanted to shout, but she couldn't because she barely had enough air to keep crying. Her daughter, that moment, might be getting murdered by this man—this man she'd met—and there was nothing any of them could do about it. She felt like she'd delivered her daughter into his hands. The man had been in her office—without any dog—and he had confessed his intentions. But she'd done nothing about it.

She'd been too worried about Aaron and his stupid car. Oh God, that too; she needed to update Aaron; someone needed to text Aaron; Aaron needed to be here. But she could not stop herself from crying. All these other considerations were secondary to the fact that her daughter was being murdered, and there was nothing they could do about it.

Then Byron Johnson left the room too, saying something about phone calls. A female police officer came in, took the girl's seat, and tried to calm Elizabeth. The officer put one arm around her shoulder, then another across her front, but Elizabeth just pushed her away. She didn't want comforting. She didn't deserve any. She deserved to be punished, to burn in hell, staring up into her daughter's eyes as Jeannine watched from paradise. She used not to believe in hell—something she had confessed to no one: not to Max, not to Nettie, certainly not to the bishop—but there was a hell, all right. She was in it now. And she was headed for one even worse.

The female officer tried again to comfort her, but Elizabeth leaned as far away as possible. She was practically prone. Right now, she just needed her own pain, her own pain; no one had a right to try to take it away from her. The female officer reached over and gently took Elizabeth's hand, but Elizabeth yanked it away and then struck the woman on the face. "Stop it!" Elizabeth screamed.

The officer stood up. "All right," she announced to no one in particular, "I'm done with this bitch." Then she walked out. *Good riddance*, Elizabeth thought, even as she continued to cry.

At some point, Johnson came back and kneeled in front of her. He was inches away, but being very careful not to touch her, as if Elizabeth herself were now a risk. She appreciated his staying away, but she resented the implication. *I only hit that woman because she was trying to hug me; she was trying to stop my pain.*

"Elizabeth," Johnson said softly, "I think we should let you sit in another room. Is that okay?"

She wagged her head yes. Yes, she'd like to get out of this terrible place.

"And we need to ask you some questions. I've found out a few things, but I need to ask you some more questions. About the man, what he said to you. Do you think once we're in another room, you can do that?"

Elizabeth didn't respond, so Johnson said, "Okay, let's get you to the other room. It's quieter there." Carefully, he insinuated a hand beneath her underarm, to help her up. She let him help her. Elizabeth trusted Johnson enough to allow it. Then they were in the narrow hallway and then in another office, one empty of all people. Johnson turned on the light. Elizabeth was thankful for the emptiness. The room looked an awful lot like Johnson's room except there was a short, padded bench against the far wall. It looked a lot like a psychiatrist's couch. The irony was almost funny. Johnson led her back there and sat her down.

"Why don't you lie here and rest for a few minutes," Johnson said. "There's a couple more calls I need to make. These are really important calls. Really important. But once I'm done with them, I'll need you to be able to answer some questions for me. Do you think you can do that? For me?"

She realized of course that this was the same question he had asked her a minute ago. She still didn't feel like answering. She shrugged.

"We can give you something to help you calm down. Do you want me to get a nurse to give you something?"

No. That Elizabeth absolutely did not want. She didn't want some nurse injecting her with anything that would make her more out of it than she already felt. They might as well shoot her. She shook her head.

"Then you'll need to gather yourself," Johnson said calmly, "so I can ask you the questions."

After a long pause, Elizabeth said, "Okay." She thought she heard Johnson sigh in response. Then he left the room. She lay on the bench. It actually was comfortable. In another situation she might have let herself fall asleep. She certainly needed sleep. She could feel in her arms and back and her thighs how the tension and the sadness had racked her. But she couldn't sleep. Instead she lay and thought again of her mistake from the afternoon and let her body empty itself of tears. When she couldn't cry anymore, she sat up. She wiped her face. She wondered what time it was. She reached for her phone, but it wasn't there. In fact, there was no place to reach for it. She had literally nothing in her possession. She glanced around the room, and then thought to look at the wall behind her. Sure enough, there it was, an old analog-style wall clock. 8:17, it read. Good God, she'd been in this police station for over an hour.

Johnson walked in and stopped as soon as he saw her sitting up. He studied her face for a moment. She smiled at him. He looked relieved.

"Okay," he said, "so you're back."

"Yes."

"That was quick. Impressive."

She shrugged. She was a minister. She was used to pulling herself together, putting on a straight face when the occasion called for it. She had to do it far too often. People told her things all the time that would make anyone else stand up and scream. But Elizabeth couldn't do that. She had to keep still, keep calm, and reassure. It could be exhausting.

"What do you want to know?" she said.

Johnson was ready. "I want you to tell me exactly what the man said to you this afternoon. Exactly."

She couldn't remember exactly, especially in her current frame of mind. But she remembered well enough. She told him the gist of it. It had not, after all, been that long a conversation. And she told him how the man had just evaporated. He was there and then he was gone. Johnson nodded, not surprised.

"He didn't specify a certain person he wanted to kill?"

She was amazed that he did not soften his pronunciation of that last word. But then again, he was a cop. "No," she said.

"Or even a certain kind of person: the people who had done him wrong, bankers, gas station workers, little kids? Anything like that?"

She swallowed. She wished he hadn't said "little kids." He didn't have to do that. She understood the question without his saying that. "No," she said. "Nothing specific at all."

Johnson thought for a moment. "And he never gave you his name?"

Elizabeth's head perked up. She only then remembered it. Yes, he had, hadn't he? "He did," she said, with the first real energy she'd felt in a long time. "In fact, he did. He said his name was Rouse."

"Rouse?" Johnson looked puzzled. "His first name or last name?"

"I don't know. All he said was Rouse. Doesn't that sound like a last name?"

Johnson nodded. "Could be an alias. After all, why should he give you his real name?"

"Well, why should he tell me exactly what he's going to do to my daughter?"

Oh yes, her energy was back. She was angry again. And again, she had to caution herself. In fact, that was not what the man had said. He'd said nothing specific about Jeannine. He had not used her name.

"Did he seem local?"

"I don't know."

"Did he sound local?"

"I don't even know what you mean by that."

Johnson rolled his eyes. She saw it. She saw him do it, even as he tried to do it quickly.

"Did he strike you as a newcomer to Caddo or someone who's lived here a while?"

"Since we didn't discuss that I have no way of knowing—or even guessing. That's what you want me to do, right? Guess? We didn't discuss it at all, but if I had to choose I'd say he seemed like someone who'd been here a while. He didn't act like anything was unfamiliar."

"Anything?"

"The town." Johnson nodded now, thinking. "What difference does it make?" she asked. She realized it was a dumb question even as she asked it. Even so, she was surprised by his answer.

"What we need to determine is if he planned on nabbing your daughter all along—and that's why he came to you—or whether it was a spur-of-the-moment thing."

"Why does that matter? He's got Jeannine one way or the other."

"It matters; yes, ma'am"—Johnson was talking with a little attitude now, he was talking back to her, and she realized she deserved it—"because if he went to you on purpose, and if he nabbed Jeannine on purpose, then that suggests a connection between your family and him. And that could tell us who he is."

"But I'd never seen him before. I told you that. I'd never met him in my life."

Johnson looked away, looked back. His wide, thick face was clouded, tense, furled. He was running out of patience. "Mrs. Riddle, on the day he kidnaps your daughter, this man goes and talks to you in person and essentially admits to what he's about to do. That can't be a coincidence. He had to know who you were, and that to me suggests some connection. Maybe you'd never met him before, but he knew who you were, and that has something to do with what he did."

Now Elizabeth went cold again. A new realization hit her, maybe worse than the earlier ones. Worse. Her daughter hadn't just walked into the arms of a stranger who wanted to kidnap a young girl. The stranger had wanted her daughter. The stranger had it in for *her*. So much so that he also decided to tease her, toy with her, announce it to her before he even carried out the deed. He wanted her to feel as much pain as possible. This man Rouse loathed her. Somehow, she'd made him an utter enemy, so bad an enemy he wanted to hurt her in the worst way possible. This, she thought, was what came from being a female Episcopal priest. You made such stern enemies that they wanted to kill your children.

Johnson was studying her with concern now. He looked like he wanted to put a hand on her shoulder, give her a pat. He didn't. "Oh," he said, "there is some good news. Sort of. I've spoken with some of the other people at the school, and with some other parents. They've confirmed Miss York's description. The assistant principal says she talked with a man earlier in the day who fits the description. He was watching the kids during recess from a side street. And he was holding a small dog on a leash. She said that he spoke for a few minutes with her and also with Jeannine. Jeannine was playing nearby. She said Jeannine didn't seem to know who he was, and she wasn't sure if he knew who she was." Elizabeth felt her heart lift. Could it really have been a coincidence? That big of a coincidence?

"The other people I talked to confirmed that he was the one who walked off with Jeannine. So, I feel good releasing the picture to the press. Once it gets out there, things should start happening."

"Wait a minute. What picture?"

Johnson blanched. "I haven't shown you the picture," he said. "Wait here."

Elizabeth could barely stand the tension, the sick, sad, foreboding sensation in her gut, but Johnson returned in only a moment. He was carrying a piece of paper. He handed it to her. The half-ruined face of the man called Rouse stared up at her from the page. There he was: hair, forehead, nose, eyes. Those frightening eyes. Tears returned without her even beckoning them.

"That's him," she whispered.

"Thought so," Johnson said and took the picture back. "I've given out copies to everyone around here. I just need to make it public."

"Do you know where my phone is?"

Johnson stared at her, nonplussed. "Did you bring it to the station with you?"

"I can't remember. Did I have a purse with me?"

It was clear that he didn't know, but he was trying to remember. "Let me go look."

He returned with her purse in hand. She searched through it wildly for a few seconds and felt the rectangular metal object before she even saw it. She pulled out the phone, turned it on. The phone told her she had eighteen new text messages and twelve new voicemails. She didn't care. She only had one message to send: to Aaron. She typed: *You need to get off work right now. Jeannine has been kidnapped. I'm serious. I need you.* She hit SEND.

Suddenly another officer, a man Elizabeth had never seen before, came into the room. He had short hair—like they all did—and a round, boyish face, light eyebrows. His face, meanwhile, was on fire. "Byron," the man said, "Darrell knows the guy. He knows who he is. He just saw the picture, and he says he knows him. He knows where he lives."

Byron Johnson ran from the room. Elizabeth prepared to send her son another message.

13

He still hadn't decided. He came within an instant of severing an artery, but then he stopped. This wasn't how he had imagined it happening—even if he hadn't yet imagined exactly how it would happen. This wasn't it. He didn't want to cut a girl's head off with a kitchen knife. Too bloody. The idea of any part of her staining any part of him was disgusting. So, he managed to pull back the knife and set it on the counter. Then he dragged her across the kitchen floor and found, in the same cabinet where he kept the spaghetti, the rope he had bought. He dragged her back to the dining room and forced her into her chair. She offered surprisingly little resistance. If anything, she seemed exhausted from fear and shock and crying, from the realization that her escape attempt—that ridiculous and futile act—had failed about as badly as possible.

She sat as still as a possum as he circled her body with the rope. She surely knew—she could probably feel it—that if she put up a fight now he would simply have to kill her. Get the knife and run her through. She must have sensed that because, in fact, it was precisely what he had decided. But luckily—for both of them—she didn't fight, and he was able to tie her ankles and her wrists to the chair, securing them with three knots each. By the time he was finished, he was sweating and sore—about as tired as she must be, he thought. The girl, meanwhile, said nothing, nothing sensible at least. She issued a bauble of a whimper and quiet, high-pitched words that sounded like the formation of prayers. She cried too. Mostly, though, she let her chin fall to her chest and stay there: a picture of abject despair.

It was, he thought, a beautiful sight. A righteous one. The girl knew she was going to die. And maybe she even understood why. Which was probably why she didn't talk back anymore. All that tough talk from before. All those stupid questions. Gone. She knew she was going to die. Beautiful. Had Paige, he thought, been allowed to contemplate her death? Had Murphy given her so much as a minute to prepare herself? He doubted it. No, he was certain Murphy had not. Murphy, he imagined, took her away to where he took her and immediately began his business. He wondered if Paige had even had a second to breathe.

The irony of Krystal pushing and pushing to take control of Paige, even after a court of law had decided to put raising the girl into Baine's hands, pushing up until the very end with an abruptly planned meeting to hash out once and for all a solution to their "problem," was that Krystal had always paid far more attention to the other aspects of her life than to Paige. In truth, considering how loud and showy the hugs Krystal gave her daughter and the exclamations of love were, especially when visitors were in the house or a camera was turned on, Krystal always found excuses to avoid being responsible for the girl. She constantly cited either her waitressing duties or some important celebration at church or a bible study class Reverend Hooker was initiating, or a television program her girlfriends talked about that she had to see, as reasons for why she could not stay home with Paige on a given night or take Paige to a birthday party or take her to the doctor or meet with her teacher.

Most of the time, Krystal just ignored whatever duties needed doing, with the unspoken assumption that Baine would take care of everything. Despite the fact that Baine made three times as much at his job as Krystal did at hers, and worked more hours at it, he was unquestionably Paige's primary caregiver. As much as his love for his daughter, or the running argument his relationship with Krystal had become, it was the burning realization of this fact that had motivated him to win sole legal custody. After showing such expansive indifference to the many little facts of their daughter's life, Krystal could not simply show up and expect to take Paige away from him. He wouldn't allow it. The court agreed. And when Baine left for that last fateful meeting, he was determined that she finally come to accept how abiding was his total legal authority for their daughter. To make it clear to Krystal that Paige was his forever.

But then what happened happened, and Paige ended up paying the ultimate price. The whole thing was so monstrously, ludicrously unfair; and someone, Baine decided, would have to pay for it. Someone somewhere had to pay, because so far no one had. Not for the act itself or for the fact they had let the murderer slip away. It was as botched a police effort as he'd ever seen. It had happened right before his eyes and right to him. Someone would have to pay.

o o o

He noticed again the bit of red on the girl's neck where he'd been rough with the knife. The blood had started to clot, an iron-colored mess, with two streaks leading from the incision down the side of her neck. The collar of her shirt had absorbed part of the stain and turned brown-red at the edges. The girl's face was whiter than before, but Baine didn't think she was white from being close to death. No, it seemed more like the white of fear.

He hadn't meant to do it this way. It was her fault. She took off running, forcing him to act. He'd meant to wait, to feed her, and maybe even make pleasant small talk with her; to let himself decide later how to do it. Now, he realized, he would have to decide sooner. He couldn't dawdle anymore. Two things of which he was certain: 1) he would kill her and 2) her death would not be a secret.

No matter what manner he chose to carry out the deed, he intended for her body to be found quickly—within a day—and her identity to be comprehensible. Her face must be undamaged and her figure left more or less the same. Her clothes would stay on, even if he had to put them on afterwards. He wanted her parents to know her at once, sooner than he had known Paige when he had been called into the coroner's office. He wanted them to feel immediate, devastating, and abiding pain; suffocating loss. No doubts, no hopes, no questions. There must be no escape for them. He had nothing against the lady priest who had talked with him about her church, and he didn't even know her husband. But they were parents. That was all that mattered. It might just as well be their daughter as anyone's. In the cosmic equation of suffering, the balance sheet would be made a little more equal.

And just like Murphy had, he would make a complete getaway. He would disappear to where no one could ever find him and he needed almost nothing to get along. This part, indeed, Baine had figured out. His trunk was packed; his wallet was full. He could get to the Mexican border in thirteen hours, maybe twelve. After they found the girl's body—because once across the border he would call them and tell them where to find it—it would take some time before they traced the murder to him. How long? A day? Two days? A week? It didn't matter. He would be out of the country and moving farther south; eventually east, all the way to Belize, where homes were cheap and the natives spoke English. Did anybody to whom the police might talk know that he'd always wanted to see Belize? Impossible. Baine couldn't remember mentioning this dream to a single soul in Caddo. Maybe to no one else his whole life. Not even to Krystal—and she was dead anyway.

The girl raised her head. She was looking at him, her eyes red with fluster. She could be a little devil.

"You should have eaten your spaghetti," he said. "You would have felt better."

She didn't react. "You wouldn't have wanted to run."

"I didn't like it," she said.

"Why?" he said. "It's a national brand."

She shrugged but didn't say anything.

"What?" Baine said. "What does that mean?"

"My dad makes real spaghetti sauce."

Did she want to die right now? Baine stood up, not sure why. Maybe he needed to slap her again. "Your neck is still bleeding," he said. "Let me put a towel on it."

"It's okay," she said. "It doesn't hurt."

Obviously, it did. How couldn't it?

"You're a mess," Baine said. "Let me clean you up. Don't you want to be clean?"

She shrugged.

"Of course you do," he said. "Stop lying."

He proceeded to the kitchen where he found a dish towel and ran it under hot water. He let it air for a few moments, the temperature fading to comfortably warm. Then he returned to her and laid the towel against the knife wound. She gasped, more from the expectation of pain than actual pain. How could there be pain, after all? It was just a towel. He heard a low, steady hiss escape her. He lifted the towel away and started wiping in little daubing motions. The congealed blood loosened into liquid and then he took the blood away. The wound looked clean now, but also open. A thin line of bright clear blood appeared on the incision.

"You need a band-aid," he said. "I don't know if there are any." He opened five or six kitchen drawers at random. No luck. Maybe in the bathroom? Without thinking, he started that way. He stopped. What was he doing? He ran back, down the hallway. His breath was short; his heart was beating. This time, however, he saw her tied to the chair, her eyes a dull simmer, her hair matted, a cut on her neck, unable to move. She looked at him curiously, as if she couldn't imagine why he'd run back.

"Okay," he said out loud. "Okay." Then, in a murmur: "Let's make sure to keep it this way." He walked again, with deliberate slowness, to the bathroom. He was not going to give her the satisfaction of seeing him in a panic. He opened the cabinet mirror. He saw a small vial of eye drops and a bottle of stool softener. He pulled open the drawers beneath the sink. Almost nothing: a tampon; a tube of Chapstick, a toothbrush in an unopened package. He was about to give up but figured he should try the towel closet anyway, behind him. He found it behind the first door he opened: lying there, prostrate against the white painted wood, the background of blue cotton towels: a box of adhesive bandages, mostly full. And not the crappy generic kind either. But the actual Band-Aid brand. Tough Strips, no less. These would adhere to the skin of the girl's neck and stay there. Against her will, she would begin to heal.

He walked back out. When he saw her tied to the chair he forgot his former fears. She was not going anywhere with anyone. He couldn't imagine there had ever been a moment he suspected her.

He wondered what kind of girl Paige would have been if she had been allowed to live to Jeannine's age and enter seventh grade, if she'd been granted those extra six or seven years of life. Would her dark hair have lightened at all or only grown darker? Would her brows have come in and a figure start? Would she have lost that edge of introspection that had always marked her character and become, like this girl, a person of the world? It always seemed to Baine that Paige had inherited more of his own inward, murky character than Krystal's fierce, uncompromising energy. She was timid around them—too timid really—or was that merely a matter of Krystal beating her down with imperious righteousness? Would Paige eventually have been able to stand up to Krystal and even to him too? Baine liked to think he would have welcomed that day. Would she have accepted him as her only available parent, accepted that as normal, the way some kids from broken homes do, or would it have lingered like a sting in her soul, a feeling of difference, of loss, of lack? Might she have started to act up and act out?

So far, this girl Jeannine didn't seem anything like his dark, quiet, tender Paige, his dreamy, isolated child. He tore the filmy paper package off the Tough Strip and pulled backed on the two sides, opening it like an orange. He placed the sterile portion against her neck and pushed. He heard her let out more air, like a bag being squeezed.

"What?" he said. "That can't possibly hurt."

"It doesn't," she said. "It's just a surprise." He wiped her neck again; a residue of thin blood entered the towel.

"I'm trying to help. Can't you get that?"

"I don't know," she said in a thin, off-center voice.

"You'll see," he said, "I'm not so bad." She grunted softly. "Maybe you should just trust me."

That gave him an idea. He grabbed a fresh plate from the kitchen cabinet, took it into the dining room, and plopped on a couple more scoops of the spaghetti. He removed her plate from before and stuck it in the sink. He found a clean fork. An unbroken piece of white bread. *Wait a minute*, he thought. *Wait a minute*. He put the plate in the microwave and punched one minute on the timer and told it to go. He stood, hawkishly watching as the sauce began to bubble and steam. Then he took it out.

"Okay, darling," he said. "Second try." He brought the plate over and set it there in front of her with the fork. "We can get it right this time."

She looked at him, her eyes encased with a broken, helpless sadness. He stepped away. Nothing happened. She didn't open her mouth. She didn't eat. She didn't even talk. In fact, it looked like she was trying not to talk. *Oh yeah*, Baine thought. *Right*. "How about I fork it into your mouth? You can eat it at your own speed."

She shook her head.

"What's wrong? It's warm now." He started to glow with anger again. He couldn't help it. She was insulting him, rejecting his food. "I'm not giving it to you cold. Maybe it was cold before."

She shook her head.

"It wasn't cold?"

"No," she mouthed.

"And you still didn't eat!" With one hand he rent open her closed mouth and kept it that way. Into the mouth he stabbed a forkful of clotted brick-red sauce with visible bits of red bell pepper, onions, and mushrooms inside. Good stuff. He let go of her mouth. "Chew, damn you." The girl's eyes were big, too big. He saw her panic, as if she couldn't breathe. But she had to be able to breathe. He wasn't choking her. Then she pursed her lips and pushed out the pulp of red mulch onto the table. It didn't look like chewed food; it looked like vomit. Dark red, as if mixed with blood.

"What the hell's the matter with you?" he shouted. "Why are you making this so difficult? Why do you keep making it worse? Are you insane?" He was leaning over her, his presence as looming as a shadow, hands on both of her shoulders. He wanted to stick her face in the vomit, punish her, push her cheek into the puddle like Murphy had done to him with hydrochloric acid. Maybe he should. But instead, he pushed her back so hard that the front legs of the chair lifted and it tilted, almost to the point of spilling over. But then it came back, all four legs on the floor. He saw a new alarm in her eyes. A deadly fear. He liked that. He hated her, hated her actions, hated her life, hated her existence; but he liked the fear he saw. He liked what he could inspire in her. He liked the new power he felt coursing through him. He was a powerful man, after all.

"You don't want to eat what I make you. It sucks, huh? Well, too bad. Nothing for you then. Nothing. You can starve for all I care. You can die." Then he slapped her again.

She began to weep, crazily, worse than before. As if she had no mind. Terrible sounds. They hurt his ears. He wanted fear, not crying. Fear, not crying. Fear was bright and dry and exciting. Fear was powerful. Crying confused him.

"Shut up," he said. "Be quiet. Shut up."

But the girl kept crying, and as she did her mouth opened, and in little spurts she ejected the remains of the watery red sauce. It dribbled as pink saliva down her chin.

"I can't take you," he shouted. "I can't take you." He covered his ears with his hands and pressed hard. For a second, he heard nothing but a kind of windy, interior noise in his skull. But the crying broke through. No matter how hard he pressed, the crying got worse.

"I can't take you," he said and ran down the hallway again, this time to the master bedroom. He closed the door. He prostrated himself on the bed: hands over his face. Maybe if he concentrated, maybe if tried to blank it all out. Maybe he could force her full away, and he wouldn't need to hear her terrible gasps. Maybe she wouldn't be in the house at all—or him either. Maybe he would be back in his own house, with his own daughter, and he would tell Murphy no. He would tell Murphy to go to hell. But he heard and heard and heard. He pressed harder with both hands. He heard and heard and heard and heard.

14

The house had been completely dark and still when they arrived. Except for a few lights the officers had turned on when they entered—they didn't have to force an entry; the door opened just by turning the knob—it was cast in blackness and seemingly unoccupied. Angel didn't like it. Dark meant completion. Dark meant hopelessness. Or at the very least an attempt to keep something hidden. Like a girl's body? She stood next to the squad car on Thacker Street, not far from Elizabeth Riddle, and waited for the two policemen—Officer Byron Johnson and the younger one, the baby-looking one, Officer Hunter Reid—to emerge with an answer. The officers had not been happy that Angel wanted to come. The mother they had been willing to bring, out of a sense of debt; also, to take back her daughter and identify Baine, if it came to that. But to them Angel had exhausted her usefulness. It would be easier and safer if she simply returned home.

But Angel was not going to abandon one of her students, one of her few smarter, with-it kids—one of the few who seemed to like her—to whatever would happen. She was too involved now: with the girl, with the case. She needed to see how it would turn out. She cared how it would turn out. She pressed the two officers, she begged to be allowed to accompany them; she told them she deserved to be there because, after all, without her none of them would have identified the man. As soon as she said it, she could see that this argument struck a chord. Their bluster and their insistence deflated. They couldn't deny it. They looked away, looked at each other, and then they relented. As long as she stayed safely inside the car, they said, and out of the way.

But as soon as the two officers had entered the house—815 Thacker; one of the bigger and older homes on the street, a classic white four square with a big porch that extended across the front of the house and down one side; only three blocks from Virginia McKinley—she'd opened the car door and stepped out. The mother—a tense, almost haggard-looking, but obviously intelligent woman—had done exactly the same. Now the two of them stood there on Thacker Street, afraid to move a step closer. But at least they had a clear view.

Angel didn't know what to say to the mother. She'd said nothing at all in the car. She had the feeling that Elizabeth Riddle detested her from the first, as if the mother thought she was the kidnapper. Angel guessed she'd been convincing enough, and helpful enough, that the suspicion had gone away, but the mother's disapproval—bordering on disgust—had remained. *Maybe she's angry because I was the last one to see Jeannine alive. She thinks it should have been her.*

Of course, that made no sense. If Elizabeth Riddle had been the last one to see Jeannine, Jeannine would never have walked off with that man. There would have been no crime to investigate. So maybe that was why the mother was blaming herself. And, in this irrational accusatory stew, blaming Angel as well. But it was Angel's description that led to the drawing, which led another police officer—Arsenault his last name was, she remembered it because it sounded French Canadian—to recall a case the year before of a girl gone missing and then later found raped and murdered. And because of Arsenault's recollection the group was gathered at 815 Thacker, acting with the first real hope any of them had felt since the case started.

Arsenault had recounted the case to everyone there, only one of whom—Jeannine's mother—remembered much about it. Hunter Reid had not been on the force yet; and Johnson had been living in Arkadelphia, working as a policeman there. It was a bizarre situation, Arsenault explained. A man and his girlfriend, who lived together in Caddo, split. They had a six-year-old daughter, a girl named Paige Baine. The man decided that instead of letting the mother raise the daughter he would take her to court to win legal custody of the girl. He succeeded. It was not a hard decision, Arsenault said. He had a good job at Entergy; he owned his house; he had no criminal record. She was an unemployed former waitress with a drug arrest post-high school and no permanent address. She was living temporarily with a sort-of friend from her old job, but word was the friend was set to kick her out as soon as the case concluded. The friend wanted no part of raising a child.

The ex-waitress seemed to have left behind her wayward period and become quite religious—maybe even crazy religious—but even so there was no comparison between their life situations. The man won the case. He was awarded full custody. But the mother didn't give up. She threatened him, legally and otherwise. They met a few times to try to come to a new, extra-legal resolution. But a resolution never came.

She threatened and bullied more. Then, one morning, out of the blue, she called the man to apologize and plead with him to meet her one more time. That morning. Just once. Just once more, that morning, she said, and then she would stop bothering him forever.

The man agreed to the meeting, sudden though it was. He figured he would say whatever he needed to say to her, and then be done with her. The problem was what to do with the girl while they met. Fortuitously, the man's neighbor, whose last name was Murphy, happened to come over. Murphy volunteered to watch the girl, for several hours, if necessary. The man, claiming later that he felt he had no choice, agreed. But the meeting did not last for hours. In fact, the meeting proved unusually brief and, to the man, completely inexplicable. Only twenty minutes in, no agreement reached, the woman had simply stood up, smiled, and left. "I guess I can't win," she'd said, and that was it. After months of anger, accusations, and determination, she simply gave up, and with a smile.

It became more mysterious when the man arrived back home to find his daughter and the neighbor both missing. The Caddo police were called. A frantic search began. Two days later, Paige Baine's corpse was found near Lake Cedar. That would have been the end of the story except, bizarrely, six days after that, and after her parents had managed to cooperate enough to arrange a nondenominational funeral and put their daughter in the ground, the kidnapper—one Gavin Murphy—pulled up with his truck into the driveway of his own house. The father happened to be home next door, grieving his lost, dead child and his misplaced trust. No one ever knew for sure what Murphy had come home for, but a confrontation happened in Murphy's garage. Apparently, the father tried to beat Murphy to death with a hammer but Murphy fought back, finally submerging the father's face in a barrel of hydrochloric acid, which for some never-explained reason was sitting, open, on the garage floor. Finally, Murphy released the father and ran to his truck. He drove off and was never found.

Several days after the confrontation and Murphy's second disappearance, the mother, whom the police had repeatedly and ever more aggressively questioned, revealed that she'd paid Murphy $500 to take Paige Baine from the father's home. It had all been a set-up. Another $500 was supposed to be paid to Murphy when he delivered her safely to the mother. Except of course Murphy never did that. What he actually did with the girl was apparently worth more to him than $500. The mother was arrested on charges of conspiracy to kidnap and accessory to murder. She was virtually certain to be convicted of the former charge, and depending on how the lawyers spun it, and given the public sympathy for Baine, might get the latter too, but she died of a heart attack while being held in a cell at the Caddo courthouse.

With this information it was clear that the man in the drawing, the kidnapper of Jeannine Riddle, was none other than Paige's father, Larry Baine. The unique discoloration of his face—creating two separate faces, really—was unmistakable. And so more than an hour before the drawing of Baine hit the 10:00 news shows, they knew exactly where to go to look for Jeannine Riddle. They didn't even need to hunt through the old police reports. Baine's home address was in the white pages.

A car's bombastic headlights filled Thacker Street as it approached from the south. Just another passing motorist with a passing life, Angel thought. He'll see us standing here next to a police car and wonder about it for a second, but go on. To whatever was waiting for him. He'd never know the pain and the fear and paralyzing tension of the moment; he would never understand that a girl's life hung in the balance as he drove by. But then the car slowed. A gawker, Angel figured. Then it slowed even more, as if it intended to stop. Angel saw the mother's head rotate mechanically. She looked at the car. She seemed to be studying it: a midsize American vehicle, maybe a Chevy, maybe ten years old, probably blue, although it was hard to tell exactly with the headlights, now so close, shining in Angel's eyes. The mother's hand went up: a signal, oddly stiff. Then her head turned back to the house and she stayed fixed on it.

The car's door opened and Angel saw a kid get out, a boy. He had thin, droopy hair that hung long over one side of his face—it was the style now—a style she thought was stupid, like most styles were. He walked around the front of the car, into the headlight lights. She saw he wore a zippered black hoodie and light-gray corduroys. He was focused entirely on the mother. He looked scared.

He stopped beside Elizabeth Riddle's shoulder. "What's the news?" he said.

The mother said, "That was Gregory?" The boy nodded. "Kind of him," she added.

In an awkward second, the boy gathered himself. "Well, when your sister's been kidnapped . . ."

Then to Angel's shock, she saw the mother—this squirrely, angry, guarded person—reach her arms around this boy and cling to him. Angel could not tell if she was crying or not, or consoling him while he cried. She certainly heard the murmur of low voices. When they broke the hug, neither person seemed in good shape. The car drove off.

"Just waiting, right now," Angel thought she heard the mother say. Then they both looked at the house: expectantly, worriedly. No, more like scared out of their minds. Angel would have liked to be introduced to this boy, to put stranger awkwardness aside, but of course there was too much else for his mother to think about. So, Angel looked away. She would try to pretend not to realize that he was there, or maybe instead pretend that he'd always been there and thus did not need speaking to.

Now Angel saw that Johnson and Reid were coming out of the house empty-handed. Were they done? How long had they been in there? And, oh my God, Angel thought, did that mean they'd found no one alive? Her heart began laboring and labored more when she saw Johnson signal to the girl's mother. *They're taking her in to see a dead body.* Did they really need to do that? The mother grabbed the son's hand and they began to walk very slowly to the front steps, their heads stiff, their tensed bodies revealing what they were trying to hide. The boy hid his anguish better, but Angel had no doubt he was feeling it all the same. Byron Johnson waited, and they kept walking until they stood next to him and Reid on the porch. Johnson extended his hand to the boy; the boy squinted for a moment and then shook it.

Johnson leaned in, murmured something to them both. Then Reid said something: a quick, low interjection. Johnson spoke more; then he shrugged. Angel tried to read the mother's expression, but in the absence of daylight it was impossible. There were the streetlights, and the new light shining out from the living room. But this wasn't enough. She saw neither relief nor tragedy on the woman's face. She saw nothing at all. Nothing new. Finally, she saw the woman nod her head slightly. Then she and her son went inside with the two policemen. Angel could not imagine what that meant. Except she doubted it meant anything good. On the other hand, if the woman had just received the worst news any mother could hear, she would not have reacted so calmly. Angel wanted to run over and follow them inside, but she had a pretty good idea what Johnson and Reid would say to that. They were being kind to allow her to stand there on the street next to the patrol car. Her best strategy for finding out anything was to just watch and remain invisible. Come to think of it, she realized, that was how she'd identified the kidnapper in the first place.

With nothing to do but wait, she checked her texts; she checked her Instagram; she checked her SnapChat; she checked her email. Nothing of interest in any of it, except for an email from Rene Hurd. It could be important—something about the teaching job—or it could be nothing—a minor detail related to her graduation. Angel didn't open it. She didn't feel like reading it, or reading or viewing anything really. She just wanted those four people to come out of the house and tell her Jeannine Riddle was okay. Then she saw them: the mother first, then the son, then Johnson, then Reid. All four had lowered heads; all four looked disappointed. Disappointed—but is that the same as devastated? Angel checked the time: 9:18.

When the mother and son drew close they said nothing to Angel. In fact, they refused to even look at her. They stepped away a few steps, as if contemplating a stroll down Thacker, and whispered to each other. She looked at Johnson. He, at least, met her eye. "Nobody inside," he said.

"Nobody?"

He shook his head. "Nobody."

"Any clues?" Listen to her. *Clues*.

Johnson glanced at Reid. They shared the same look: muted amusement.

"Nah," Johnson said. "This guy is pretty slick. He must have known we would come here. Didn't leave us nothing."

"Nothing?"

"Nada," Reid said.

"What now?"

"I don't know," Reid said, smiling at her. "What do you think, Chief?"

Johnson chuckled grimly: once. Then he put the noise away. He glanced at the mother and son, who were still huddling together, several steps away. Johnson put his game face back on. "Something will turn up," he said. As if on cue, the little radio unit on his shoulder went off. He pressed the talk button. "What?" He released the button.

"It's Darrell. You guys find anything yet?"

He pressed the button again. "Nothing. House is empty. No suspect. No girl. No dog."

"You checked everywhere?"

Johnson rolled his eyes. He pushed the button. "Don't even need to ask that."

No reply. Johnson tried again. "Yes, we were thorough."

"Found out something," Arsenault said.

"What?"

"I talked to his old bosses at Entergy. He worked there until about six weeks ago. They said when it first happened, he managed to act completely normal on the job. But after a while, he started getting strange. Then he just quit. They were going to recommend a leave of absence for him, but he quit instead."

"Okay." So far Johnson seemed unimpressed. "What else?"

"They told me he was really interested in the Lake Cedar area. Said he wanted to buy out there, or just try renting. Apparently before he quit he said something about renting a house out there for a week, for a vacation. They asked him if he didn't maybe want to go vacation at another lake instead—given what happened—but he insisted that's where he wanted to go."

"How do we find him?"

"One of the bosses told me he told Baine to talk to this other guy, a realtor: Taliaferro is his name. James Taliaferro."

Angel's ears came to attention at the first sound of the name. That was Shelby's boyfriend's last name. Another weird thing about him. She had thought he was possibly the only Taliaferro in existence anywhere on the earth.

"And?"

"I've just got done knocking on his door. 1770 Mooney. In Caddo."

"And?" Angel could see Johnson's naked impatience. With good reason. He had to keep tripping this information out of the other officer, when Arsenault should have told it all: right away, without being asked.

"Nobody home," Arsenault said. Johnson's face collapsed; expectations overturned. "Everything dark."

"Sorry to hear that. You think he's involved?"

"No reason to think that. But he might know where Baine is. I'm going to wait here for a while, see if he comes back."

"10-4," Johnson said.

Angel had her phone out already. Her thumbs flew through the text: *Tell me what Jess's dad does.* She didn't know if Shelby was even near her phone. She couldn't be sure the phone was on. She couldn't be sure that Shelby and Jess were not in such a state of savage coitus that answering a text would be the last thing on their minds. Worst of all, she couldn't be sure that even if Shelby's phone was on and she wasn't preoccupied she would in fact reply. This was the sad truth about her relationship with her roommate. She wasn't sure the girl was even willing to text her. Angel tried to remember that last time she had texted Shelby, but she kept coming up empty. Maybe she never had.

Then it happened: the telltale noise on her phone.

Shelby: *Why?*

Is he a realtor?

Why?

Please.

You looking to move out?

Just ask him. Please.

Wait.

Seconds went by. More seconds. Johnson and Reid were talking, but Angel could tell they were ready to leave. "Ma'am," Reid said to her, "we need to get these people back to the station. Or home. Wherever they want to wait."

"No," Angel said. "Just wait a minute."

"Ma'am?" Johnson said: louder, gruff. A statement not a question. "No ma'am, these folks have been through hell. I'm not going to make them wait while you play with your goddamn phone, excuse my French. You can walk back to the station then." He moved to the car and opened the driver's side door. He descended into the seat. Reid hesitated, looked at her, but started around to the passenger's side. Angel felt the mother and son drawing near. They were going to get in as well. She felt their eyes, their heavy, newly suspicious glances.

"No, you have to wait. I might be able to find out where James Taliaferro is."

Johnson got out immediately. "What?"

"Please, just wait, and then I can explain."

Johnson glanced at the mother, asking her. The mother looked back at Johnson, at Angel, at her son. Angel couldn't tell what look she gave the boy, but then she turned to Johnson and said, "Do we have anything else to do right now?"

Johnson hesitated. He looked almost bewildered. "Afraid not. But that could change."

"Then we'll wait," the mother said. She looked with new hope at Angel.

Angel looked at her phone. She couldn't imagine what was taking Shelby so long. She didn't know how long these people would wait. The *bing* sound.

Yes dad is a realtor.

Is he James?

What????

The dad, is his name James?

"Miss York, maybe you could step into the car." Johnson's voice. "I'm sure your phone will work just fine there."

Angel looked up. Two people—the mother and her son—were staring at her with a longing so intense she felt the skin pulling back from her face. "Sure, but if I find out won't you want to go to him?" Johnson looked away. The investigation was moving out of his control, because so far it had led to only dead ends; she sensed how frustrated he was. But that didn't give him any right to try to intimidate her.

Johnson threw his hands down. "Whatever. I'm waiting in the car."

"Come on, Shelby," Angel whispered. "It's a simple question." *Bing.*

My dad's name is James. So what?

Is this Jess?

What do you think?

Your dad is a realtor?

Yes. So what?

Angel took a breath. Her thumbs flashed over the phone.

Police want to talk to him. About someone he rented a house to. Bad guy.

There was a decided pause.

What bad guy?

I can tell you later. Where is your dad?

Another pause.

I don't think I want to tell you.

It felt like a knife to the gut: sudden and deep.

Please!!!!!

I don't think I want to tell you.

Can you show me?

Her last chance. She didn't know why she thought it would matter to Jess, but she thought it would. He might not simply want to pass on information about his father, but leading them to the man might give him some illusion of control.

Where are you?

She typed the address. Then she added, *Crime investigation.* She thought that might catch him.

She waited ten full seconds for a reply. Then it came.

Wait there.

She brought her head up and looked for Johnson. "James Taliaferro's son is coming here. He's going to take us to wherever his dad is."

The mother and son both let out squeaks of grateful noise. Reid tilted his head to the side, like a dog trying to better understand human speech. "How is it that you know James Taliaferro's son?"

"I didn't know I did," she answered. She lifted the phone to show them. "Until he told me a minute ago."

The mother took one step Angel's way. Angel knew what was coming and welcomed it: the gratitude hug. After all, she deserved it. Hadn't she made the case her own? But before the mother could take a second step, a car's rampaging tires lit up Thacker Street. The mother stopped. She turned. She stared. She squinted. The car, a new-looking Nissan, squealed to a stop on the curb, not four feet from where the mother and son stood. A man emerged: fortyish, with a nose that traveled rod straight for an inch and then bent a hard right; also, hard-cut cheekbones, ruddy brown hair, thoroughly overgrown (for a forty-year-old), and bad boy retro sideburns. Yuck. Angel couldn't tell what color his eyes were, but she could see they were on fire—and completely focused on the mother.

"Where is she?" the man said.

"She's not here," the mother muttered tonelessly.

"Where is she then?"

"We don't know yet."

The man turned a near complete 360°, as if the mother's words had the physical force to spin him. When he faced her again, his arms were extended in a question and his voice was at a scream.

"Why didn't you return my calls? You send me a message that Jeannine's been kidnapped, and then you stop communicating with me? What the hell is the matter with you, Liz? Did you have something to do with this?"

Angel watched as the mother, Elizabeth Riddle, covered her face with her hands and began to sob.

15

Under the force of Max's accusations, she broke down again. Of course, when he accused her of "having something to do with it" he meant something particular, something other than what she felt, but what she felt she felt deeply and more urgently every moment. As the afternoon turned into evening, and then nighttime, she had an inkling that she was to blame for the entire situation. Perhaps the crime had not been initiated by her, but she had allowed it; no, even more than that, in the broadest sense she had made it inevitable: her marginal response to Baine's plans for murder (How come she had not felt instinctively, from his very first word, that her daughter was in danger?); her losing track of time and consequently stranding Jeannine with the devil himself; her insistence in the first place on the divorce from Max, her unwillingness to give him or the marriage another chance. That had been the truest root of today's events, their primary causation. Moving to Florida had been Max's idea: a petty, wicked, vengeful action meant to complicate her life. But she had brought him to that, hadn't she? Rightly or wrongly, she had insisted on the divorce. And if she hadn't, Max would have been present that afternoon, not just in Caddo but in her home, ten minutes from Virginia McKinley. Or he would have been at the Bistro, which was even closer.

She was at fault. She was at fault. And now Jeannine was paying the price. Staring at Max's tortured face had brought it all home. There was no point in even asking him "What are you doing here?" because the answer was all too obvious—and once again her fault: *Because coming was the only way to get answers from you after you turned your phone off.* Coming was the only way to help save the daughter he still loved. He must have found a direct flight from Tampa to Little Rock and then rented a car at the airport. She didn't know how he could have afforded all that. He cooked for a place called Señor Billy's!, after all. Señor Billy's! He most certainly could not afford what the trip cost him. But she wouldn't ask him, because she didn't want to hear the answer. And she knew what he would say, in a plaintive, sarcastic, but truthful whine: *How could I afford not to come?*

She heard Max talking with Aaron, asking him for more information, apologizing for not coming sooner, explaining that he'd been waiting for a message from Aaron's mother. Elizabeth didn't want to look at the two of them. She didn't want to see them getting along, understanding each other. Max showed up out of nowhere—his naturally curly hair thoroughly overgrown and sporting ridiculous, mammoth sideburns—and now he would proceed to steal her son from her. Her son's heart, that is. Possibly her only remaining child. And why wouldn't Max succeed? He'd have every incentive to, and, because she was the parent at home, every day Aaron experienced a veritable parade of her shortcomings: her temper, her forgetfulness, her inability to cook, her devotion to her job, her hopelessness with automobiles, her frightening lack of a grounded spirit.

Elizabeth wondered if she became a priest with the hope that doing so would create a center in herself that heretofore had never existed. So far, the plan wasn't working. And some days she was sure Aaron saw her as nothing but a hypocrite, a pious phony. All she could offer the boy was the fact that she was there. And that she hadn't slept with someone to whom she wasn't married. Initially, she thought those two advantages would be more than enough to outweigh Max's smoothness, his subtlety, his ability to always look like the cool-headed one even when he wasn't. It would be enough to keep Aaron permanently in her corner, and spiteful of his father. But now she could see that she had overestimated her advantages. The calling of a boy for his father might be stronger. And she might very well be alone for the rest of her life.

Byron Johnson was at her elbow. She didn't know, and didn't want to think about, how long he had been standing there. "Mrs. Riddle—"

"I'm not married anymore. Can you please just call me 'Reverend'? That's what I should be called anyway. You wouldn't call Father Joe at St. John's 'Mr. Kohler,' would you?"

Johnson paused, held her stare coolly. Finally, he nodded. "Okay," he whispered. "I'll do that. Reverend, this girl's friend is going to be here any minute. If the boy can tell us where his father is, we're going to find him. As soon as we possibly can. And if it turns out the realtor rented something to Baine, we're going there right after." He held fire for a second. "I wonder if you're up for this. You could go home and wait there. Then we can call you when we know anything."

Elizabeth reared her head. "You think I'm not going to be there when you find my daughter?" She nodded at her ex-husband. "*He'll* be there."

"Not about you," Johnson said. "Not about either of you."

Of course he was right, but his insistence angered her. Why, after all, was everyone else—this incredible growing multitude—allowed to have a say in finding her daughter, even her cheating ex-husband?

"I know it's not about me. I just never expected to see him here. Especially not in these circumstances."

"Neither did he, I'm sure," Johnson added.

Elizabeth turned away. Fine. Whatever. She was guilty of something, certainly, but her anxious feelings had nothing to do with Max experiencing any discomfort. She was not going to waste any pity on him.

She walked over to him directly, catching him off guard. "I turned off my phone because I didn't want to hear you blaming me—and that's what's happening anyway."

Max didn't hesitate. "Of course I'm blaming you. For not talking to me. Because you didn't."

"Plenty of women would not have sent you that text in the first place."

"What good does it do to send someone a text if you're not available to answer their questions? Come on, Liz."

She started shaking her head. She was not going to let him do this. She had to fight. She couldn't let this man put her in a box or she would never get out of it. Never. In fact, even after divorcing him, she would be in the box worse than ever.

"I'm not the one who ran away to Florida like a little child, leaving me to handle everything."

"Because that's how you wanted it! That's how you've always wanted it. Are you going to try to deny that? Because

I can recount about two dozen times without even thinking where you insisted on doing everything with the kids your way—and you left me totally out of it. This is just desserts, baby."

Elizabeth's face went white. "Our daughter is missing. She's been kidnapped, Max."

"Yeah, on your watch."

"It could have happened to you too, if you had—"

Aaron was talking. Elizabeth didn't know when he had started talking, but when she heard him it seemed like he had been talking for minutes. "Please, Mom. Dad. Stop. I don't want to hear this now. It's not helping."

Johnson was at her elbow. She'd forgotten the police were still here. Where did she think they'd gone?

"Sir? Ma'am? You can argue about this all night, but I can guarantee that it won't make you feel any better. And it's not going to get us any closer to rescuing Jeannine. Can we focus on what we're focusing on?"

"Sure, we can," Elizabeth spat before she could stop herself. "But we're not focusing on anything right now. We're waiting for"—she gestured with her thumb to the dark-haired girl, whose name had seemed patently ridiculous all evening—"her 'friend' to show up. The friend who could just tell us where his father is, but he refuses to. In the meantime, my daughter could be dying."

The girl made a noise. Elizabeth felt bad about that, but only a little. She hadn't trusted that one from the beginning; there was something staged, something self-aggrandizing about her. When she claimed to know who and possibly where James Taliaferro was, Elizabeth couldn't help but feel grateful. Moved really. But this waiting was ridiculous. Where was this girl's friend? Why—because her daughter's life was at stake—couldn't he just tell them what they needed to know? Why was he making them wait for him? It didn't smell right.

They heard a car approaching on the street. All heads turned. It was a small vehicle with a rearing engine, like it was being pushed too hard from the inside. When it stopped on the other side of Thacker Street, not far from the house, the rearing noise became worse. Elizabeth wouldn't have been surprised if the engine just exploded, casting shrapnel all over the lawn—and at them.

"That's him," Angel York said firmly. Elizabeth noticed the girl send her a bitter, accusatory glance.

Don't even try, sweetheart. Your pain doesn't count. Whatever pain the girl might be feeling—pain about Jeannine, that is—it was just not the same. It was not even real.

The rearing engine turned off and two young people emerged from the car: a girl, about the same age as Angel but much thicker, much broader, and a boy. The boy was almost as skinny as Aaron. Dark hair. Pale face. Indifferent eyes. No, not indifferent. Reluctant. Petty. Self-involved. He approached them slowly, letting the girl go ahead.

"Hi," Angel said to the other girl. Elizabeth heard something hesitant, even anxious, in her tone, as if she did not know how to rightly welcome this person. Some recent history, she imagined.

"Hey," the girl answered neutrally. Oh yes. History galore.

Johnson was ready to get going. "These are the friends we've been waiting for?"

Angel told him their names. Elizabeth didn't catch the girl's last name, but she didn't care.

"You're James Taliaferro's son?" Johnson said.

The boy looked at Johnson wryly. "Yeah," he said gradually, as if the answer were cash he'd rather not give away, especially not to Johnson. "So what?"

"We need to know how to contact your father."

Pause. More studious scrutiny from the boy. "Why should I tell you that?"

"Because my daughter has been kidnapped, you little prick," Max shouted, his face flaring to a red that was perfectly obvious even at nighttime. That was Max. Everything from excitement to disgust went immediately to the front on his face. "And from what these people tell me, your father knows something about it."

The boy seemed genuinely stunned to hear this. Clearly, felony crime and his father were two ideas that did not usually go together, no matter how the boy felt about the man. His mouth opened, in a completely new manner: one in which he demonstrated no control. Finally, he said, "My dad doesn't do kidnapping."

"I'm not saying he did," Max followed. "Listen to me. I said he knows something, like where the kidnapper is."

"Mr. Riddle," Johnson broke in. "Let me explain things to the kid."

Elizabeth saw the realtor's son react. He didn't like being called a "kid." The prickliness of adolescents: determined to prove they were adults, but so willing to slough off adult responsibility when it didn't suit them. Elizabeth watched as Johnson, hitherto professionally cool and expert as one could want, put his hand on Taliaferro's shoulder and kept it there. "Look, dude. We're in a situation, and your father can really help. No one suspects him of anything. He's a realtor. It's what he does. Apparently, someone he rented to—or might have rented to—is a pretty messed-up character. That's not your father's fault. All we want to know is the address of the place he rented—if he rented it."

The boy nodded. Elizabeth could see that Johnson's hand and his tone were working. The boy was about to relent.

"Why are you asking him for this information?" Max shouted. "Just demand it. He's putting my daughter at risk. Isn't that against the law?"

Elizabeth saw Johnson turn a murderous glare on her ex-husband. Maybe, she thought for the first time, it was a good thing Max was there. She wouldn't be the bad one anymore, the one who let her daughter get kidnapped because she couldn't keep track of time. Because she was too busy trying to save other people's souls.

"Mr. Riddle," Johnson said, "I'm going to advise that you calm down, for your daughter's sake." Reid took a couple steps in Max's direction, a strategic decision, a smart read on the emotional tenor of the scene.

"And I'm going to advise you," Max said, "to get an answer from this jerk."

Now the boy was smiling, enjoying being at the center of this urgent and angry attention, enjoying being able to make this man scream.

"I was about to," Johnson said and turned back to Taliaferro. "Now," he said.

The boy hesitated, his eyes darting from Johnson to Max to his friends, even to Elizabeth. *Taking it all in.*

"I don't want to tell you, but I'll show you. If you let me lead you."

"Son of a bitch," Max said and charged the boy, attacking him with a strange, physically illiterate move halfway between a right cross and a karate chop. It landed somewhere in Taliferro's shoulder area, and the boy crumpled. Max proceeded to kick the boy in the side, in the back, and in the ass before Johnson had his arms around him and Reid was ready with handcuffs. Elizabeth couldn't watch anymore. She knew what this was about. That blow, and those kicks, were meant for her. They were a revelation of Max's pent-up anger. She understood this, but what could she do about it? Should she stand there and tell Max to swing at her instead? She could, she supposed. The idea ran through her head for a second. Maybe she deserved it. And if it helped them get an answer out of Taliaferro . . .

But then she saw that Reid had Max on the ground, one knee in his back, handcuffs on his wrists. Max had easily overwhelmed the unsuspecting college student, but he was helpless against a young, fit police officer. Max was a chef, for God sake. An ex-seminarian. Getting in fights had never been his habit. Not fistfights, at least. Arguments, yes. Fistfights, never. The boy clambered up off the grass and glared anew at all of them. Uh oh. He was not a naturally helpful, naturally cheerful person. Elizabeth could see that. He struck her as even more closed-down than most young people. But he'd been about to help them anyway. *About to.*

"Fuck you all," the boy said. "My father can mind his own business. I'm minding mine."

He took off in a run, past Reid struggling with Max, past his two female friends, past Aaron.

"No!" Johnson shouted. "You can't let a girl die."

But he reached his car before anyone could get to him. He locked the door instantly and turned on his engine. The car started to pull away. As if in a nightmare, Elizabeth saw Aaron run straight at the vehicle and splay himself across the hood. The car jerked to a halt. Elizabeth thought she heard shouting. Shouting from inside the car. "Get the fuck off! Get the fuck off!" Aaron didn't. He stayed there, holding, holding, and finally crying. Then Elizabeth realized she heard words.

"Please," her son was saying. "Please, help me."

16

He came to as suddenly as if a bell had rung or a light flickered angrily in his face, all at once but with his mind whistling: a high-pitched crackle as if from passing electricity. He pulled his head off the pillow and felt a drop of saliva hanging from his chin. Gross. He wiped the area with the webby expanse of skin between his thumb and index finger. He blinked, and then he remembered how he had come to be in this room with its king-size bed and that night table, upon which stood a lamp that sent a dank, lemony illumination over a few yards of space. He remembered how he had come here, but not where he had gone in his mind once he shut the door. He had no memory of turning on the lamp. He had slept—apparently—but he could not recall a single image—fleeting or static, colorful or dim—from that period. It was as if for an indeterminate expanse of minutes his mind had simply gone black. Nor could he decipher why he had awakened with such a startle. What did it?

He sat up, shifted to the right, and put his feet on the floor. He looked around the room for clues. It was not his room;

it was not his home; he couldn't ever love it, but it was not unfamiliar to him: the walls with their purposefully rough texture, like scores of tiny sand mountains glued together; and that odd color, not quite earthy and not quite sandy—both of which might be appropriate for a lake house—but more like a coppery mustard. The bed beneath him was not merely comfortable but substantial: a newish mattress resting upon a solid sleigh bed frame. The side table was almost—*almost*—the same color as the bed: dark walnut with a sip of red. The lamp was of a fussier shape than Baine liked, but at least he understood it. What he couldn't understand was the green plaid shade. The closed bedroom door, six feet away, was a woody brown, an entirely different brown than the bed or the table, and nothing like the coppery mustard tone of the walls. It was a very strange room. All the individual pieces were of high quality, and yet the texture of the walls and the colors of the different components made it seem that the scheme had been vomited into place by a crazy person.

He heard a noise of something move behind him. He jerked around and saw Cocteau splayed across the mattress, revealing his underbelly to the world. So, the dog had slept beside him. The fact made Baine bitter. As much as he was good at acting like a dog owner, he secretly detested the species and had never owned one. Never in his life. He had not been one of those children who pestered his parents for an animal. He had been content with what they happened to collect: a fat, mangy, long-haired Persian gray that in his recollection had existed unchanged for the first eighteen years of his life before dying suddenly while he was at college; a few forays into goldfish; a rabbit his sister had brought home from a friend's and kept for two weeks; three chickens his father had insisted on for six months, hoping for fresh eggs every morning, but which had been mauled one summer night by God knows what.

Never a dog. They were too loud, too slobbering, too obvious. Krystal had wanted one during the time they lived together, but Baine refused with the threat that both she and the dog would find themselves homeless if she ever surprised him with the animal. The only reason he'd been able to stand to keep Cocteau was because the Pomeranian was no bigger than a cat and about the same weight. Even so, Cocteau was not allowed in bed with him. At home, he never slept in Baine's bed. So why, in this room, hadn't Baine felt him there?

Baine shoved Cocteau off the bottom edge of the bed. Cocteau recovered by the time he hit the wood-paneled floor. Then he shook himself and stared at Baine quizzically. He settled into a dozy sitting position for a moment and then stretched out, stomach down, on the floor. How long had Cocteau's hairy body been pressed against his own? Time as an idea seemed to have stopped; or rather, to have died. Perhaps if he opened the bedroom door and walked out he would find himself in an alternative universe. Maybe one where Paige was still alive.

No. The idea was too painfully hopeful. He whirled instead, looking for a clock, until he saw one in the oddest place: on the wall behind the bed, about a foot above the lip of that headboard, a round, gray-faced thing with black hands and only four numbers—12, 3, 6, and 9. What was the point of putting a clock up there where no one could find it while they lay in bed? Especially such a minimalist one? Baine stared at the clock and decided that it read 10:32. But could that be right? Had he been asleep that long—and with Cocteau beside him? Could a dog press its body against his own for four hours and he not be aware? It seemed impossible. Perhaps the clock was simply wrong. Then again there was the telltale whistling of his brain, that period of utter blackness. He decided the clock must be right.

Baine turned and again faced the bedroom door. He wondered if it was possible that he had killed the girl already. He seemed to remember an argument, becoming violently angry with her. Completely sick of her. Had he done it then, perhaps with a kitchen knife? Had he slit her throat? He dearly hoped so. Killing her was the only part of his plan he didn't like. He would do it—he had always known he would do it—but he didn't like having to. The struggle, the shouting, the mess.

He loved the idea that he could claim a measure of revenge on the world, on the police, on other parents, on fate. On God, if you will. He loved the idea of setting the balance sheet right. He could not wait for that to happen. He couldn't wait to know that the girl's parents had found her dead body and to know how badly they were suffering. How bad was their shock and their grief and their disgust. As bad as his own had been when he heard what happened to Paige. How deep their loathing for him would be—like his for Murphy. How newly hopeless their view of humanity and of civilization. What wasn't civilization, they would now understand—because human beings were not the least bit civil—but a finely articulated system of rationalized murder. He could not wait to inflict that pain. That would be the retribution; that would be when the scales of crime and heartbreak in the world would finally be set equal. Because, like Murphy, he would be nowhere anyone could find him. He would be 1500 miles away, in another country, in an alien legal jurisdiction. No one would find him; and even if they did it wouldn't matter, because they couldn't try him. He would sit there in some shack with a drink in his hand and know the completeness of his victory.

But he had first to get from here—this house, this situation—to there. And he could only do that by killing the girl. If he'd already killed her—well, that made matters perfectly easy, didn't it? That made matters wonderful. Was it possible to kill someone and not remember it?

He stood up and felt a dead ache behind his knees, inside his calves, on the back of his neck, in a certain stiff space on his spine. He may have slept, but his body had not slept well. His body hadn't liked it. He didn't know what that meant. Baine hobbled clownishly to the door. He heard Cocteau get up and patter over.

"No, stupid," Baine said. "Don't even think about it." Cocteau was staying in this room. There could be no other way. Yet, based on the eager, hopeful look on the Pomeranian's face, staying in the room was not the dog's expectation. Baine kicked at Cocteau, a clumsy sore-legged move that missed at first, so he tried again: quickly. The second time his foot landed in Cocteau's belly and the dog screeched. It scurried away to the far side of the room. "Stay there," Baine said.

Then it occurred to him that if the girl was dead his next order of business should be to kill Cocteau. He could not have the dog hanging around here, making noise and making a fuss, calling attention to the corpse before Baine was ready for it to be discovered. Cocteau would have to die too. The prospect of this murder bothered him far less. He considered whether drowning was a good option. Was it very difficult to drown a dog? He didn't know, but the lack of blood made it an attractive idea. When he opened the door, he decided to just leave it open. Better yet, he walked over to the lamp and turned it off. That would do it. Cocteau wouldn't want to stay in a darkened room. Let him come. He'd only be coming to his death.

Halfway down the short hallway to the kitchen, Baine was overcome with the certainty that he'd killed her already. After all, why would he have let it go this long? And why else had he suffered such a strict, absolute blackout? While he had always wanted to do it, he didn't want to have to remember it, which was why—he saw now—he'd delayed taking any real action. But his mind, clever thing, had hit on an eminently workable solution: kill her and then instantaneously eliminate the action from memory. Replace it with blackness.

Sure enough, even before he reached the kitchen he could see the table and her there still tied to the chair: her shoulders slumped forward, her head stuck in a dropped position. Not moving. Dead.

Good. Good.

Even more: *Thank God.*

He congratulated himself on his daring, his unremembered capacity for violence. He had no recollection of actually ending her life, but clearly he had. Somehow. He thanked himself for that. And in a manner that did not entail blood. For that, he congratulated himself too. Because that was the most amazing fact of all: no blood. *Well done, Baine. Extremely well played.*

Then he wondered if it was possible she had died accidentally. No, he didn't think so. How, after all? She'd been tied to a chair the entire time. What would she die of? *A broken heart?* No. People did not die of broken hearts in the actual world. If that were true, Baine himself would have died long ago. Jeannine could not have died accidentally; only by Baine's own hand. Besides, if she died accidentally, that would have been so unfair. Unthinkably unfair. No one had a right to deny him what he had to do. After what had happened to him, no one had the right to deny him anything. Of course, to her parents, death would be death, right? The tragedy would be the same. Right? No, it wouldn't. And this was what bothered him most of all about the idea of accidental death. To the girl's grieving parents, the notion that she had died not at her kidnapper's rough hand but in some other way would be their sole consolation—and not a trivial one. That was not a trivial consolation. Not trivial at all—he knew. And Jeannine's parents had no right to that consolation.

A memory rose up without any struggle from the lockbox he had stored it in, formed it seemed out of nothing, at least nothing he could control. The memory surged and smacked him on the forehead, hit him in the throat. Like any fist to the throat, it made his eyes water and his body ache: that singular, too-familiar pain that for a terrible stretch of months had been his sole bodily feeling, indistinguishable from his body itself.

He remembered Paige looking at him doubtfully as he explained that Mr. Murphy from next door would keep an eye on her for an hour. Mr. Murphy had kindly volunteered and would be a lot of fun to hang around with. Her eyes: so dark, so brown, so probing, just stared at him as he said all this. Stared at him, without words but with some kind of message he was trying not to decipher because if he had been able to it might mean he couldn't meet Krystal. He had to meet Krystal. One more time.

And yet there was Paige: keeping her eyes on his, clearly trying not to look at the figure of Murphy who lingered near the front door, strangely impatient for Baine to be gone, completely deaf to the delicate work of taking leave of one's own child. This wasn't surprising. As a man without children there was no reason why Murphy should be the least bit sympathetic to Baine's guilty leave-taking. For Murphy, Baine knew, this was just a chore, a good Samaritan gesture to be gotten through as quickly as possible so that he could go back to his afternoon. Murphy was an odd duck but not a bad neighbor. And this was only an hour or so. And Baine needed to go to this meeting. So, he kept taking his eyes off Paige's, kept hoping that when he looked back at her, her stare would be less gruesome, less determined, less exculpatory. But it wasn't.

"Why?" the girl said, when he said she had to stay behind.

"I've got a really important meeting with your mom."

"I can go," Paige said. "I can be with you and Mom."

"I'm sorry. You can't."

"Why?"

"This will be a very involved meeting."

"But I can be there, right?"

"Normally, yes. Yes. Just not today. Not for this meeting." As much as he would rather have brought the girl than leave her behind, her presence would only keep what needed saying from being said. And that meant nothing would be resolved. He would never be free of Krystal.

"I bet Mom wants me to go."

He shook his head. Slowly, gently, but he shook it. "No, baby, she suggested I get a sitter." This was true. Unusual, especially given the short notice, but true. "It's really important this time."

He worried that the admission that even her mother didn't want her at the meeting would ruin Paige, but she stayed just as calm. She didn't even blink. Instead, she studied his face carefully. For a lie? For a better explanation? There wasn't any. He had to do this. That was the only explanation, and of course it could never be good enough for a six-year-old.

"Don't get mad at me," Paige said.

"Why would I be mad at you?"

"I mean with Mom." The full meaning of what she said slammed him an instant before she spoke again. "You and Mom get mad at me when you are with each other. You talk about me. You get all red." To Baine's way of thinking, this described Krystal pretty aptly. Krystal was the first one to go nuclear in any argument, the first to lose any sense of care with her words. To Baine's way of thinking, their discussions were mostly a matter of his keeping calm against Krystal's paranoid accusations, his trying to navigate a way through to safety for himself and his daughter. He didn't appreciate Paige suggesting otherwise. There was so much this girl didn't understand about her mother. When would she finally realize what he'd done for her?

He felt a defensiveness—just shy of anger—rise in his throat, an oniony taste, almost like bile, but he swallowed it down. His daughter just wanted peace, after all. Her parents at peace. What kid didn't? She wanted to know what she could count on. "I'll try especially hard this time, all right? And I think Mom will too. Without any distractions we think we can really work everything out this time. Okay?"

Finally, Paige lowered her head and took those dark, staring eyes off him. She nodded numbly. Then she turned away, back to the television she had turned on an hour earlier. Baine knew he shouldn't have waited so long to explain to her what was happening. He knew the suddenness would make her take it worse, make her resist it. But he'd waited anyway. He took the easier path, and now he was paying for it with her sadness, her refusal to accept his solution. That nod was not a nod of understanding but of acquiescence.

Murphy, over by the door, made a noise, some unsatisfied grunt that sounded a bit like boredom and a lot like scorn. He almost wheeled on the man to yell at him. He almost decided to take his daughter along anyway. But when he turned, he saw Murphy, dressed in the usual sloppy white tee, jeans, and work boots, waiting with his hands behind his back, a placid stare fulminating out of flat brown-hazel eyes. It looked like the man had actually shaved today; maybe brushed his hair. Baine had to appreciate these tokens of respect for his duty. Murphy was impatient because he knew how long the meeting might take, and it would only take longer the longer Baine delayed.

"Don't hesitate to call me," Baine said to Murphy. The man nodded neutrally. Baine looked at Paige too. "If you need anything, Paige, tell Mr. Murphy, and he'll call me." She was staring at him in that way again, still refusing to see Murphy even when Baine referred to the man by name. Even though he was four feet away. "Or if anything happens," Baine added.

"Like what?" she said.

"I don't know. You never know, baby. If we knew that we could stop it, right? If I knew that, I wouldn't leave until I'd taken care of it—whatever it is. I wouldn't need Mr. Murphy because everything would be worked out in advance. But unfortunately, it doesn't work that way. I can't predict the future." It might have been his imagination, but he thought he recognized a certain new strain, a new discomfort to Murphy's impatience. Maybe, he thought then, the man didn't like being referred to as if he were a necessary evil. Especially when he volunteered to check in on the girl. Paige, meanwhile, seemed sadder than ever.

"I love you, girl," he said. He squatted beside her and wrapped his left arm around her body. To show that what he said was so. Paige was still against his arm, her body stiff, caught in thinking. He thought it was time to stand up again when she rolled herself into him and said, "Please let me go with you." The bottom nearly fell out of Baine then; all his determination turned to nothing. His guts were streaming from his abdomen, hanging down around his toes, grazing the floor. He closed his eyes. Could he take her? After all, he didn't really want to leave her behind; even if he had come, after several months, to trust Murphy, to decide that his earlier suspicions about the man had been clichéd and unfair.

It wasn't really about Murphy. It was the fact that his daughter seemed so strangely out of sorts, even terrified. Terrified to the point of paralysis, to the point of not being able to say exactly what it was she feared. Maybe she herself didn't know. There seemed no other, better way to resolve the impasse except to give in to his daughter and somehow make that work.

But even as he considered the action, he knew he couldn't take it. Krystal would be aggravated, even incensed. She would claim—perhaps rightly—that he was sabotaging their negotiations, purposefully making them impossible. After all, she had specifically asked that Paige not attend. No, he had to leave her. He would leave her this one time, and then the issue would be resolved forever. He would never have to leave her again with anyone, not if he really and truly didn't want to. It was finally for her own good to make her suffer through this: just once, one little hour with the neighbor, as a payment on the more peaceful future they would enjoy. "I can't," he started to say, but the words stuck in his throat.

Instead he said, "It will all be better—much better—when I get back. I promise."

Baine shook his head to push the memory away. Where had it come from anyway? What right did it have to come now to torture him? It was so unfair. So unfair. To blister him out of nowhere, to devastate him, to reintroduce that electrified soul agony that caused him not just sleepless nights but months. To the point where he had found himself one bitter December morning trying to make the decision between killing himself by overdose and killing himself by hanging. Hanging, he had decided. Hanging would be the surer method. He walked to his garage, found the 100' extension cord he had long ago abandoned there, and brought it back into his living room. He was staring at the coil, staring at the ceiling, trying to gauge heights and support mechanisms, when his phone rang and his machine picked up and he heard a Caddo policeman say that they had new information about his daughter's murder, about how and why she was abducted in the first place. Information they needed to talk over with Baine immediately.

Baine had stopped in the kitchen, his eyes on the girl for well over a minute as his mind replayed the moments of his worst shame. He had stared at the girl the whole time without noticing, but now he saw it. He saw it again: Her chest was rising and falling. *He hadn't killed her.* God, how he had hoped he had already done it. How badly he had wanted that. But now he saw that it was still in front of him, it was still what he had left to do. Moreover, she wasn't just alive but sleeping. How could she sleep? How could anyone sleep, tied to a chair, in a house with a man who wanted her dead? Had Paige slept? Jeannine's sleeping was defiance. It was obscene. He could not let her get away with it. She needed to be punished. In fact, the whole situation needed to end.

"Are you still here?" he shouted.

The girl's head came up; her eyes opened; in a millisecond, her sleepy look went from surprise to confusion to horror. Her blue eyes turned a vile, gaseous silver. "Please let me go home," she said.

"Go to hell," Baine said. No, she was not his Paige.

"Please," she said.

"Shut up," Baine said. "You're being stupid. That's all you've ever been. From the very beginning."

"No." Her voice was loud, with an odd urgency, as if that word, *stupid*—after all he'd put her through so far—was the worst violation. The one insult she could not stand. Then she began, once more, to cry.

Baine was not going to retreat this time. Not now. Maybe he wouldn't kill her—not yet—but he was not going to hole himself up again in the bedroom. That had accomplished exactly nothing last time, except to waste multiple hours. Hours he dearly needed, unless he were to change his plan radically now. But he could not stand this sickening weepiness of hers. He had an idea. He went to the kitchen and found in one of the drawers a dish towel. It was clean, in fact new, but that didn't matter. He would have used it regardless. He folded the towel and then rolled it, until it formed a cylinder of cloth about an inch and a half wide. He went back to where she sat, grabbed her upper jaw with his left hand and yanked upward. She shook her head and he lost his grip. He grabbed for her lower jaw, but she shook her head so much his hand bounced off it. She kept shaking. He slapped her as hard as he could. He slapped with his whole shoulder behind it. Her head stopped, her eyes shut, her mouth opened. She wailed. He stuffed the rolled towel inside her. Immediately, she coughed—or tried to. Harsh, barking sounds came from the back of her throat. She moved her lips; she worked her tongue. She was trying to push the towel out.

"Oh no," Baine said. "No, you don't." He remembered his stash from Walmart, including the roll of duct tape. He found the roll, tore off the plastic package, and pulled up on the jagged edge of the tape to form a lip. He ran back to the table, stretched out a foot's length of tape, and stabbed it across the front of her mouth just as she was about to eject the towel. He stopped it just in time and sealed it inside her. He wrapped her mouth once, twice, three times. He stopped, studied her. *More*, he thought. To be safe. He circled her head with the tape three more times, reinforcing the gag. *Good*. He tore the tape and pressed the end of it hard against the tape circle he had made.

He saw her react: her pale, terrified face; her eyes bulging and newly lined with spidery red veins; her nostrils flaring from the effect of trying to gasp in air only through her nose, to keep herself alive, to keep herself from vomiting. She didn't know how to do that. She'd never had to do it before, Baine thought proudly. *Well, she better learn.* He didn't like looking at her. She was newly ugly, even monstrous, with her mouth gagged, her hair trapped against her skull by the duct tape, her eyes watery, noises still sounding from the back of her throat. Was she coughing again or was that a scream? Baine had another idea. He ran to the bedroom and stripped a pillowcase from one of the pillows he had slept on. He returned and shoved the pillowcase over the girl's head. There. He would not need to see her anymore: the horror and the accusation; the veins; the ugly mouth. *There.*

Paige never had it so good, Baine thought. *Paige was never extended any of these courtesies.*

Cocteau appeared then, for no reason that Baine could discern. Suddenly, he was squatting by the girl's foot, his eyes fixed on her pillow-cased head, his mouth a scar of indecision. "Go away, Cocteau," Baine said. The dog ignored him. "Go!" He pointed to the hallway behind him. "Go. Leave. I don't want you here." Cocteau didn't move. Cocteau didn't even seem to hear. "Go. Get." It was as if the dog wanted to see what would happen next, as if his animal brain had wrapped around the thought and would allow no other. Baine leaned over. "Get!" he shouted in a full voice.

He saw then that the girl had begun shaking her head: slowly and at odd, off-center, erratic angles. Then he understood: she was trying to shake off the pillowcase, a losing proposition if ever there was one. Then he had a different thought. She was trying to speak to Cocteau. She was trying to give the beast a message: *Don't go.* Of course she would do this. Of course. The dog was her natural ally. Her only ally. The only thing in the entire house—perhaps in the entire world anymore—that could give her hope or succor. They had been in league together, hadn't they, from the beginning of this expedition? He remembered how closely she had held Cocteau in the car; he remembered her stroking the soft chunky hair on its back. They were a pair now: these two mammals that existed for the sake of his use. Fine, he decided. Why not now? He had never liked dogs anyway. Time for the dog act to be done.

"You want Cocteau to stay, is that it, Jeannine? That's what you want?" Her saw her go stiff, rigid, afraid. Her head stopped moving, all of her poised at attention. "That's it, isn't it?" He knew that was what she wanted. Why should she not just admit it? Suddenly the girl began shaking her head wildly. Liar! She was lying! Did she think he was that stupid?

"No, no. That's exactly what you want, Jeannine. You know it. I know it." The girl shook her head even faster now. So fast. "Well, we will see what we can do about that: keeping little Cocteau here."

Baine stalked as fast as possible into the kitchen. He didn't have to worry about Cocteau making an escape. The dog had no intention of leaving the girl's side. From the Henckels set he extracted the eight-inch-long, non-serrated knife and brought it back. With his left hand he grabbed Cocteau's collar: a simple brown leather strap with the requisite badges and name tags attached to prove what a good owner he was. He held the collar fast as he plunged the knife into Cocteau's side.

The dog shrieked and jumped away, a mere few inches given Baine's firm control of the collar; then Cocteau went rigid with surprise. Baine yanked hard and the knife came out, oozing with yellow intestinal innards and cherry-dark blood. Back in he plunged it, as far as it could go, as far—he hoped—as Cocteau's heart. This time he left the knife in and just moved it around, ripped as much as he could of the dog's inner tissue. Its black eyes were shiny and shining, dazed and begging. Blood moved across the wood floor; gore greased the area underneath Jeannine's chair. He heard sounds of some sort: human sounds, from somewhere. He guessed it must be the girl, but he didn't stop to check. Instead he watched as the look in Cocteau's eyes went from surprise to disappointment to consternation to nothing. In maybe a minute, Cocteau's blank look was frozen in place and his heart had ceased to beat. Baine pulled the blade out of Cocteau's side and set the knife on the table.

Well, well, he thought. What he'd failed to do with the girl he carried out rather easily against the dog. *That's a start.*

He picked Cocteau up and set him on Jeannine's lap. "There," he said. "Since I know you love him so much." The girl reacted immediately. He could hear her screaming beneath the pillowcase, despite the towel that was duct-taped into her mouth. He could see her squirming and twisting, at least as much as was possible with both of her legs tied to a chair. She wanted the corpse off her, naturally enough. Too bad.

"You feel sad for the dog, I bet, don't you?" Baine said, and immediately the girl stopped squirming. She stopped all sound, all motion, and just listened. *Yeah, I have her attention now*, Baine thought. *Of course I do.* Whose thoughts wouldn't race ahead with a dead dog on their lap? Who wouldn't make the connection, such an easy and natural one: this minute a dog; maybe the next a human. Who wouldn't be scared out of her mind and scrambling for a solution? Baine saw the girl begin to move again slightly. To tense the muscles at the top and insides of her thighs. She was trying to push off the corpse: the corpse he had deliberately made and purposefully laid atop her.

He slapped her hard, this time with the back of his right hand. From the way her head started back, he knew he'd found a sweet spot, even through the camouflage of the pillowcase. He'd smacked her good. She stopped wiggling. She let the dog lie in her lap. "There you go, smart girl. Be smart for once instead of stupid. After all, the dog liked you."

Baine went to the kitchen then and washed his hands. He was relieved he'd found an answer for Cocteau. He might have accidentally enabled everything that would follow. He might have made it possible for his plan to succeed. After all, he never had any intention of keeping the dog. How to dispose of him had been the question. And now, just like that, it was done. When he came back he saw that the corpse was literally gluing itself with blood to the girl's blue-jeaned lap. Good. He looked at the blade on the table: slick with mucous, blood, and intestinal runoff. He wondered if he should clean it before he put it back. Or should he put it back at all? It occurred to him he could do the other thing just now, just like he had with Cocteau. He had the weapon; he had the knowledge; he even had—and this surprised him—the desire to get it over with. He'd seen how easy it was to just act. How blissful it felt afterwards. All he had to do was plunge this knife directly into Jeannine's heart. He didn't even have to clean it. Just stab hard enough and she would get her due. *I bet her heart is beating so fast right now. I bet it would make her shoot blood.*

Just then a car's headlights—two broad, hard beams of brightness—passed through the long, fat windows beside the front door and broke the seal of the silent dining room. Baine had never turned on the overhead lights in the tv area or the sitting room. The only light on in this part of the house was the rather weak one above the table. It was dim enough that the headlights were evident. Someone was parked outside the locked front gate. There was no other direction from which the beams could have come.

As if to prove his point, the beams stayed exactly in place: sending blistering rods of light across the far edges of the room, close to where the tv was. For the first time all night, and for the first time since they left the neighborhood of Virginia McKinley Middle School, Baine felt real fear. Then, as if sensing the fear in him, as if able to read it through her open pores, the girl began screaming louder than ever. Loud enough to be heard by a car outside, parked sixty yards away? He didn't know. He didn't know. He didn't know if he could trust his own ears anymore. What should he do? What if they came closer: with flashlights and pistols and handcuffs? What if they began firing? What should he do? Should he take Cocteau's body to the bedroom, get it out of sight? Should he try to clean up the blood? What if they rang his doorbell? Could he just not answer? Could he do that? And would it work? If he just didn't answer it, if he didn't let anyone in, wouldn't they finally have to turn and leave? It wasn't possible that whoever was in the car knew he was there and with the girl. That wasn't possible. No one knew. Wouldn't they have to go, as long as they didn't hear her screaming?

But the girl was screaming. She was. Baine retrieved a second pillowcase and pushed it down roughly over her head—he had to work to get that one on, what with her screaming. Then he grabbed the duct tape and circled her neck several times with it. He tried to create a seal. He duct-taped the pillowcase so tightly that nothing could get in or out. Nothing at all: certainly not sound. A perfect layer of insulation. As soon as he accomplished this, the girl stopped wagging, stopped screaming, stopped everything. As if she was too stunned to know what to do or how to do it. Good.

He set the duct tape back down on the table. Then he moved backwards, into the kitchen, where a light switch was fixed to the nearest wall. He hit the switch and the light above the dining room table went out. In the brand-new darkness, the beam from the car's headlights was bolder and fatter than ever, practically dissecting the room. The girl, meanwhile, remained still. And completely soundless. This was good. This was good. With the lights off, they would see nothing.

With the girl no longer screaming, and with Baine staying back in the kitchen—and with Cocteau dead—they would hear nothing. There would be nothing to arouse suspicions of any kind. Whoever this was, they would have to give up. They would have to turn around. They would have to go back. He could see it. He could visualize it perfectly in his mind's eye: the headlight beams shifting direction, sliding across the walls as the car backed up, then disappearing altogether. The sound of a car engine growing quieter as it drove away. Then nothing. He could see it all in his mind's eye.

Then he heard pounding on the front door.

17

The tall black fence was an unexpected development. Taliaferro had said nothing about that. When they'd finally managed to track him down—at a rally at the South End Baptist Church, following the Wednesday evening worship service—he told them he couldn't remember which of the lakefront properties Lawrence Baine had rented. It was one of three he'd been showing, Taliaferro said. Should he just tell them all three? Johnson—who'd been acting increasingly anxious all evening—rolled his eyes and asked Taliaferro if he could just take a moment to think and to remember. It would save them crucial time.

Taliaferro nodded at the comment, but Elizabeth could tell he was only half hearing it. Flush with a righteousness that Elizabeth recognized and feared, his head wrapped around a victory of another sort altogether, it was hard for him to put aside the meeting he'd just been pulled from and to focus on a different problem. They stood with him in the lobby—the two policemen, his son, his son's girlfriend, the Angel girl, and Elizabeth (the policeman had left Max and Aaron in the squad car)—while inside the worship hall a speaker was shouting about how every person in the hall needed to call their state representative, a man named Davin Gates, and urge him to vote for the anti-adoption measure. The man's voice didn't need to carry through the closed sanctuary doors into the lobby; a series of speakers were placed in strategic intervals, so that it was impossible to escape the voice. It made their shoes rattle.

"We all know how this game is played," the man said. "The State Supreme Court keeps siding with the gays—because that's the kind of people they are. They're shameless liberals who somehow snuck though our system before we could catch him. And time after time we see them adopt the most un-Christian, anti-family positions. No one is holding them accountable, certainly not our governor. The Court has already said that we can't create a law that forbids gays from adopting as that's discriminatory. Well, of course it is. That's the point. It's like saying that you can't pass a law against murder because that discriminates against murderers. I don't care what is or is not discriminatory; I care about what's right." Lots of muted and not-so-muted applause. Comments: "Tell it." "You said it, brother." "Finally." Elizabeth felt her stomach curdling and her anger rising as Taliaferro smiled at the man's comments instead of answering the question they'd put to him.

"Sir," Johnson said, "we are under a severe time crunch here. A girl's life hangs in the balance."

"The beauty of the new law is that it makes adoption by any unmarried person impossible. The Court can't claim anti-gay discrimination, because there's not a word about gays anywhere in the document. Not one word. All it says is 'unmarried persons.' We all know that unmarried persons come in all stripes." Caustic laughter. "But because gays can't legally marry in the state of Arkansas, it means they are by necessity 'unmarried persons.' Every last one of them." Cheers.

"Mr. Taliaferro, should we go somewhere else?" Elizabeth said. "I'd rather my daughter not die while we stand here and listen to sanctimonious bullshit. Or is murder okay in your playbook?"

Taliaferro's smile was gone. He reared back and scrutinized Elizabeth as if through a telescope 300 light years away. "Who are you to say what's sanctimonious?"

Elizabeth didn't have to think about how to explain herself. Certain aspects of her identity were better left unsaid around a person like James Taliaferro. Others were not. "I'm a mother whose daughter has been kidnapped and who would like her found. Preferably alive."

Taliaferro's eyes cleared and his cheeks went white. "I'm sorry," he said. "Of course." He turned to Johnson. "If you don't mind going with me to my office, I can pull the file and tell you right away which house it was. I'm sorry I can't remember. I'm"—he looked at his son next—"well, I've been accused by certain people of losing my memory. I am sixty-four, after all." He certainly did look sixty-four: the ashy quality to his skin, the age spot—or whatever it was—on his neck, the obvious lines around his eyes, the balding top, the tall glasses. Elizabeth had thought that maybe he merely looked older. But no, there it was: sixty-four. He must have been past forty when his college-student son was born; perhaps as old as forty-three. Her own age.

"We can do that," Johnson said. "If you're absolutely sure you don't know which house it was."

Taliaferro hesitated, opened his mouth. "Well, I can take a guess at which house it was."

"A good guess?"

"Maybe."

"Ninety percent?"

Taliaferro frowned. "Fifty." He thought about it. "Yeah, fifty."

Johnson's head dropped. "In that case, we're going to your office."

Taliaferro's office was on the other side of Caddo, back in the direction of Baine's home. More and more of this infernal crisscrossing, Elizabeth thought. Her adopted hometown had never seemed so large to her as on this night. Never had she realized how many stoplights there were on an ordinary Caddo street. And how long it took to wait at a red. She was not in the squad car anymore, but riding with the college students, but still she wondered why Johnson didn't just sound his siren and run through them all. Wasn't her daughter's life worth that? The man himself seemed annoyed and anxious at the delays. Maybe there was a rule. Some arcane Caddo ordinance dating from eighty-five years earlier, because of one time a police car hit someone: *No chasing unless you're on a criminal's tail.* Well, weren't they? Elizabeth thought. Weren't they? Still, Johnson stopped at every red light.

At Taliaferro's office, he found the file easily enough and located the paperwork on the rental: 989 Lake Cedar Road. "I thought that was it," Taliaferro said. "I just didn't want to get it wrong." Elizabeth wanted to slap him, except that she wanted even more to run to the car.

Now they were stopped, both cars, in front of a wrought iron fence, just over six feet tall, that extended across the entire face of the driveway and then down the sides of the property as far as she could see at this time of night. Elizabeth and the two officers had left their respective cars to examine the situation. With the help of the squad car's headlights, it was easy to see the gate door in the middle of the fence. When the latch was unlocked—probably there was a switch inside the house to enable this—the door would swing back to allow cars through. Johnson and Reid each tried it, shaking as hard as they could. No luck. Shut up tight. Of course.

Elizabeth looked through the gate to the house. It was a regal structure. Not tall but broad and apparently deep, with several attending buildings on either side —a sizeable garage and mansion of a toolshed on the right; and what looked like a miniature house on the left, turned to run north and south, not east and west, as the main house did. A grandmother's apartment? No, not an apartment. An edifice. To the immediate left and right of the front door of the main house were long glass panels. With the squad car's lights, and one light that was on deeper in the house, she could see the shadowy resemblance of a foyer; and somewhere in the background, perhaps, what looked like a living room. On these grounds her daughter was being held—either in the big main house or one of the others. Elizabeth thought she ought to sense something. Her mother's radar ought to be able to tune in to her daughter's frequency. She ought to be able to feel Jeannine here. But she felt nothing except a growing panic.

Ever since she'd learned about the profile of the kidnapper her despair had gotten worse, even calcified. There was no way to know what to expect out of a man whose daughter has been stolen, raped, and murdered. Who knew how badly he had taken it, whom he had blamed, and what he thought he was owed. Likely he blamed himself, but Elizabeth knew that stabbing guilt could often manifest itself as accusations cast broadly and adamantly upon others—a defense mechanism, a way to keep living, a way to not despise yourself, or not too badly. She remembered some ideas she had read in a book by Parker Palmer, the educator and spiritual writer. In the moment, she couldn't remember Palmer's precise words, only the paraphrase she'd used in a recent sermon. Grief, Palmer explained, would break one's heart. That couldn't be helped. But how one's heart breaks made all the difference in whether one survives the grief. And what you do with it. If the break amounts to shattering your heart into a million pieces, future happiness becomes impossible. A shattered heart can never be at peace. But if the break turns the heart inside out, if it opens up the heart to the wounds of others, then sympathy—even beauty—can result.

It was one of Elizabeth's favorite analogies. There was almost no life tragedy to which the analogy could not be made to apply. She just never imagined it would apply so directly to herself. As soon as Officer Arsenault had told her about Baine losing his daughter, she understood. He was suffering from a shattered heart. By no means was he irredeemable, but he was, without doubt, completely unpredictable.

She knew that losing a child in the way Baine had did not guarantee a person turned criminal. She thought of how many parents of lost or murdered children had been motivated by their experience to help other parents and other children. They started television shows and milk carton campaigns; they lobbied for new statewide missing-children notification systems; they volunteered to answer phones for hotlines. They brought food and consolation and perspective to parents suffering through the worst torture imaginable. They came ready with their knowledge of what to say and—even more important—of what not to say. Elizabeth was willing to bet that 99% of parents whose children had gone missing or been murdered had found a way to turn their pain into productive use. Almost none of them—almost none, she'd bet—turned into kidnappers and murderers themselves. And yet, *almost none* was not the same thing as none. *Almost none* meant that some—if only one sad man—reacted that way. *Almost none* meant that at least one child and at least one parent was at risk from a former victim. The parent was herself. The child was Jeannine.

Something happened. Some change. She'd been thinking of wounded and shattered hearts, gazing haphazardly at that overlarge toolshed, not quite listening to the tense, quick conversation of Johnson and Reid, when something changed inside the main house. Or about the house. What was it? Then she realized: A light went out. There had been that light on in the back-center part of the house. Now, it wasn't.

"Did you see that?" she said to the two policemen.

They didn't reply directly, but their renewed scrutiny of the house told her what she needed to know. "Somebody's home," Johnson said.

"Maybe we should introduce ourselves," Reid said.

Johnson nodded once. He returned to the car, pulled it forward as far as safely possible, so that it was almost grazing the metal gate. He turned off the engine, doused the headlights. Then he jumped onto the hood and grabbed the top of the gate. He hoisted himself up and over. Reid did the same. Johnson was about to walk forward when he stopped suddenly and turned back.

"All of you will need to stay out here, behind the gate," he spoke in a stage whisper. "Got it?" Elizabeth nodded and felt accused. She was the only one, besides the officers, standing there. "Safer," he said, directly to her, "if you stay in his car." He motioned his head toward Jess Taliaferro's Ford, parked several feet away. Reluctantly, Elizabeth gave in, but not before seeing Johnson signal to Reid to circle the house and approach it from the back; not before she saw both men remove their guns from their holsters and take long silver flashlights from their belts. They turned the flashlights on. Then they went.

She returned to the car, opened the rear door. Angel York was in the back staring at her apprehensively, as if she feared Elizabeth would take her head off. Or maybe it was a simpler anxiety: worry for Jeannine. "They want me to stay here," she said.

Angel nodded. "That's probably a good idea."

"Yes. But I don't know if I can."

"I can't say I blame you."

"I don't blame you," the boy added.

"I'm so sorry about this," the other girl said, the bigger one. It was the first thing she had said to Elizabeth all evening. Heretofore, the girl had just seemed annoyed that her nighttime ritual had been disturbed.

Elizabeth couldn't help herself. Her daughter was in there. She stepped out of the car and back to the gate. She saw Johnson move swiftly to the front door of the house, his flashlight opening a portal for him into the darkness. When he reached the door, he seemed to do nothing for several moments; then he knocked. Hard. Elizabeth held her breath. She could not believe Baine would simply open the door and let a stranger enter. It could not be that easy. In fact, she hoped he didn't. If Baine didn't mind letting Johnson in the house it might mean he had already done what he intended to. On the other hand, if no one came to the door that might mean Baine was not there at all. Or, worse, he might have fled with Jeannine. No, there was still one other worse possibility—much worse—but Elizabeth refused to let herself consider it. Not when they'd gotten this close. Elizabeth felt torn, waiting for some sign from Johnson and Reid. She didn't know what to expect; she didn't know what to want.

The door did not open. No one appeared in the glass panels, even though Johnson shone his flashlight through. Johnson knocked a single time more and announced himself as a police officer. He waited several moments and then turned around. He walked back to the gate in a straight, sure path, as if he didn't care who saw him. That could not be good. Before Johnson reached the gate, Elizabeth saw Reid appear at his left. The two men stopped, talked in low voices. Then they kept walking.

When he saw Elizabeth standing on the other side of the gate Johnson kindly did not mention his earlier instructions to her. "No signs, no sounds," he said.

"I saw the light go out."

Reid started. "I know, but neither of us heard or saw anything. So far."

"He's hiding," she said.

Johnson nodded. "Possible. Hunter said the side door to the garage is open. Baine's car is parked inside. He radioed in the plate number to be sure. Hard to know anything for certain though. The curtain is closed across the back door, so there's no way to see in. Question is, where do we go from here?"

"I'm not going anywhere," Elizabeth said.

Johnson smiled grimly. "That's not what I mean. I mean, do you want us to bull rush the house? If he's in there, we get him, but it might force his hand. You can guess what that means."

"I'm not leaving here with my daughter inside that house."

"I know, ma'am," Johnson said. "I'm not suggesting we do that."

"What then?"

Johnson looked at Reid. Reid issued the answer. "We could call in a SWAT unit."

"You have one of those?"

"One," Johnson said.

"And that's not the same as a bull rush?"

Johnson and Reid passed another look. "Actually," Johnson said, "it's a lot like a bull rush, but with better shooters than Hunter or me. And much more specialized training."

"How long?"

"Half hour maybe. Maybe quicker."

She didn't know why the decision was hers, but apparently it was. And she had no idea what the right call might be. She thought that these two men were paid to know the right call. She thought they should tell her. She heard shouting from the squad car. Why was someone shouting? She turned. Max.

"Let me talk to my husband," she said. Then: "I mean my ex-husband."

She yanked the door of the squad car hard.

"Stop it," she said to Max. "Do you want to ruin it for her?"

Max, typically, even with his hands forced behind his back by the cuffs, even in a state of abject powerlessness, went on the offensive. "What's going on? Why aren't they busting in?"

"They're afraid he'll act. Act bad."

"He might act bad if we stand around here doing nothing."

"We're not talking about doing nothing," she said firmly, with a cupful of exasperation purposefully added in. In the moment, she knew how the police must feel, speaking to panicked relatives of victims. She understood how they felt talking to her.

"What are we doing then?" His voice was jagged but at least his eyes were calmer. It was an actual question. Aaron sat beside him, blank-faced and silent, trapped between his two warring parents, deathly scared for his sister. All over again, all at once, Elizabeth felt for him, for what she'd put him through. For what they'd both put him through.

She lifted her head, looked at Johnson. "Officer? Byron?" He came quickly. He looked like he was expecting a decision. "Can you take the handcuffs off?"

Johnson stiffened. "Is he going to stay calm?"

Elizabeth looked at Max. Max breathed out hard, stared at the house for a moment, and nodded. He looked at Johnson expectantly. It would be easier for him, Elizabeth considered, if he hadn't grown those ludicrous sideburns. They made him look like nothing but trouble, even when he wasn't saying anything.

"All right, but you cause us any trouble, especially now, I might have to shoot you." Elizabeth couldn't tell if Johnson was making a joke. It was a very bad time for a joke. But his face didn't look like he was joking. Johnson motioned Reid over. Reid, not without a doubtful look, removed the cuffs.

Elizabeth squeezed in the back of the squad car, next to Aaron. In order to fit she had to keep the door open. "Now we can talk," she said.

"About what?" Max said. "Wasting time?"

"They want to call in a SWAT unit. They think that might be a better bet than trying to break in themselves."

"Why?"

"They seem to think that if they bust in he could react badly. They say the SWAT guys have more training with this kind of thing. But they're willing to go in right now if we want them to."

"Are we even sure she's in there?"

Elizabeth shook her head.

"Don't you think they should be sure first?"

This, actually, struck her as a good point. "Officer Reid said Baine's car is parked in the garage. And I saw a light go out in the house right after we pulled up."

Max started to speak, then nodded instead. He glanced once out the window and came back. "But that doesn't mean she's in there. Don't we need to find out where she is?"

"I don't know how you find that out without going in."

"Maybe they can ask him," Aaron said. They were the first words her son had spoken since she'd opened the door. It was almost a surprise to hear his voice.

"Who?" Elizabeth said, although she knew of course. She just was shocked that Aaron, as distracted and frightened as he was, had thought of that. It hadn't occurred to any of them. She watched as he pointed softly at the house.

"How would they ask him?" Max said, his tone on edge but not dismissive either, not ridiculing.

"I suppose they have bullhorns," Elizabeth said, "but that's the same as barging in, isn't it?"

Aaron shrugged. Max, however, was looking at her; in that way that said he was thinking, not really looking. "Maybe not," Max said. "I mean, if they tell him they won't hurt him and they won't enter—as long as he lets her go. Whereas if they bull rush, he's more likely to panic."

Johnson stepped over, lowered his head to look at them in the backseat as he spoke. His feet were nearly tapping with impatience. "Folks, I realize this is an incredibly difficult position for you to be in, but I need to do something. We've wasted enough time just getting here. I don't trust this guy. I'm going to suggest to you—rather urgently—that we radio for SWAT."

"All right," Elizabeth said, "go ahead, but I'd like you to do something before they get here." The plan was forming even as she spoke it, and then it happened: She realized who should talk to Baine. "Get me the phone number for this house."

Johnson stared at her for a moment. Then: "You think we can just dial him up?"

"I think it's worth trying."

"Why should he answer?"

"Because you're going to get on the bullhorn and tell him that if he's willing to talk to me, no one will force their way into the house."

Johnson startled. "You're going to talk to him?"

"I talk to people all the time."

"We don't let mothers get involved in hostage negotiations. I've never seen it."

"I'm not going to negotiate with him; I just want to talk to him."

He kept his eye on her: the same doubtful, frozen look. She knew what he wanted to ask—*About what?*—but he held back, and Elizabeth was grateful. Because she didn't know how she would answer the question. Or, rather, she didn't know how she could answer without sounding like a lunatic. Because the only answer she could fairly give would be, *I want to talk to him about his pain.* "But you'll need to explain first, to tell him we're here."

"Oh, I expect he knows we're here, what with your husband shouting his damn head off."

"I'm not her husband," Max said. "And you'd be shouting too if everyone was standing around chatting while your daughter was in the hands of a kidnapper. And I think driving up with your headlights on might have tipped him off about ten minutes before I ever started shouting. So don't blame that one on me."

Johnson gave Max a look as if he was considering putting the handcuffs back on, but then he shook his head and climbed into the front seat. Reid did the same.

"What are you doing?" Max said. "Where's the bullhorn?"

Johnson tapped the dash. "Don't need one," he said. He radioed headquarters to ask if there was a landline at 989 Lake Cedar Road; he copied down the number he was given. Then he requested the SWAT unit. Then he flipped a switch on the dash and spoke once more into his radio. This time, however, instead of communicating with the station in Caddo, his voice was broadcast into the night, into the wide, dark space between his car and the house.

"Lawrence Baine?" he started. "Mr. Baine?" Then he changed it from a question. "Lawrence Baine, this is Officer Byron Johnson of the Caddo police department. We are parked in the driveway, on the other side of the gate. We have reason to believe you're in the house now, along with a girl named Jeannine Riddle, who you took, without authorization, from Virginia McKinley Middle School this afternoon. We are going to call you on the house phone, and we want you to pick up. We've alerted our Special Weapons and Tactics team, and they are on their way. However, if you answer the phone, no harm will come to you; no one will enter the home without your permission. If you do not answer the phone, however, we will have to force an entry. And that could get ugly." Johnson took his thumb off the button.

"How do we know he hears you?" Max whispered. "I mean, how do you know he understands?"

"Tell him to flick a light on and off," Elizabeth suggested, "a light we can see from out here."

Johnson turned and looked at her, studious now. Elizabeth had the feeling she was constantly surprising him, one way or the other. Maybe just now she'd surprised him in a good way. He looked at Reid. Reid shrugged. Johnson pushed his thumb in. "Mr. Baine, if you have heard my message and understand it, please turn a light on and off, a light we can see from the driveway."

Sure enough, a few seconds later the light that Elizabeth had seen before turned on, then off again.

"Bingo," Reid said.

"All right," Johnson breathed. "We're closer. At least he's listening."

"Give me the number," Elizabeth said. Johnson handed it back. Immediately, she began punching it into her cell phone. "Pray for me," she said to no one.

"You sure you want to talk to him?" Max said.

"Positively," she answered.

She felt something in Max's stare and looked over at him. She saw what was very familiar, but at the same time long lost. She hadn't seen that expression in years: a bemusement mixed with amazement and sly, subtle pride. She saw that expression constantly when she knew him in seminary. He was four years older and a year ahead of her in his studies: a handsome and intelligent and fiercely confident man, but also erratic, given to occasional depressions and bouts of self-pity. He was perfectly masculine—an avid follower of NFL football and NCAA basketball, conversant in the political arguments of the day and eager to talk about them—physically strong and immaculately healthy from a childhood spent working on a central Florida farm; and yet with a kind of feminine expressiveness around his chin, along his cheekbones, and across his forehead. And he had those intense, almost painful, underwater eyes. Not surprisingly, he was never at a loss for female companionship. He had dated what sounded like an endless string of women in his young life, including, the year before she met him, both of the female seminarians in his own class.

The look she recognized was the look that wondered where in the world a strange creature like Elizabeth Brogan had come from, how she had materialized into his existence and what exactly that meant. The look that asked who she was finally: genie or harpy, angel or scourge? Elizabeth always knew she confounded him; she took pleasure in the fact. Without question it was what attracted him to her and what kept him there; finally, what urged him—at the end of their one year together in seminary, the year he decided he did not have a genuine calling and wanted to go to culinary school instead—to propose.

Finally, he'd admitted to her, he didn't want to let such a one-of-a-kind person escape. He'd marveled at how she would battle anyone and everyone—including her teachers, even if they were renowned visiting scholars—on matters of biblical interpretation, and yet always with a tomboyish smile, a laugh, a veneer of carelessness that was both off-putting and useful. She claimed to be worried about this test or that one and swore that she messed up on some crucial essay question, but then she never failed to score highest in the class and be saluted by the teacher as *extraordinary*.

For pocket money, she worked weekend nights as a barmaid in a dive in downtown Austin, yet she almost never drank. She had no fashion sense—actually, she dressed like a slob—but she liked to shop. In fact, nothing seemed to please her in a childish way more than grabbing coffee and conversation with girlfriends at a mall. And yet this same person could churn out a fifty-page term paper about the feminist implications of the unrecorded narrative of Abraham's servant Hagar. She was perfectly squeamish about movies or television shows that showed too much flesh, but she was just about the most passionate kisser he'd ever dated. And yet as convincing as her passion was when she was expressing it, it never kept her from picking a theological point with him a second after they'd broken an embrace.

It was the look of a man in awe and a little afraid and a lot proud that apparently this wunderkind was content to date him, to talk speculatively if casually about children and a future. It was a look of shocked admiration and complete befuddlement. And even if it predicted many of the misunderstandings they suffered through and the battles they fought in their seventeen-year marriage, it was at its root a sweet look. She had missed it. She was glad to see it again, especially now.

A voice answered the phone. It both was and wasn't the voice of the man who had sat in her office earlier that day—what felt like a thousand years ago now—and told her what seemed like a wild, self-aggrandizing fiction. This voice in its outer aspects resembled the other one—its low pitch, its emotional blandness—yet the earlier confidence was gone; she heard strain, perhaps even a cracking of identity. That could be good. In her heart, she felt that was good.

"Who is this?" Baine repeated.

"Mr. Baine, my name is Elizabeth Riddle. I believe I spoke to you this afternoon in my office at St. Thomas's Church."

A long pause. It went longer: second after second. Finally, Baine said, "Yes, you did." His voice cracked off the last part of the sentence, as if someone had brought down a hatchet on his throat. He seemed surprised to hear from her. He seemed scared. Good. Scared was very, very good. Scared created an opening she could work with. And—she reminded herself, in the hardest, most unnatural reminding she'd ever have to issue—she would work with it by healing it. *This is all you have to offer the man. Take it seriously.* If she didn't take the task of healing seriously—if she let her natural anger and her complete loathing of him take over, and it was brimming right now just behind her words—there was no other option for her but to become a ranting lunatic. She might as well do the bull rush herself then. She might as well buy a gun.

"I didn't understand you before, Mr. Baine. When you came to see me. I apologize. I don't think I realized what you were trying to tell me."

A sigh. "No, you didn't."

"You said your name was Rouse. Why?"

Since she'd found out who the kidnapper really was, Elizabeth had been wondering about the meaning of the name. After all, he expressly chose it. It was an alias, yes, but he chose it. Choices weren't accidents.

"Why should I give you my real name?" Now he sounded tired. This too was good.

"Well, I know it now anyway, don't I?" She tried to take all victory, and any mocking, out of her voice. Victory wasn't what she was implying at all. She meant to suggest a comic, situational irony he might find interesting. This was a dangerous game she was playing. But that was what Max's look was about, wasn't it? "I mean, after someone realized it was you."

"Who realized that?"

"It's complicated, Mr. Baine. But, basically, one of the policemen—"

"Which one?"

"I think his name is Arsenault."

"I don't know him. I never talked to him."

"Okay. That's okay. I believe you. But he knew about you. He knew what happened to you."

"Lot of good any of them did me."

"I certainly can understand your frustration."

"It's not frustration, Reverend. That's just altogether too reductive. It's rage; it's disgust; it's nausea. I get sick to my stomach thinking of what that man did, and how little the police did to stop it, or to catch him. Even if they couldn't have stopped it, they could have tried harder to find him. That's what we pay them to do. That's what we count on them for." Pause. "They even let Krystal get out of it, by dying. She completely got away with it. She never had to stand in a court and admit what she'd done. Someone should have noticed. Someone should have caught that. But they completely fucked it up."

"I think you're right. I think you're totally 100% right."

There was a silence then, one filled with surprise. "You're just saying that."

"No, actually, I'm not. It sounds like they completely botched your daughter's case." Elizabeth looked up. She saw Johnson giving her the evil eye. Reid too. Too bad. This was her daughter, not theirs. She would say what she wanted. Besides, the man was right. The case was botched. That was the truth. She found herself moving off the seat and through the door. She needed out. She needed air. She needed space, not watchers, to carry out this conversation. To really hear and really respond to this man.

She knew from her fifteen years as a priest that there was no way she could effectively counsel someone without first opening up her own empathy. If all she did was listen to words and respond with more words, nothing ever happened. Things only happened, the right words only happened, when she connected spiritually with the other person. In this moment, therefore, trying to forge an improbable bond with her daughter's kidnapper, the police had become the enemy and Baine her ally. The only question left was how good of an ally he would let himself become.

"Yes, they did," he said, and she hoped that she heard some appreciation in his voice.

"So," she said after a moment, "Rouse."

"It's my grandmother's name."

"Oh." That was a surprise. Elizabeth didn't know what to do with it. She imagined a vengeful axe-wielding grandma with a bad wig and silver eyes and a lantern jaw, one that open and shut with automatic delight as she murdered her enemies.

"She treated me better than anyone. Better than my own parents."

"Really? I'm glad she did that for you."

As he admitted a desire to kill an innocent person, Baine had summoned the idea of the best person he'd ever known— or at least the person who had treated him best? Maybe this was merely a revelation of his sickness, but Elizabeth sensed there was something hopeful, even useful, in it. What exactly about his grandmother had Baine been trying to emulate? That was the question.

She heard the doors of the police car opening, men exiting. They were getting impatient, as men tended to. Too bad. You couldn't hurry counseling. Healing happened at its own pace. Even so, she cut to the chase, what she'd been skirting for minutes now. "Mr. Baine, what happened to you and your daughter was truly horrific. Please accept my sympathies for your pain."

Seconds went by. "Thank you."

"I'm guessing that you felt so angry with the police that you decided you needed to do something; you needed to strike back."

"That is exactly right. I need to strike back."

Okay, here was the crucial moment. She had to be careful how theological she went on him because that might only make him angrier. Any logic coming out of a system of belief he didn't share was automatically useless; it might even be repugnant to him. And even though he voluntarily came to her office and seemed to profess to a Christian background, she couldn't be sure that added up to belief, or curiosity, or respect. On the other hand, Elizabeth couldn't deny who she was, how she'd been trained, what she believed, how she counseled. If who she was—and who God was—wasn't enough to save her daughter, she wasn't sure what was.

"But do you think that will do much good, Mr. Baine?" She almost held her breath as she let loose the question. She heard how it came out: too high-pitched, too nervous, too wobbly, like a leaking balloon. She desperately hoped it would not crash-land on jagged rocks.

"I don't care about doing good, Reverend. That should be perfectly obvious."

She almost hung up on him. She almost turned and said to Johnson, *Go in and eight ball the motherfucker.* Instead, she took in a breath and kept her control. Who she was, was all she had. She couldn't throw it away yet; not with Jeannine's life on the line. The final issue she would have to confront, even during this telephone call, was forgiveness. If she was going to effectively counsel a man who had done her such a naked wrong, she was going to have to forgive him first. This wouldn't work otherwise. To deal with his pain she had to move past hers. The only way she knew to do that was to forgive. But she couldn't. Not yet. Not without knowing Jeannine's status.

Is that what forgiveness depends on? It was the voice of one of her seminary teachers. *Getting your way? If you get your way, what is there to forgive? Forgiveness only makes sense—it's only heroic and not self-serving—in the face of the worst possible loss.* Was she up for it? No, not yet. She still wanted to know how her daughter was doing.

"I don't know," she tried. "I think you do care about doing good. I think you want good to come out of your daughter's case, and it hasn't yet, and that's what frustrates you."

There was a pause, a lurch, a breath. Something. The next time Baine spoke, and it was only one word, he sounded different. He sounded broken. He might even have begun to cry. "Yes," he said.

"Right now, you're innocent in God's eyes, Mr. Baine. You've done nothing wrong. The man who did the terrible wrong was named Murphy, and we all need to do what we can to find out where he's gone. Once we find that out, things can begin to change for you." She almost said, maybe she should have said, *And I can help you.*

"He's gone," Baine whispered. "I know it."

"If he's alive, he can be found. And if he can be found, he can be punished. Meanwhile, you are innocent. And my daughter is innocent. And I am innocent. And everyone here outside this gate is innocent. We are all loved by God. We are all the loved children of God." She hesitated before the kicker: "And we can keep it that way."

"What do you mean?"

"We can stay innocent by trying to keep death back for another day. And another day after that. And another after that. 'Death shall have no dominion,' Dylan Thomas said. That's us, right now, Mr. Baine. We don't let death win. We try to keep living, no matter what that means."

"I don't think I want to live," Baine said.

Uh oh.

She heard more noise behind her: vehicles. She wheeled and saw a boxy-looking truck rushing down the driveway, followed by a regular police car. Their sirens were off, but their lights were pulsating: red and blue, red and blue, red and blue. They braked to a halt not far from the two cars. Dark-suited men jumped out: helmets and boots and thickly padded shirts. Body armor, she realized. This was SWAT. The men went immediately to the back of the truck. Weapons. She turned to Johnson and signaled: *No. Get them back. Good God, not now.* Johnson and Reid both hurried to the SWAT men and started explaining.

"Mr. Baine, can you tell me if Jeannine is all right?"

"What's going on? What are those lights? I hear voices."

She looked toward the house. He must be staring out a window right this second. He might be staring right at her. Her eyes, without knowing it, might be on his.

"It's some help we brought in if we need it. Don't worry. I promise you that no one is going to hurt you. Officer Johnson already told you that."

"He said no one would come in."

"That's right. We are not coming in. I promise you. As long as you stay and talk with me, no one is going to rush the house. I would much rather talk to you. I promise you that."

"I don't believe you," Baine said. "I mean, them. I think they want to barge in."

"They won't. They're not in charge."

"Who's in charge? You?" She heard the snide tone. It was the first time he'd used it.

"Yes," she said. "In fact, I am in charge."

After a long second, he said, "Good. I wish they'd have let me be in charge. You know. With Paige."

"Yes."

"Instead of keeping me in the dark, telling me nothing, not telling me if they had any leads or what they were doing with the leads. Because as it turned out they were doing nothing whatsoever."

"I can hear how painful that was."

"You have no idea. No idea whatsoever."

Actually, Elizabeth thought, *I know pretty damn well, thank you.*

"Mr. Baine, I can hear in your voice how you've suffered. You've suffered the worst thing a parent can suffer. It's broken your heart." *Shattered it into a million pieces.* "I think it's time that we all get to the work of making you feel better."

He made a noise. "No one cares about how I feel."

"I care about you." Oddly, in the moment, it was true. "I want to make sure you get help: help for yourself and help finding Murphy."

"Murphy's gone."

"He's got to be somewhere."

"Not here. He's not somewhere here, and even if he were it wouldn't matter, because the police don't care."

She felt a tap on her shoulder. She turned. Max. A different look. Not so admiring anymore. Johnson was behind him.

"Mr. Baine, could you give me an update on Jeannine. Just a little word?"

That sounded more like pleading than she had wanted.

"She's okay. Don't worry about her. She's eaten."

"Can I talk to her?"

"Actually, she's kind of busy right now."

Elizabeth felt that Max and Johnson wanted to tell her something. They needed to, from their point of view. "Hold on, Mr. Baine. I want to talk to you some more. I want to talk to you all night, but first I have to answer a question for my husband. I mean, my ex-husband. He'll be happy to know about Jeannine." She lowered the phone to her stomach and held it close against her shirt. "What?"

"These guys are ready to go," Max said.

"Go where?"

He winced and looked at Johnson. Johnson said, "Ma'am, it will take them just a minute to get into position—and then . . . they're fast."

"Then what?"

"They take him out," Max said.

"Jeannine's in there. She's alive."

"Have you talked to her?"

"No. He says she can't."

Max threw his hands up. "How do we know he's not lying!"

She turned to Johnson. "You said as long as he answered the phone no harm would come to him."

Max's head reared. "You're talking about the guy who kidnapped our daughter, right? The guy who told you he planned to kill her? Or is there someone else you have in mind?"

"I think he's ready to break. I really think he is."

Johnson studied her for several moments. He nodded. "A couple minutes. Then they have to do something. But first they have to get into position."

"Why? Why can't they just wait?"

"If they have to act on behalf of your daughter, you sure as hell want them where they need to be. Reverend." He almost spit the last word.

This was a complete violation of what they'd agreed to, of what they'd told Baine, but Elizabeth saw she had no choice. She nodded. "All right. But give me a couple more minutes."

Max started. "You could tell him that if he doesn't give up Jeannine we have enough fire power out here to blow his head up seventy times."

"Seventy times seven," she said. Max blanched, lowered his eyes. He understood, and she saw he understood. Yes, seventy times seven. She hadn't thought of that in a while. "Just let me handle it, will you?" she said.

"I don't want our daughter to die," Max said.

"Of course not. Why would I think that?" She brought the phone back up. "Mr. Baine, are you still there?" There was a heart-stopping empty moment before he answered: "You got me."

She tried to cover her relief. "Thank you for staying on the line."

"Yeah," he said, more desultory than ever. She didn't know what that might mean. "You know," he said then, "I didn't know who you were when I came to your office."

Elizabeth moved her head. She opened her mouth. What did he mean?

"I didn't know she was your daughter."

Ah. She was so glad he'd said that. She was so glad. Because it seemed to her that it was a form of apology, and thus a sign of a conscience. Most of all, it cleared her head of the nightmare notion of a kidnapper nabbing her daughter and then coming to her office and secretly taunting her. As it turned out, it was just chance. Chance was lighter than evil.

"Well, the thing is, even if she wasn't my daughter, she'd be someone else's."

She heard him breathe in again, painfully. "I know," he said. And she believed he did. He knew and understood, and yet he had been prepared to kill her anyway. A man with a conscience would have killed a twelve-year-old girl who'd done nothing to him. It was almost impossible to conceive of the anger, the roiling despair he must have felt.

"Mr. Baine, you're obviously a good man. You're a man that's been hurt. And I don't think you want to cause any more hurt. I really don't think you do. I think you're just looking for an answer. We can help you find one—all of us can. We can find an answer that's better than what you planned on doing."

Another long pause, and then she heard him say it. He actually said it: "Okay."

"How about we just put an end to death? We try to keep the good people alive."

"Okay."

"So, do you think you can let Jeannine go?"

When he spoke next it was with a strained, nervous voice. "She's tied up."

Elizabeth's stomach flipped. New nightmare images came to her. What had this man done to Jeannine? What was happening right now? Somehow, she controlled herself enough to say, "Well, untie her, please."

"Okay," Baine said. "I will."

"And then let her come out, please."

He hesitated. "All right."

She heard nothing for several moments. "Mr. Baine?" She wheeled around to find Max still behind her. She covered the phone with her hand. "He's letting her go!" Max's face broke into a grin. Hours of worry fell off his brow in a second. His eyes shone at her with something like that original adoration she had seen so long ago. But maybe, oddly, it was even purer now.

"Oh my God," she heard Baine say.

"What?"

"Oh. Oh—oh my God."

"What? What's wrong?"

The line went dead.

18

Neither Angel nor Shelby nor Jess went inside. They knew they weren't really supposed to be at the house in the first place. Their only excuse was that Jeannine Riddle's mother needed a ride. Thus, while the police tried to decide whether or not to go in and take the girl out, they had stayed in Jess's Focus: waiting, silent, hoping they might witness a heroic rescue. As long as they stayed out of sight, that is, as long as they gave the police no reason to notice them and tell them to leave.

When the SWAT truck came, it looked like things were about to get very interesting. They craned their necks to follow the movements of the police-soldier guys as they rushed to the back of their truck, retrieved serious-looking military-style rifles, and rushed to the gate. Byron Johnson, the police officer nominally in charge—although with each passing minute that appeared to be less the case—began talking urgently to one of the SWAT members, who then talked to the other men—eight or nine total—who in mere seconds were over the gate, rifles in hand, and shuffling with quick but guarded steps to different locations around the outside of the house.

"This guy's done for," Jess said, not quite able to contain his excitement.

"Unless he hands her over," Angel said. "I wish he would just hand her over."

"I don't know," Jess said.

"What do you mean 'you don't know'?" But his meaning was clear enough: Jess would rather see a gun battle. "The point of this whole thing is to save the girl's life."

Jess didn't answer for a second. Then he shrugged.

"Relax, Angel," Shelby said. "For Jess this is like one big, hot video game."

"But it's not," Angel said.

"Oh, yes it is," Jess said and smiled.

"I can't believe you guys."

"Hey, baby," Shelby said, serious now. "Don't go all righteous on us. None of these people would even have found this dude if not for Jess and me. Especially Jess. So lay off."

She had a point. It really burned Angel to have to admit it, but Shelby had a point. The girl hadn't had to answer her text. She could have told Angel to fuck off and let them have their evening. But she didn't. And then Jess led them to his father. And Jess's father, after that annoying trip to his office, instructed them to come here. Better, Angel figured, to just shut up now.

The mother was still on the phone with the kidnapper. That took some guts. It also took an unimaginable level of self-control. A man stole your daughter and talked about killing her, and you could talk calmly to him on a cell phone? Impossible. For Angel, it would be impossible. If that were her daughter, her head would explode before she could manage to press her anger down far enough to issue even one word to the man. Then again, she thought, maybe that was what being a mother meant. You did whatever you had to—including talking calmly, even respectfully, to the man who wanted to murder your child. You took yourself completely out of it. You just did what needed doing.

Angel watched the woman. It was actually amazing: her composure, her focus, her careful listening, her considered replies. This while her mad-ass husband and Officer Byron Johnson stood only a couple feet behind her, obviously impatient, ready to try something else. This while eight or nine SWAT guys in helmets and flak jackets who carried rifles crossed the yard and got into shooting position. She was able to keep calm, to keep talking, to keep listening. Angel wasn't even sure Elizabeth Riddle knew the SWAT guys were on the other side of the fence now. Angel didn't have to hear the conversation. She could tell just by looking at the mother's face: she was actually concerned about this kidnapper.

Please let it work, she thought. *Please let it work.*

In the actual world, in a civilized world, this was how it was supposed to work. Calm discussion was supposed to be valued over everything. Reason was supposed to prevail over violence. This courageous woman, this religious woman, was supposed to be able to find the heart of the man who stole her daughter and win that heart over to her side, to the side of peace. But could she? How actual was the actual world?

The police were giving her time; she was insisting on it. But it was not an infinite amount of time. That was clear enough from the expression on Johnson's face and the movements of the SWAT guys. Obviously, SWAT had other plans.

Angel saw the mother move. She saw her smile. The mother looked at her husband—or former husband, it was hard to tell—with a look of unfathomable relief and said something to him. Something quick. Something happy. The husband smiled too. Good news. Good news! Then the woman's head jerked back; she re-focused on the phone. She spoke something urgent to the kidnapper. She spoke again. She looked up at her husband, newly dazed. Her mouth moved in a dumb mumble. Johnson shouted something, and Angel saw three SWAT guys rush the front door. In fact, they ignored the door and instead smashed through the glass panels on both sides. A couple blows with a rifle butt and the windows were gone. The three of them were inside. Where were the other SWAT guys? She couldn't see them.

"Here it is!" Jess shrieked and started to open his door.

"Get the fuck back inside!" Shelby screamed. He looked at her, mystified. "They've got guns. They might start shooting."

Jess just looked at her as if to say, *Yes, that's the point*, but then his expression fell; he shut the door; he stared dismally through the windshield, disappointed.

"Why are men such morons," Shelby said, and it made Angel love her to hear her say that. And, weirdly, it made her love Jess too. These two cold, standoffish people with their odd habits were really just like anybody else, any guy and girl on campus. She thought to look for the mother. Elizabeth Riddle was standing at the gate, her whole body pressed against it, her hands gripping the wrought iron rods, like a sad prisoner moaning to be let out of her cell. Angel could see that she still held her phone in her hand. That instrument of hope. Her husband stood behind her, also tense. His hands, Angel could see, were on her shoulders.

It seemed to take several hours, but eventually the front door opened and a SWAT team member appeared. It might or might not have been one of the guys who smashed the window. Angel couldn't tell. They all looked the same with their equipment on. The SWAT guy waved for someone to come. The mother and father started, but then Johnson spoke to them harshly.

"Lower the window," Angel said.

"What?" Jess said vaguely. He was still smarting from Shelby's rebuke. He was being deliberately obtuse.

"Open the window!"

He did it in slow motion, but he did it, so Angel heard the last of what Johnson said to the parents: "When it's safe for you to come in, you can come in." Johnson signaled to Reid. Reid came over and stood by the parents. Then Angel heard a surprising buzz. The buzz seemed to surprise Johnson too. He studied the gate for a second, then realized what was happening. He pushed on the gate. It swung open. SWAT was fully in control of the house. Johnson passed through. Then he ran for the front door.

Even before the parents came back out, Angel, Jess, and Shelby had decided they didn't need to hide any longer. Whatever happened was over. Why else would they have let the parents go inside? What's more, as soon as they stepped out of the car, a news truck arrived with its big satellite dish on top and its big gold number 5 blaring from the side, along with the station call letters: KDYL. A couple of technicians hopped out, along with a petite, tired-looking brunette woman who carried a microphone and a notepad. Angel was confused. It was late, wasn't it? The evening news was over. The brunette had probably been working all day. Maybe they felt they had to have something for the morning shows. That must be it. Either that or risk getting smoked by the competition. Indeed, even as Angel thought this, she saw a second van come rushing down the driveway. It pulled to a stop next to the first. She could guess which station this one belonged to: channel 9, KCAR. Eventually the local Fox station might show up too, although they always seemed behind on everything, from tornados to school scandals. They existed, it seemed, only for the purpose of broadcasting national Fox programming. Whatever budget the local news was given must be miniscule.

In any case, if the news vans were here, surely everything was over. It was just a matter now of telling the story. She could only hope the story had ended with rescue and not tragedy. It occurred to Angel as she stood there, outside the gate, in the cold, that no ambulances had arrived. That had to be a good sign.

Then she saw the father and mother come out through the front door. She couldn't see them that well at first, but then she did. She was certain that they both looked white. They looked spent. The father had his arm around the mother's waist. He was literally carrying her along, step by step. Her face was gone: racked with tears and something worse—a gut-level, brutish agony that the tears could not wash away. Johnson walked beside them, head down, as if ashamed of himself. As if chagrined. As if guilty. When they came a little closer, she could see tears were streaming down the father's face as well: cool, silent, and painful. Angel could not know yet what had transpired inside, but one thing was certain: Jeannine Riddle was dead.

19

After three weeks away, she still does not know if she can ever return to her job. For the first nine days she was immobile with grief and with guilt, utterly senseless; the next five or six she began to respond to questions, however glumly; also, she began to eat. In the last six or seven days she has started taking long walks around Caddo, usually in the afternoon, usually when Aaron is at school or at his job, leaving Max behind to fill his own hours, reside with his own grief, make his own decisions about what he must do. There is so little of her right now that she has nothing whatsoever to spend on Max; barely anything for Aaron, either.

She leaves her neighborhood and keeps going. Where there is no sidewalk, she walks along the hilly sides of roads while fast-paced Caddo traffic buzzes by; when there are sidewalks she follows them wherever they go, turning as they turn, drifting finally into cul-de-sacs in neighborhoods she's never seen before, not in six years of living here. Eventually, she realizes she is tired. She looks up, and she has no idea where she is or how she arrived or what is the quickest way home. Not that it matters. She has no particular business at home or anywhere anymore. Home or here, it doesn't matter. Her heart is shattered. So, she starts walking again with no fixed direction in mind, only a vague notion of where her house might be. Sometimes the return trip is fast; other times quite long. Once she arrived to find Max and Aaron overwrought and angry. She had been gone four hours, Max said. Where could you possibly walk for four hours? Four hours? Elizabeth couldn't believe that. It seemed to her that she had just left.

For now, Max is staying in her house, sleeping in the living room, minding Aaron and trying to act the role of the strong one, simply because someone has to. She appreciates beyond words what he is doing—she realizes of course that in order to be the strong one he has to deny or at least put off the largest portion of his own grief; he has to answer the telephone and buy groceries and text Aaron; he has to communicate with the ongoing particulars of life—but it is simply impossible for her to be strong right now. It is barely possible for her to stay sane. Max has not suggested that they share the same bedroom. She's not sure he even wants that; she's not sure she does. Technically, he's not returned home; he's only on leave from his job at Señor Billy's! Indefinite leave, that is. Elizabeth doubts there will be a job for him when he goes back. He does not seem to care. She suspects that, in one capacity or another, he is here to stay, and for that she is grateful.

What floored her during those first nine mindless, hopeless days wasn't only the fact of her daughter's death— although that was bad enough—but the certainty she felt that she had caused that death. She was the one who had insisted on calling Baine, then on staying on the phone with him, on slowly prodding him to hand over her daughter, while all the while Jeannine was asphyxiating underneath pillowcases taped to her head, her mouth jammed with a towel, her hands tied to a chair, a dead dog bleeding over her pants. How in the world Baine could not have realized that would happen, Elizabeth doesn't understand. Maybe he did realize, and passive as he was, he was willing to let it happen, if that was how things went.

Yet, she simply cannot help asking herself and her God whether if she had insisted that Johnson and Reid invade the minute they arrived at the lake house, they would have found Jeannine still alive, even if barely: her eyes panicked, her face white and sweaty, her breathing labored, her mind a lamp of terror. Instead, that is, of the blue-faced corpse with a slaughtered dog on its lap that the SWAT men found when they finally entered.

It is her fault. All of it. She is virtually 100% certain and was certain from the first moment she spied her daughter's dead body. Baine had merely been a player, but Elizabeth had been the originator. Who had insisted on the divorce? Who had let Max drive away to Florida—secretly glad, in the moment, that she would have the kids to herself—instead of pleading with him not to go, appealing to his conscience, reminding him what his leaving Caddo would do to Aaron and Jeannine. Because that's all Max really wanted: for her to plead with him to stay. For her to stop ignoring him. Stop pretending he didn't matter. A single sentence might have been all it took to keep him there. And if she had spoken that sentence maybe he would have been the one to pick up Jeannine that day. And he would have been on time, because Max was always on time. And, therefore, Baine would have had to prey on someone else.

Oh, an unholy thought. But she can't help it. Her loss is so acute, her guilt so vast, it seems to her current state of mind that it would be a wildly beautiful fantasy—the most gorgeous imaginable—for some other mother's daughter to have died. Sometimes in her long walks around Caddo she manages to pretend this is the case. She manages with her mind to rearrange circumstances so that it is pint-sized Ava Roop—she of the kinky brown hair and oversized glasses and pixie shoulders and tiny feet—who has been stolen and murdered. Yes, Ava is gone, not Jeannine. Jeannine, in fact, is waiting for her at home, eager to see her and eager for her father to finish with dinner, the one household chore he has never resented; waiting for Elizabeth so that they can be a family again for a few minutes that evening; a family instead of a collection of driven and isolated people sharing a house together. Don't worry, she will tell Jeannine when she gets home, everything's fine. Your father and I are fine.

She doesn't really believe the fantasy. It kindly entertains her for a while, gives her mind a break from the guilt, that oppressive and constant blanket of self-loathing. But fundamentally it changes nothing. The police are working with the courts to hurry Lawrence Baine's case along. At the very least, the lawyer told them, he'd get kidnapping, reckless endangerment, and manslaughter. Possibly murder, depending on the jury's mood. Given Elizabeth's standing in the community, the lawyer said, he'd bet that the jury's mood would be to call it murder.

Max seems to take some consolation in these discussions, but Elizabeth doesn't at all. Oddly, Elizabeth finds herself not caring about the upcoming trial and the eventual sentence. Lawrence Baine is a sad man with a shattered heart who acted out of a desperate, irrational need. She can almost—

almost—understand him. And then there is the fact that he held Jeannine for seven hours at the lake house, and at the time the police arrived he hadn't raped her and hadn't killed her, although he easily could have managed either. Maybe he would have raped and killed her eventually, if left to his own devices. If the police had never come. Maybe. But, if anything, his behavior suggested a latent wish not to hurt her.

And now he is more broken, more shattered than ever. Already he has attempted suicide in his Caddo jail cell, using his jumpsuit as a crude noose. He never had a chance. The ceiling is not tall enough, first of all, and, besides, he was found out by a guard before he'd even gotten the suit around his neck. Now he is shackled to his bed for twenty-two hours out of twenty-four, released only for daily exercise and to eat and to shit; and on those occasions he is supervised 100% of the time.

She knows that some people think that her primary challenge as a Christian and as a priest is to forgive this man who kidnapped her daughter. But, in truth, for Elizabeth, Lawrence Baine has ceased to matter. Her anger toward him has burned away in the chemical solution of her own guilt. The person she needs to forgive but cannot is herself. She is fairly certain she will never be able to forgive herself. Because she is fairly certain she does not deserve forgiveness. It does not matter that if it were someone else this had happened to, and she were counseling this person, she would say with confidence: *There is no human being alive who cannot receive God's forgiveness, and there is no action so heinous that it cannot be redeemed, provided you feel sufficiently sorrowful, provided you express that sorrow, provided you make whatever reparations are possible, and provided you commit yourself to never ever undertaking the action again. What's more,* she would say, *if you believe in God, you have to believe that such forgiveness is possible. Otherwise, what exactly is it that you believe in?*

The thing is, for Elizabeth, now, God has nothing to do with it. For Elizabeth, God's forgiveness isn't what's impossible—she hasn't even thought about it—but her own forgiveness. Her own forgiveness will be very hard won and will quite probably never come. Because it seems to her that making one's children pay for one's own bullheadedness, one's own pride, one's own internecine and puerile skirmishes with one's husband is about the lowest thing a parent can do. Especially a parent who likes to think she tries to be a good one; one who ought to know better. And yet that is exactly what she has done. She has made Jeannine pay with her life.

There will be no forgiveness. Not yet. And because of that she knows she cannot go back to St. Thomas's Episcopal Church and stand in front of a group of worshippers and speak to them about the gospel of Jesus Christ. As if she had any wisdom at all, as if she weren't anything but a hollowed-out, pretend preacher, a selfish and self-righteous blowhard, prancing through the service in her alb and stole and chasuble. Worse would be the hours spent in her office, meeting with parishioners. Oh, she could handle soulless chores like ordering new bulbs for the lights in the sanctuary or going over the budget with the Finance Committee or meeting with the Junior Warden about the new floor that is needed for the Food Pantry. What she cannot do is merely the substance of her position and the center of her existence: advising and counseling and listening to and crying with and praying for and praying to and praying about: that is, nursing souls. Her heart is shattered. She has nothing to bring to such conversations. She cannot forgive herself.

Actually, she feels more of a kinship than ever with Lawrence Baine. Sometimes on her long walks it occurs to her to ask the police to just let him go. Sometimes it feels that they are partners in this, co-conspirators and mutual victims. They each have endured the worst possible fate. She thinks about her smug appraisal from before, what she had hoped to raise with Baine on the phone that evening if she had been given time and opportunity: *Okay, so your heart is broken, it is shattered in a million pieces, but wouldn't you rather turn that heart outward, with a knowing sympathy for others?* As if she had any right to lecture anyone about how to handle the loss of a child. When your heart is shattered, it's shattered. No one has a right to expect anything different, to ask anything higher or purer or more selfless. No, she would never think to kidnap a child and put that child's parents through the same torture she had endured; she would never want to do that; but for the first time she really does understand *shattered*. And she understands how almost any reaction from a shattered heart might be possible.

On this day, three weeks since she and Max were led into the house at 989 Lake Cedar Road to see their daughter blue in the face and cold, she extends her walk another fifteen minutes. She decides not to turn down her street and instead continues on a broad, square loop around her subdivision. For the first time since she started walking she knows exactly how long she has been away: fifty-seven minutes. Not enough time. She needs to go sixty at least. Seventy. Ninety. This is her need and her punishment. She will be punishing herself for several months to come. Possibly forever.

When she gets home, Max will be glad she wasn't gone for hours. Aaron will look at her with heartbreaking hope, the hope that maybe she's returned from the abyss. They'll ask her how her walk went, and she'll say fine, because she won't know what else to tell them. Because it was fine, first of all. These days, any minute that's a minute in which she doesn't actively wish she were dead must count as fine. But, also, because the ways in which it was not fine are so profound and so numerous she does not know where to begin.

They will insist—even Max will insist—that she is being too hard on herself. But she knows she is not. Only she can know how much she is not being too hard on herself, because only she knows the full extent of her weakness and her ego and her pettiness. Even Max never realized this, the whole time he was deciding to take comfort in that nineteen-year-old waitress. Max never knew; Aaron never knew; Jeannine did not know. But Elizabeth knew. Oh, she knew. And she acted anyway, out of all that weakness, all that pettiness. And now if she is ever to care about anything ever again—if she is ever going to be good for anything again—she has to stand still and begin with herself. With God's help, with God's help, she must sweep herself clean.

John Vanderslice teaches both undergraduate and graduate students in creative writing at the University of Central Arkansas. His stories, essays, poems, and one-act plays have appeared in dozens of literary journals, including *Sou'wester*, *South Carolina Review*, *Crazyhorse*, *1966*, *Exquisite Corpse*, and *Seattle Review*. His recent books include the historical novel *The Last Days of Oscar Wilde* (Burlesque Press, 2018) and a linked short story collection called *Island Fog* (Lavender Ink, 2014).

Author photo by _____.

CPSIA information can be obtained
at www.ICGtesting.com
Printed in the USA
LVHW030928110821
694575LV00001B/101